Drax

Ikenna Nwimo

ISBN: 978-0-244-30968-8

Blaque Falcon Publishing prides itself on delivering social narratives that challenge the norm. Our stories reflect the tales that we see in the everyday person's perspective and enhance it with natural creativity and, most importantly, imagination.

The falcon is a symbolic animal for victory as well as visionary power, and with that, they are able to point themselves to their prey – their life purpose.

'Men who are in earnest are not afraid of consequences'

Marcus Garvey

Part 1

Genesis

1

Friday 15th December

My name is Luke, and as of this week I hate my job. I work for Turnbull and Partners as a planning junior, and today I was asked to investigate a site for refurbishment or even potentially a demolition of a school in Bethnal Green. The local council here have struggled up to this point in obtaining funds for the school and it's currently involved in a massive redevelopment scheme. It's unlikely we'll do anything with it anyway. The building itself isn't in the best condition, so that justifies why it would be taken down. Recently, the enrolment percentages have been dropping due to the building's current state, which in turn has significantly reduced the amount of money the school receives from parents and, more importantly, the government. No wonder these tight bastards want to start work on it now.

More and more, as each day passes, I witness the hypocrisy of everyone around me. We have the local authorities, the building contractors, the developers (us), the investors and the blah, blah,

blah. I witness that, although everyone *claims* they do it for a good cause – the community, the future of our children (they love that one) – as long as everyone still gets their payslips at the end of the month, they couldn't give two fucks about it. The sad thing is, neither do I.

I went to the University of Berkenshire to study building surveying hoping I could get out and get a job with my degree, and I did. Luckily, my mate Jimmy is in line to take over T and P one day. The chairman, Johnny Turnbull, didn't start his property career with much. I read online once that after secondary school he wasn't particularly sure what he wanted to do for himself, so he eventually started labouring for a few construction companies, learning the tricks of the trade before saving up enough capital to put his father's house on the market back in the mid-eighties.

The recession of the early nineties didn't deter him from aiming high, and he built up a prestigious clientele to make himself into the property tycoon that he is today. That rags to riches story alone is why I was more than happy when Jim presented me with the opportunity to join the company. My parents weren't intelligent enough to build up a portfolio of their own, such as Johnny's, so I have the constraint of a student loan to contend with, unlike Jimmy.

Our head office in Central London consists of only two floors, the ground floor for the project team, and the first floor for the CEO, his PA, and Johnny Turnbull himself, as well as an office for his son/heir. I've only been in Johnny's office once, and, I think, serene is the right word to describe it, simply because it was so quiet in there: full-height double doors, along with Gothic columns, and the only sound you hear is the wailing from the CEO and the keyboard typing of his PA.

Every footstep in there comes with an echo. You could drop a pin and probably see the sound waves coming from it. I do whatever I can to avoid that office, just in case the CEO (whose name I'm not bothering to mention and probably never will) asks me to do something for him. He can be as democratic as he likes, but he is, and always will be, an arse. The only time I see Jimmy at work is if he comes down to let me know when he's having lunch, and that's it.

3

Goodness knows what godforsaken contraption they're all planning up there.

Anyway, I digress. Winter is the time of year when everyone wants to feel snug with their families, or to brace themselves before having to endure their families, so Friday evening happy hours at London bars just feel that much more upbeat, especially seeing as Christmas is around the corner. Yoyo's is our designated Friday after-work bar, and I usually expect Jimmy to give me the inside scoop about what his dad is planning, but you'd be surprised at how little he gives away. Since there's no Christmas do for the office this year, tonight's pretty much the night where we can sign off work for the new year.

'I want your money,' Jim says dramatically.

'What?' I say.

'Time is money and money is time, meaning that if you want some money you need to make the most of the time. And I would like your time.'

'Ooooookaaay?'

'That's the type of bullshit my dad always says during interviews. Any worthless suckers who want to fall prey to his charms usually get drawn in using that line. Always works,' Jimmy says.

'How do you know?'

'I sit with him during the meetings.'

'Really? He never used that on me.'

'That's because you know me, you bellend, ha ha.'

I've known Jimmy for roughly three years now, and I'll never get used to that laugh. Usually when I'm put into a corner like this, I make an attempt to change the subject.

'Have you ever had a Kolo cider before? Mate, this is outstanding.' I say, while Jimmy gives me a real concerned look.

'You have two things wrong here. NO ONE drinks summer fruits cider in winter, especially during Christmas, and since when did you use big words like outstanding?'

'You know I don't drink lager – never have, never will, Jim.'

'You read November's *Alpha Digest*, didn't ya?'

'Of course. I give it another month before they ask me to be on the front cover of those things,' I say, then he graces me with that laugh again.

4

'Lukey?'

'What? I hope it's not another bloody *Star Wars* reference, you prick.'

Jimmy laughs hysterically again and then orders another round at the bar, a Kolo cider for me and a Coke and rum for himself. It's Friday evening, so yes, we can say what we want and let it out. We haven't got work for two days now. *Yabba Dabba Doo!*

There's an air of nonchalance in Yoyo's tonight. The majority of people in the bar are either having their last drink with colleagues before they use up the rest of their annual leave for the year or are just looking to drink themselves under the table to quell the pain of dealing with their own existence.

'I'm trying out this new moisturising cream called Joule – you heard of it? It's this new type of cocoa butter that keeps the sheen on a little longer. Those two birds in the design meeting today couldn't help but stare, mate,' I say.

'What's the point of using coconut oil if you have stubble?' Jimmy asks.

'It's cocoa butter, not coconut oil – that's different. It shines my face, especially under the office lights,' I say. Jimmy would never admit it, but he's jealous of me because I never suffered from acne like he did. That's why he stays clean-shaven. Gives him that extra shine when required to suit those perfect white teeth of his. Believe me, Joule's cocoa butter moisturising cream is more than just another skin moisturiser. It is an energetic face protector, helps my skin feel stronger. Time to insert my off-hand comment here to check how short his fuse is tonight.

'So which blackhead cream do you use then?' I ask.

'You're a cunt,' he replies.

Fuse blown. However, the intoxication of the Coke and rum that Jimmy drinks calms him down a little. He can't react with as much venom when he's a little tipsy.

'All I'm saying is moisturising cream is for people who don't have our faces. Men like you and me, we gotta start looking after ourselves now. You know the metabolism goes turtle when we reach thirty,' Jimmy says, and he's right. I'm twenty-three years old, and I'm fucking shaking to bits at how I'll look when I reach thirty.

Muscle gains? Rock-hard abs? A Victoria's Secret Angel for a wife? I've got all three of those in contention, with the exception of my girlfriend Susie. She's been asked to do Ann Summers twice now and has rejected their approaches, although something tells me I think she rejected them just to boost her ego a little.

'Yup, the family album is pretty fucking depressing. It's like as soon the kids start popping out, mum and dad don't give a shit about ab crunches, do they?' I say.

'No, they don't, mate. Anyway, hang tight, sweetheart, Pill should be here soon.'

It makes sense to fill you in a little bit on this. I first met Jimmy during freshers' week in university. It's supposed to be a period when everyone's supposed to get to know each other through cheap alcopops, weed, and casual sex. Bit of an upgrade from handwritten name tags from secondary school. I kind of already heard about him from my time in sixth form, but I knew he was a popular character because of the summer barbecues he would host and all the boat parties his dad would organise in Tenerife and Ibiza.

Back on campus, there used to be summer party flyers all around and girls wearing promo T-shirts. If Jimmy wanted you to know he was doing something, he wouldn't hesitate to tell you about it. A lot of people just thought he was a flashy bastard, but I liked him. He did what he wanted, when he wanted, and we always had something to do on the weekends.

'It's Pill's birthday soon. We're gonna go down to some bar in Bank, meet the lads over there, then head down to Eros.'

'Eros again?' I ask, because we've been there before – same DJ, same drinks, same girls, same old bullshit.

'I'm getting us a table over there, all-inclusive, champagne, wine and … erm, all the Kolo cider you could ask for.' *Very Funny*. He says this with a smug grin and a wink, but I can't complain if he's paying for it all (he is).

'Who's coming?'

'Mike Ward and his mob are all coming down, some girls from your sister's uni uptown – London Heath Uni – I think, and Tamera. Doesn't your Susie tell you anything? Better get your *Alpha Digest* beauty sleep the night before, mate.'

'I couldn't give a shit if Tamera comes, bro.'

'You mean if Susie brings Tamera again?'

'Mate, I don't have to remind you how much that woman's presence infuriates me.'

'All right, all right, geezer. I'll make sure you two share a hotel at the end of the night, ha ha.'

That laugh once again. Do I really want to endure the demeaning presence of Tamera all just for Pill? I've known Pill just as long as I've known Jimmy, and I don't like that guy. Ahhh, Fuck it, why not?

Phillip 'Pill' Parsons is a snivelling little bastard who's been trying to be Jim's best mate since uni. He has a similar haircut to us but is hairier than I am. It takes me about two weeks to get a decent length of stubble on my face to look good, while it takes him a couple of days.

'Mate, if it's for Phil, you know I'm there, son,' I say, actually trying to sound excited about it.

'Good man, he should be here any minute. I was only joking about you and Tamera though. You know, if you two ever did shag, Susie would never know.'

'I know,' I say.

Tamera and Susie. Suspicious, subliminal and sexy. In that order. Susie has been my girlfriend since our fresher year in uni, and I swear, both of those girls, as much as they're supposed to be close to each other, just love to keep secrets about each other. I'm sure they have a bitch gossip fest meeting every other night just to catch up on who's sleeping with who.

Anyways, before he arrives, let me fill you in a bit more on our 'mate' Pill. You're probably wondering why we call him this. When me, Jim, Pill, Susie, Tamera and another girl, Sarah, all went to Marbella in the summer after our final exams, Phillip had broken up with his bird Maria. Jim and I thought it would be an idea to get him absolutely wasted every night we were there. Since he was so intent on getting laid and forgetting about Maria, he brought a box of Viagra, which is stupid because young people like us don't need anything like that, unless he has a little finger for a penis (which he has).

'I've always liked the name Maria. Has a kind of fiesta feel to it. I'm sure she has a sister called Catalina,' I said during lunch at our penthouse hotel suite, doing a questionable Spanish 'José' accent.

'Fuck off, Lukey. Maybe if you weren't so hung on Susie, your body count might rise,' Pill said. *You have no idea.* But give him a round of applause, guys. At least he had some testicular fortitude to bite back. I laughed because I could tell he was offended by my comment – he was and still is incredibly insecure.

The highlight of the holiday was when Jim and I found the Viagra in his bedroom and slipped three pills (you getting it?) into his food. Ten minutes later, he had a gargantuan erection for the rest of the day until we managed to get the ambulance. It was about thirty-five degrees, the perfect temperature to bronze skin, for them anyway. Unfortunately, our prank ended up with us catering for this sorry bastard for the rest of the day.

Jim and I couldn't help but giggle in the ambulance on the way to the hospital throughout the whole ordeal, wondering how we'd explain all of this to the girls without damaging Phillip's social life. Both of us were still relatively high on the weed I managed to smuggle over there. Too bad the marijuana smoke hadn't lightened Pill's mood, but at the time I could tell the two Spanish doctors were resisting the urge to cry out laughing themselves. One of them, Dr Hernandez, expertly tanned, asked us in pretty good English if he'd had this type of thing before. At that point I hadn't experienced so much laughter for quite a while. Was it Doc Hernandez' questions or the size of Phillip's ding a ling?

'Oi, Lukey,' Pill called out to me.

'Yes, mate?'

'Where's your sister Molly?'

'Why?' I asked.

'She hasn't chosen what she's doing in uni yet, has she? Maybe she can do med science and sort this out then,' he said, gesturing to his crotch area, laughing on his own, with Doc Hernandez grinning, understanding us well. *British men complain about immigrants to their country, but they come to ours and make fools out of themselves.*

Right then and there a flash of internal rage overtook me. I would have been happy to grab the good tanned doctor's scalpel and slice this cunt's throat and ask him to repeat what he'd just said, but rational, sane thinking doesn't condone such behaviour, does it?

A minute later, he had the smuggest grin on his face.

'Go fuck yourself. We're only having a laugh,' I remember saying.

'Oi, oi, lads, for fuck's sake, it's just a holiday,' Jim said.

*

I'm bored of my cider, so I order the next round with a Coke and rum and get Jim's drink too, while he goes into the little boys' room. The hazy noise around the bar increases as the time passes, which means that for me it's getting a little late now. The majority of people that come in now are more than likely having a pre-drink session before they hit the major nightclubs in the city. People around this part of town do this without a care in the world. It's what's involved in being a part of London's nightlife – the drinks, what make-up to apply, more drinks, what to say to a female at the bar, etc., particularly in the West End. That's the price of having a good time in such a metropolis. Everyone wants to come here for a new scene, for better education, an exciting job, but this city can't house everyone.

We're enthusiastic about stamping our patriotic foot to the ground and making a noise about how great it is here, but we're more than happy to sell ourselves to some Russian oligarch, an Arab sheik or some sell-out religious preacher. I vividly remember this city once being beautiful, and I still see some remnants of it, but we're all now chasing after one thing and another, and are too embarrassed or scared to admit that we genuinely want the best for ourselves – no matter the cost.

My miserliness towards my girlfriend's best friend Tamera – the fake smiles, blushes and false flirting – is something that I don't intend to endure during Pill's birthday night out. I may not like Pill that much, or Tamera for that matter, but at least it'll keep me away from home or keep my mind away from work. I'll more than likely be hovering around Susie throughout the night anyway. There are many reasons why some people just don't get on with each other.

Their smell, their voice, whatever it is, it's difficult to get a clear idea why disliking another human being provides such a safe haven sometimes.

'Bloody hell, that was quick,' Jimmy comments, returning from the lavatory.

'What, your piss?'

'No, you twat, your drink.'

'Oh.'

'Is this mine?'

'Yeah.' *Who else would it be for?*

'So you decided to drop your bollocks in the time that I went to the loo then?'

'Ha ha, mate, I was just thinking about that time in Marbella again ...' I say.

'My dad's gonna go mental if we don't hand over Cliveden Place on time. He can't stop talking about it.' And just like that, Jimmy changes the tone. *If you don't like the conversation, change the subject.*

Great. Work stuff. Precisely what I wanted to hear. We only just came out of work and we're now talking about work even more. Usually when Jimmy says *'my dad'* and *'can't stop talking about a project'* it means everyone in the office needs to be on code red to avoid getting a rollicking from him. Or worse. It's as if everyone just dances to the tune of one man, à la Johnny Turnbull. If he's happy, then the office is happy. You can tell that he's angry and in a fiery mood when everyone is quiet and staring even more deeply at their computers. It's like a game in there, about who can avoid facing the wrath of Mr Turnbull. Everyone at the office is of the opinion that Jimmy will be much worse than Johnny, and somehow they all expect me to tell him this, but I don't see me doing it at any point soon. As long as you're getting your money at the end of the month, why would you care anyway? Thank goodness there were no team Christmas drinks this year. I heard last year was a real cringe fest.

'Any reason why he's always on edge with things like that?' I ask.

'Because it's HIS fucking company,' Jim snaps, with a strand of blonde hair straggling its way across his forehead. 'Are you always on call for stupid questions?'

10

'Mate, I'm just asking. Did anyone piss in your drink?' I ask sarcastically.

Jim sighs to himself, readjusts the strand of hair and pulls it back, probably snappy because of his frustration with his father. This is one of the uglier sides of Jimmy; he can easily snap at anything, and he doesn't even have the humility to say sorry.

'My dad's been … real distant lately. He's just a prick, keeps going on about me taking over the company, its assets, but he isn't there to show me the ropes. Keeps going on about bringing that Alexander Pierce bloke in.'

'Alex Pierce is a big player in the investing world, Jim. It's inevitable that someone like him would want a piece of the pie. Sorry, mate,' I say.

'Fuck off.'

I do agree with him on one thing, although indirectly, and that is that most dads are pricks. At least mine was, here and there. Not much else positive to say about the sorry bastard though.

'All I'm saying is that it's just unrealistic to expect the handover of all those apartments by the summer. Yes, the market would be good for potential investment, but it's not going to be met without any resistance from Bethnal Green council. Maybe bringing Pierce in closer would make sense. You know how strong that community is?' I'm fully back on work mode here, trying to explain to my dear friend of the reality, trying to console the poor guy. *If only he saw things my way.*

'Why are we talking work stuff anyway? How are you and Susie? Completely forgot to ask.'

'She's OK. Her parents are doing a loft conversion. They're getting her to move to a hotel temporarily so she doesn't have to put up with the builders. We were thinking of—'

'We're thinking of Vegas next summer. We should do it, mate. It'll be a shutdown,' Jimmy says, looking over my shoulder.

'Who's we?' I ask.

'Me.'

The Pill has arrived. I must admit I'm bemused by Phillip's appearance here, and also just about fathoming the idea that I wasn't privy to this idea of Vegas before tonight. *When were they planning on telling me about it?*

'You all right, mate?' Pill says.

'Fucking hell, you two planning a wedding together without me as well?' It takes a fair bit of effort to not try to sound offended about this in any way.

'Yes,' Pill says (he wishes). 'No, my mum got that new job as a travel agent, didn't she, so she's managed to find us a good deal for Vegas. Five star hotel. Walking distance from Caligula's Palace. We should do it!'

'I don't see why not?' Jim says.

'Lads, only us this time though,' I say, thinking of Marbella last summer.

'Of course, mate. No need to explain,' Pill says.

Jim puts an arm around him, walks up to the bar and orders him a drink, leaving me to sit on my own and wallow in my pit of self-hatred and jealousy.

Just so you know, Pill did not find a random deal from his mother. This is a lie. His baby brother won it in a competition online, but he's just turned twenty, and since the age of consent in the United States is twenty-one, and the expiry date of the competition is in two weeks, he's had to give the prize to his dickhead brother. I know this because Pill's mother told me when I bumped into her at our local off-licence.

'Which hotel are we staying in exactly, Pill mate?' I ask.

'Err … The South Rock.'

'The South Rock Hotel?' I ask.

'Yeah.'

'What about the other casinos? That'll be the main reason to go there, right? Didn't you also fantasise about marrying Maria over there?'

'Just be happy for the news, man. Pill's gonna sort everything out, aren't ya, Pill?' Jimmy says.

'Yeah, lads on tour, son!' Pill says, smiling.

This is so predictable. Funny how he'll more than likely be using the #LadsOnTour thing already, but it's OK. I'll use the online competition thing as my trump card for another time. Cue the

'Whatever Happens in Vegas, Stays in Vegas' printed T-shirts and the sun-kissed selfies online.

My mind feels a little too vaporised now to listen to Pill's fake boasting, so I act interested, turn my phone to airplane mode and adjust myself to get going home. Pill notices this, and then, with a smug grin, he says, 'You doing a grandad on us then?'

'Yes, mate. Got an appointment at the barber's tomorrow.'

'See you later, bruv,' Pill says condescendingly to me.

'I don't talk like that.'

'See you around,' Jim says, with an arm out like I've been dismissed from my duties today.

'Cheers, mate.'

Go fuck yourselves.

2

There's always a subtle, tender beauty that comes with winter. The crispy iciness on the London streets seems almost unrelenting, but there's that snuggled-up feeling, the urge to have a warm, hot cocoa while watching *Home Alone* (the first two) or *The Wrong Trousers* (Wallace and Gromit) because that's the type of stuff that'll be on television this time of year and it only feels right to watch it. Every Christmas advertisement would have Mariah Carey's 'All I Want For Christmas Is You' playing in the background somewhere, while you see a family full of actors cut a turkey and pretend that they love each other, while the voice-over convinces my dear stepmother Julia to buy that extra set of candles just to make our house look like the advertisements.

I'm on my way back from Yoyo's bar on the Central line Tube back home to Loughton and Pill's voice and comments are still ringing in my ears. Anyway, I've got the hairdressers tomorrow so I'll let Pill torture Jim with his goofball presence before I shutdown the office on Monday morning with my fresh haircut.

My Undercut haircut, as I like to call it (others call it a fade), always looks good on me. Somehow I see all these footballers, teen pretty boys and pretentious women wearing it, and it just doesn't look as good. There are, of course, challenges to maintaining a haircut as sharp as mine. Maybe's it's my hairdresser, or maybe it's just me. Either way, you know it's the glacier season when your fresh haircut deals with that icy breeze that screams at the bottom half of your head.

Now that it's winter, I go to the barbershop every two to three weeks; it's simply not as busy this time of the year. During summer, however, I have to make sure I style it so that it maintains its sharpness. This is because of the extra pores on the skin that open up from the heat. I remember seeing a couple of other guys try and flaunt my cut, but it looks absolutely horrendous on them. Sorry young bloods, brethren or homies or whatever. Now, just to get Pill's voice out my head, I put my headphones on and put on one of my favourite albums of all time.

Tha Dogg Pound

Have you ever listened to Snoop Doggy Dogg's modus operandi: *Doggystyle*? Jim and Pill hate listening to rap music because to them it all sounds the same. I tend to listen to this in my own free time. How embarrassing would it be for them to recite rap lyrics and … erm … let's say 'accidentally' say 'nigger' right before the best segment of the song comes in? Especially infront of me? Can you imagine the outrage? Anyway, what makes this album so unique is that it makes you want to embrace and understand how it was to experience the G-Funk sound of the early nineties properly. Dr Dre's *The Chronic* did indeed offer a sense of freshness to the hip-hop scene at the end of the 'Golden Age' era, and there've been multiple discussions about which album is stronger: *The Chronic* or *Doggystyle*? It's been a subject of debate for quite a while now, and I'll give you my reasons why I much prefer *Doggystyle*. To digress a little, despite the prison industrial complex investing into the music industry like it did, I guess gangsta rap was inevitable.

Originally derived from the legend that is George Clinton's P-Funk, parliament funk was a distinctive type of funk music that has been kept relevant today partly thanks to G-Funk, otherwise known as gangsta-funk. The P-Funk and soul samples that Dr Dre uses in both *The Chronic* and *Doggystyle* broke down doors as to how urban music was to be approached. Dr Dre himself, fresh from the heyday of the N.W.A, decided to use the drawling synthesised sound with upbeat baselines, live vocals and even live instrumentation, to perfect the sound that was created back then.

Dr Dre's mastery of composition and direction, along with Snoop's magnetic West Coast vocal drawl, showed everyone that this combination could rival that of Boogie Down Productions, Gang Starr, DJ Jazzy Jeff & the Fresh Prince, Pete Rock & CL Smooth or even Eric B. & Rakim. Snoop gave signs of this earlier in 1992's *The Chronic*, from his lyrical dexterity, particularly on one of the later tracks 'Stranded on Death Row' and 'Bitches ain't Shit' (my personal favourite). This then raised the question as to what it would be like if he had his own album. It did not disappoint.

Doggystyle, from 1993, kicks off with a skit of Snoop taking a bath with a lady friend before he's interrupted by his homies. In my opinion it was tongue-in-cheek skits like these that made *Doggystyle* an entertaining album rather than just an exceptional hip-hop record. This intro track is immersed by an introductory verse by The Lady of Rage, topped off by some vocals by the funk legend, none other than George Clinton himself. This just lays the whole album out and sets the tone for a gangsta-themed party for the rest of the album. This theme is cemented by the street anthem 'Gin and Juice', where it's extravagantly detailed about what happens when Snoop hosts a party when his parents are away. Songs like that never get old because it delightfully articulates what young people really want to do in their spare time. What also strikes the listener straight from the off is the audacious nature of the album. This is adequately detailed in 'Lodi Dodi', with Uncle Snoop respectfully honouring fellow legendary emcee Slick Rick. The darkly humorous tone of the song showcases his street storytelling ability as well as his intimate wordplay. The P Funk samples are very much evident throughout the whole album, but is epitomised through the street anthem, Who am I (What's my name). A classic that will surely go down in history.

Yes, in terms of genre and lyrical content it is very much similar to *The Chronic*, but listen closely at how the sound quickly developed between both albums – *Doggystyle* doesn't fail to tell you directly what's happening. Whether it's hanging out in the club or chilling with your homeboys, you are never lost about what Snoop is actually doing.

You can argue that the album's themes touch on black American stereotypes, but you can only adequately detail experiences that have actually been imposed on you in art form, and it's this that confirms the perfect blend between keeping Snoop's rawness and hunger in check while also keeping on track with the authentic production. So, of course, the lyrics are about bitches and hoes, gang-banging in the streets – oh, and also a substantial amount of profanity too – but seeing as this kind of content was endorsed at the time, you just have to admire the art above the explicitness. This is what makes the album so damn good. The composition and the adroitness in which Snoop was able to switch flows from the smooth seventies Blaxploitation-themed 'Doggy Dogg World' to the hard-core gangsta 'Pump Pump' proved why he was able to maintain a glittering career.

What pisses me off the most about people (especially Pill, because Pill does this all the time) is when they mumble their way through a song and then get all excited when the chorus comes in. Can't they take a big step back and just appreciate good music and lyrics when it's around?

3

The day's search had been an absolute shambles. It couldn't have any gone worse. McIntlock was going to have Frank for this. He and his team were searching for a suspect from the Romanenko crime family. There had been multiple whispers about them, but for Frank, it's all been smoke and mirrors. They had been making more noise recently, though, hence the sudden urgency to bring them down. *What a superb time of the year to start a narcotics investigation though*, Frank thought.

The Christmas season had got everyone in Frank's narcotics department in a jolly ol' ho, ho, ho mood. In past years, Frank had never been in the Christmas mood or spirit before, but today gave him every reason to be in a 'bah humbug' mood. The cup of tea he'd made ten minutes ago had gone from hot to lukewarm, which would turn almost anyone irritable by the minute. Somehow Frank knew he was expecting a lump of coal from St Nick's fire stove at home. *Uncle Frank's been a bad boy this year.*

He never really believed much in self-help books, vegan diets, or any of the new trendy herbal tea nonsense – *Just another hustle into your pockets*, he always thought. Especially as it reminded him of what his partner had done when she really got into the whole yoga movement thing. She used to wake up, go straight into the living room and start meditating. An early morning cup of tea used to be the ritual before '*Namaste*' came along. '*Bye, sweetheart*' she would say. A kiss on the cheek. '*See you later, namaste.*'

His young Detective Sergeant, Marlon, knocked on the door cautiously, unable to tell what mood his new superior was in, then walked slowly up to Frank's desk holding a hot mug of chocolate. Frank, smelling the mild aroma of the cocoa, then looked down at the now mildly warm cup of tea he had on his desk that needed some TLC. Frank also then noticed Marlon had a lipstick kiss on his cheek and a big smile on his face like his teacher had just given him a lucky gold star for best behaviour. His boyish late-twenty-year-old face indicated he'd finally had some luck with Kyra. It was the staff Christmas party that night, which meant that everyone let their hair down in the office with one eye open for any leads. Frank always took solace in knowing that he wasn't the only member of the force who allowed their job to affect their personal life.

'Hey, Scrooge, I got you something, be careful, it has cream' Marlon said leaving the mug of chocolate on his desk.

'Thanks, I take it you finally made friends with Kyra?' Frank said, while preparing to finish off his paperwork.

'How could you tell, Chief?'

'Your face is blushing and you look like your mum's bought you a new Scalextric set.'

'Ha ha, no one buys those anymore.'

'They used to back in my day.'

'You're not *that* old, Chief. You're like five years older than me,' Marlon said, as Frank grinned to himself. *The years have been kind then.* 'Anyway, Kyra's invited me over for New Year's Eve.'

Frank always took pride in being looked up to as a role model of sorts in the department. He was always the one who his peers could speak to in confidence, but today wasn't a good time after the failed raid that morning.

'That's still quite a way, mate. You both been dating then?'

'We've been going out for lunch and stuff, nothing too serious though, Chief,' Marlon said, his grin implying that he wished he could take it to the next level with Kyra.

'You're a good lad, Marlon. Just don't think about it too much.'

'Have you sorted things out with … Leanne?'

'We haven't spoken in a while now, but you should enjoy the moment while you got it,' Frank said, redirecting the conversation away from him.

'Thanks. McIntlock is looking for you. He didn't look too pleased.'

'Here we go. Thank you, Marlon,' Frank sighed.

That morning's assignment had been a raid on a suspect's location in Earlsfield, south-east of London. Frank knew that he had to provide a substantial report on today's events. It was funny to him, because the end of December was supposed to be a time of giving, family, tradition and all those clichés you read and hear about. This, of course, wasn't the case. Frank and his team were led to believe from his informant – 'Vlad' he called himself, who claimed he was a runner for Andrei Romanenko, a former Russian mercenary who went AWOL after the debacle in Ukraine – that there was a little cocaine factory in Picklesfield Council Estate.

Frank had been keeping an eye on this case for a number of months now, and he knew that after the political noise in the media died down, the real war began. He knew that there would usually be a power vacuum about who can muscle in on the vulnerable and the weak, gangs and the youth – social terrorism as a whole vying to unleash its revenge on the world in one way or another.

'Kraken' was a new drug that was flooding the streets. Either way, as a Drax operative covertly working in Scotland Yard's SOCA (Serious Organised Crime Agency) division, Frank knew that being at SOCA had its ins and outs. Although there would always be leniency towards human errors and circumstance in any other organisation, a Drax operative's consistent failure was never tolerated. Frank was just glad that the year was coming to a close.

To Frank, Drax meant almost the world to him – a safe haven for him to express his own natural talents with pride and, most importantly, his dignity. It was a classic counterterrorist/crime agency that had taken him in, and it had no judgement or discrimination towards anyone's creed or background. He was one of the few detectives of colour over at SOCA, along with Marlon and Kyra. At the very least he would continue to do what he did best. That was what compelled him to continue in the Drax agency in particular. It simply seemed right and just to be part of such a programme – an outer haven to his troubled past and relationships.

Making his way into McIntlock's office upstairs, it appeared that everyone here had already had their celebrations. The Christmas tree had been taken down and it looked as if it was ready to be put away. It wasn't even Christmas yet, but Frank safely assumed that McIntlock had ordered it so that people didn't get too caught up in the Christmas spirit and focused on the job at hand. He now understood Marlon's point of view with the whole Scrooge thing. *Bah humbug indeed.*

In one way or another, Frank could definitely tell McIntlock was in the building, as he knew that he would have more than likely sucked the life out of the occasion somehow. The floor itself was pretty empty, just a few recognisable faces. Those who acknowledged him sent a wave and a Christmas condolence. The majority of people in here would more than likely be working on Christmas Day onwards. Other than that, there wasn't anyone here who excited his attention. As Frank got older and more experienced, it became more and more apparent to him how similar his behaviour was to McIntlock's. That was very worrying to Frank, seeing how solemn and subdued the noise level was in here compared to his spot downstairs.

Frank knocked and allowed himself in, catching his old mentor McIntlock staring at his phone, his glasses on top of his head – an old caricature of the man he used to be.

'Just a minute, Walker,' he said.

Frank knew that when McIntlock addressed someone by their last name, it meant that it was serious. Frank decided to pretend that he was busy on his phone. *No new messages.*

'Take a seat, Frank,' McIntlock said, still staring at his phone.

'I'm sat down, sir. Merry Christmas,' Frank said, noticing McIntlock, still in deep concentration on his phone, look up and put his glasses back on. He was finally done staring at his phone.

'Thank you. Now, I'd rather speak to you face-to-face about … I don't think I need to ask you, but I need to see your report?'

'It's near completion.'

'At ease, it's Christmas for goodness' sake, Frank,' he said. 'It hasn't been our best year, has it?'

'I apologise for today's performance, I …'

'I'm not talking about that, Frank. Drax hasn't had a good year – no special crimes or organised insurrections. Not like when you started with us. That was all perfect experience for you.' Frank knew acutely that nothing much actually changes. Human beings evolve, modern technology becomes passé, but all in all, nothing really changes but the season, so whether or not the Drax initiative was relevant today or not was still up for debate. *Anything can happen at any time, and when it does we'll be ready.*

Something was on McIntlock's mind and it was clearly troubling him. The Romanenko case was always one that would be worth keeping an eye on, although for some reason the heads of the Drax board didn't believe it was worth chasing up.

'I've already expressed my regret about the failure of today's task. I've …'

'It's OK,' McIntlock said, 'I trust your instinct and I always have, Frank. You're taking this a little too seriously.'

'The intel we had was from a reputable source. I'll talk to him. My Russian isn't the greatest, but I was sure—'

'Listen to me, Frank. The bigwigs down in Whitehall want some action done on this. They're complaining that we aren't getting the results. Results that we were hoping you would produce.' A pang of guilt shot Frank straight through the heart.

'Bollocks' Frank exclaimed.

'I just came off the phone with them. We have a month until we bring everything together and provide a full report on the squad division – monthly expenses, members signing in and out, the lot.'

'You mean they want to see if we were doing anything dodgy?'

'You see, this is why I've always admired you, Frank. Ever the realist, seeing things for what they are, but this is also why you should take some time off, clear your head. It's Christmas. Lord knows you could do with some company this year. It's been tough, and because we both know how stubborn you can be, I'm giving you a suspension – effective immediately.'

McIntlock's words were confusing to Frank. Throughout the year Frank had endured week after week of constant nagging and angry outbursts, the pressure clearly doing a number on McIntlock. It had Frank wondering whether to feel either responsible and guilty for this morning's failed operation or to believe that the circumstances set by the suits at Whitehall would have made this predicament happen anyway.

'OK, you'll have my report soon,' Frank said.

'You planning to go anywhere nice?' McIntlock asked, trying to make conversation.

Frank smiled and then walked out of the room, knowing full well that whatever else McIntlock had to say would be useless – just banal conversation to follow the blow of possibly losing the very organisation that had helped guide him through the lonely tough years.

Frank headed back to his office wishing that the earlier conversation hadn't happened and that there would be more to it. He also wished he hadn't been so much of a big brother figure to his team downstairs, only to then all of a sudden have to disappear. All of this simply because there weren't any major crime threats to the city – all because a group of people, who no one on the Drax programme had seen, were shutting it down, more than likely to save their pockets. *Pathetic. Typical.*

Leanne would usually be there to talk to about issues like these, but now she wasn't around, Frank had to deal with the same issue he had been dealing with pretty much his whole life. Abandonment. He walked back down to his office downstairs in disgust, wondering in what way he could perhaps sort this all out. Bring down the distribution of Kraken itself? Or get on his knees and beg?

It was only ever going to be one way, but first he had to get back to dealing with the familiar emotion of loneliness.

4

My home is roughly ten minutes away from Loughton station, a twenty-minute walking distance if your walking pace is affected by alcohol. My head still feels a little hazy and I'm still agitated as to why I wasn't briefed on this whole #LadsOnTour Vegas thing. For about a minute, Jimmy poured his life out to me, and we were getting somewhere before dickface Pill McGee turned up.

Approaching the front door, I lazily grab the keys without noticing my Audi A3 hatchback on the driveway, nearly scratching the poor girl, which forces me to sober up a little quicker.

Even though we are a family of four, I live in a five-bedroom house, with laminated timber-panelled flooring complemented with underfloor heating – superb for the glacier-esque weather we have here at this time of year. My hallway has various pictures of us throughout the years, and if you observe closely, you can see how we've aged and how puberty is a clear signal and substantial proof that there is a God. My favourite photo is of my sister and me: young, innocent and hopeful about life, while we assimilate to this society thanks to our parents. *Nostalgic to say the least*. The kitchen was recently extended with a larger cooking space, supplemented with a glass patio seating area, for whenever stepmother Julia has her book club over for tea. I always like to avoid the house whenever that happens, because nothing else in the world matters than her having that book club.

There's always an argument between her and Dad because he's trying to watch TV and she wants to keep up appearances with her friends. Absolute stupidity if you ask me, but Dad cluelessly submits to Julia's antagonisms and just gets on with life. Good one, Dad.

Roman blinds occupy the patio internally, remote controlled to three different settings. Add that to an electric fireplace which happens to be right next to the six-foot pine tree, filled to the brim with decorations and you have the perfect catalogue setting for a living room. Although you hear a slight creak when going up the stairs, walking up to my bedroom always has a welcoming feel to it. I turn my phone back on from airplane mode and receive a multitude of pings and pongs but I'm too dazed to care. I then doze off on top of my bed for about five minutes before realising I can't sleep much thanks to the alcohol and artificial sugars, so I head into bustybadbitches.com on my phone and wank myself to sleep.

*

This morning, the sky couldn't be any greyer than it is now. The few trees we have along our main road are looking ever so lonely with no leaves on them. I didn't drink much last night but it was enough to create a slight knot in my stomach to remind me that I did. I hear the faint sound of medium wave radio and Blur downstairs, which means Dad's already up. Sometimes I think he's testing me with his shit nineties rock music, because I've expressed my disapproval at this before. The incorrigible white noise then turns to sport analysis. Football. West Ham United are linked with signing bright Spanish wonderkid Estaban Rodriguez. He's supposed to be the next big thing for world football, and local North East London rival Tottenham Hotspur FC are alleged to be in contact with the player. *What a surprise.*

I get up and do my stretches more languidly than usual because of my achy back, which is more than likely due to my sleeping position last night, which also reminds me to get my head straight for when I sleep tonight. I send Susie a *'Can't wait to see you'* message, then realise I haven't bothered reading the Christmas edition of *Alpha Digest* yet. This is supremely important because unnecessary weight gain is always possible during this time of year and this month it features a section just on that. Briefly glancing at it, if I keep going where I'm going currently with this, I shouldn't be shocked if I'm approached to become a cover model for *Alpha Digest*. I get my shit together, check out my biceps for about ten minutes in front of the mirror, then make my way down to the dresser's or barber shop or whatever you want to call it.

This is usually one of the highlights of every other weekend – the freshness I feel after Fabrica cuts my mop with cut-throat precision and authority. Fabrica, whom I have the utmost confidence in believing that she fancies me, listens to me all the time when she cuts my hair. I have, admittedly, never had the audacity to ask her age, but she looks about mid-thirties, maybe younger, with a smile to die for. If only I was a decade older. Oh well. *Tough love.*

'How are ya today, handsome – getting ready for Christmas?' She always has that glacier-fresh mint chewing gum when she works. We exchange greetings, and she and all the other female staff here are wearing Santa hats with 'ho ho ho' written on them ironically.

'Yeah, nearly ready, the new pine tree we got for Christmas makes the living room smell great!' I say.

'Nice, how's your sister? I haven't seen her here for a while?'

'She's OK. Just focusing on her exams at the moment. She has one straight after the holidays, then she'll be going back to uni.'

'What university does she go to again?'

'London Heath. Apparently that's the best for what she's studying. Med science, I think.'

Molly has never liked getting her hair done. She very much enjoys her hair natural and long because she wants nothing to do with what most girls at school are looking like. That's my sister for you.

'OK, what's new then?' she asks.

I wait a little bit before answering because Fabrica starts off trimming my sides. I then explain to her everything about Pill and Jimmy refusing to tell me about the Vegas holiday, as well as telling her about the latest on Susie and me. I was expecting some girl advice from Fabrica but all I got was 'OK', 'I see', 'Very interesting' and 'Hold still now'. Either way, it's still pleasant to be around someone who just listens. Fabrica's delicate hands, warm and soft, guide the clippers to get the perfect height for my hair. Money well spent every time I come here. She gives a great cut, listens and doesn't complain. Money well spent indeed.

Considering that it's Pill's birthday this coming weekend before Christmas, having this cut now will save me the effort of coming down here again, as much as I would love to grace Fabrica with my presence once more. Seeing Susie tonight will be the highlight of this weekend though. She makes everything seem sane in my life.

*

I'm back at home now and the decorations certainly like to make their presence known. I notice now we also have an abundance of lights on the front of our house and a snowman who we've decided to call 'Icey' (don't ask why), which to my mind is less and less enthusiastically received as the years go by, much like birthdays and Christmas itself.

By now, I'm sure you can probably tell I'm not a big fan of this time of year. When you're a child, everything is exciting: your birthday, going to the zoo, staying up late during time off school; it was always the little things that gave you joy and happiness. Now that I'm a little older, I know why parents used to always put you off whenever you assumed being an adult would be a better life. You not only put up with situations and people that you don't enjoy spending time with, you have to pretend you actually *like* these people, so much so that it ends up being plastic, so plastic that I can shake hands with you, look into your eyes and exchange greetings in the form of '*It's so nice to meet you*', when in reality I know fuck all about you. At least when you're a child you look forward to Christmases in the hope of a new bike, a games console, a West Ham shirt, or anything that'll shut you up until your birthday at least.

Since we have the nicest house on our road, Julia's always happy to invite the whole of Essex for Christmas, and that's not even considering family members. You must have those people, right? The ones who never contact you on birthdays but always seem to appear when free food's available in the house and ask the same questions to you every time you see them annually:

'*You've grown so tall*' (I'm only five foot ten).

'*You're looking more and more like your dad*' (I look nothing like my dad).

'*How many years of uni do you have left?*' (I've already graduated).

And so on and so forth.

I do whatever I can to avoid people sometimes. You know, those plastic members of society trying to cut themselves a piece of the action when the opportunity strikes. *Bloodsuckers*. All this just feeds Julia's ego. She *has* to be the one to throw the get-together. The very idea of being forgotten or left behind, I believe, haunts her daily. This is why Christmas has to be 'perfect' every year. The lights outside on the house, Icey the Snowman (made with real snow or not), the Christmas tree, the roaring fireplace, everything. Even the decorated wrapped-up boxes of empty cardboard under our tree would drive any ten-year-old boy to heartache and betrayal when he finds out there are no real presents under there.

The only things that seem to exist are false promises and a hope that you can be whatever you want to be on this stinking planet. *Another year closer to that reality for that poor boy*. In other words, we are obliged to show everyone that everything is working out fine, especially to Julia's mother; we have to show that we are a happy progressive family, no matter the circumstance.

Anyway, Susie sends a message to me saying that she won't be able to make it tonight and that she's getting things together with her parents to move back home. I offered to help but she advised not to. Her dad isn't in the greatest of moods because of how much it's cost him to sort everything out for her in the hotel. I don't blame him.

Room service and pay-per-view movies more than likely. You can add a spa and facials along with a manicure and pedicure to that list too. That's my Susie for you. Knows what she wants – expensive maybe, yes – but at least she's honest about it.

As I've told you before, Susie makes everything seem sane in my life. Her hair gives off a fruity smell and her eyes are so blue that if you looked at them long enough you'd imagine yourself swimming in an ocean, and she has the cutest smile, so warm it could make any iceberg melt. This is why Pill's off-hand comments don't bother me as much as they probably should, but if there's anything that I've learned about people, it's that jealously stinks, and with Pill, it reeks of shit. As she's cancelled our date, I guess today would be a good opportunity to make up for lost time at Reece's Gym. This should clear my head of the disappointment of last night and my growing suspicions over my girlfriend.

Reece's Gym

I strongly believe in looking after myself. I'm a big advocate in looking after your body and ensuring it reaches its full potential. As clichéd as it may sound to you, everyone, and I mean *everyone*, has a beast in them. I know this because if you'd been an insecure overweight child like I was, who couldn't stand being asked to change into his PE kit in front of all the other skinnier boys, to then become an Adonis and have them look at you now in envy is a feeling that cannot, and I *mean cannot*, be comprehended. In my case, the gym is the one-stop shop in today's world where you can let out the beast and not look completely insane.

Although I've already reached my summer body goal for Mallorca with Susie this year and NOT Vegas, my intention for now is to simply continue toning up. This includes strength training my core and persevering with toning up my biceps. I'm not up for those steroids or protein shakes. Jimmy has his routine because his metabolism isn't as fast as mine, and Pill is just a skinny loser. This means I can get away with the odd pizza with extra cheese, the sloppy shish kebab after a night out, the double cheeseburger with fries. Anyway, my point is that I do also like to let it go briefly. Occasionally.

Every time I work out, I usually like to do it in the evenings after work, to let off steam after working in the Johnny Turnbull plantation, or from working at all. Usually a group of geriatric men, a group of five, turn up and do their sets on the equipment here, which is oddly inspiring in a weird, wrinkly way. They tend to look at me like they want to strike up a conversation while I'm on the chest pressers, but they carry on their business like they've got my telepathic message: DO NOT DISTURB. To them I'm probably what they used to be – an alpha god with a lot of energy to burn off.

Today I'm working on my chest. I do about twenty reps of these and then I get on the mat and commence my ab crunches. I can finally do a hundred of these without fail. Then it's on to the treadmill for my cardio set. I'm on this for about twenty-five minutes on a 5.5 incline and gradually get the pace up to 8.0 and then 12.5. After this, it's a one-minute break of stretches then it's off to the leg stretcher. Nothing is much more embarrassing than having a fantastic upper body but no work done to the legs. *Nothing.* You cannot afford to not work on those legs.

This is the beauty of a Reece's Gym session: the euphoric feeling after a strenuous workout. I feel better than usual because I wasn't planning on coming here today, so I wasn't particularly pumped up for it. Thoughts of Pill's deception and Susie's continued unresponsiveness still leave me with a lump in my throat when I briefly anticipate the gains I can possibly make if I continue to work out in this fashion. I go back and repeat that set again (minus the cardio) in an attempt to get the present failings of my peers out of my head.

That post-workout feeling really does give a sense of perspective to you; my arms and chest ache now but it's not so bad because you know how bloody great it is. After taking a shower and absorbing an unrelenting force of East Anglian winter wind, it makes me wonder how cold it may be for our northern counterparts.

After parking up and walking back home, I notice a vibration in my pocket. What could this be? Jimmy's cancelled Pill's birthday? Tamera's moving country? Pill died?

No.

Susie
Hey bbe, sorry I haven't been replying, everything's been all topsy-turvy ever since I moved to the hotel. I'll make it up to you, promise. ;) xx

Molly
Mum's left some chicken korma in the fridge for when you get back.

False alarm. It's only Susie reaffirming her failure to satisfy her duties as a girlfriend once again. It's too late in the evening for making false promises now. *I've won this round, Susie, but thank you, Molly*. My anger gets too hot, too inflammatory for me to accept my own existence now, so I go back inside the car and embrace some Luke time.

The dark winter night brightens up the settled snow outside our front porch – each snowflake reminding me that it's winter, and that it's here to stay. The nonchalant nature of this arctic weather justifies the indifference that Planet Earth gives you, wherever you are. Susie will probably open her eyes and let me in about what's happening with her. Jimmy will finally find out about Pill's fraudulent behaviour and cut him loose and, most importantly, I'll have enough money to buy my way out of this house. I'll run away from Dad and Julia, away from the phoney people arriving at our home, the arguments Julia always makes out of nothing, Dad actually standing up to Julia and making his position known – like a *real* man should. This is all wishful thinking, of course, and one of the consequences of what marijuana does to you. You may be wondering what would happen if Julia smelled it on me, but not to worry, I've parked a couple of blocks away in my 'high-ding' spot. No one will notice a thing.

The enticing thing about burning and consuming this innocent plant specimen is how it tends to remind you how little almost anything in this world matters. Wars happen, populations increase, fresh new diseases occur and everyone pretends to panic – until it happens to America and Europe and then it's a 'global epidemic' that somehow always comes from Africa, apparently.

Hypocrisy is beyond comedy now. Everyone's an actor in some form. At work, everyone puts up a front that's supposed to be accepted by everyone. Then we go home and continue to eat and shit. Ever since school, the majority of my life has been to hide away the things that make me ugly, to avoid being looked at as weird. Do you think Susie would love me if I didn't have this job or this car? Do you think I'd be looked at if I wasn't hanging out with Jimmy? I went to university believing that would be my ticket out of this shit stain, get a good job and get myself settled, live the dream. Except that I dislike my job, and under this roof, I can never be settled. *I'm still young. There is time to change.*

I now have a sudden urge to eat something and sleep, the achiness of my arms and chest telling me I should've done this an hour ago. I'm going to wolf down everything I see in that kitchen. Hopefully Molly's promise of Julia's chicken korma is true, but frankly I'm too dazed and high to care. I. Just. Want. Food. I rush and park close to home. My gregarious primal behaviour in the kitchen can be compared to that of a wildlife animal in a David Attenborough narrated documentary:

'Watch and observe as the human mammal, fresh from a dose of marijuana, hunts and scavenges for food to quell his hunger. This is critical for the survival of the human race, as our protagonist, Luke, battles his way through the lactic acid of his earlier workout in the gymnasium to quell his post-workout weekend high.'

My hunger is so bad I'm tearing through Coco Pops packets, Bran Flakes – anything I can rummage through. I'm on top of the kitchen worktop now, my head inside our cabinet, surprised that, as of yet, I haven't caused a big mess that I would have to clear up.

'What the hell are you doing?'

The surprise intervention by my sister causes me a fright, and I bang my head inside the cupboard. Ouch!

'Ahh, shit, what are you doing up so late?' I ask sluggishly.

'I'm drawing. It's the only time of day where I can get some peace, plus you know I don't sleep much.'

'Right,' I say. Molly gives me an inquisitive look, her chocolate eyes and long brown hair in a cute afro style looking more browner than usual.

'Why are you drawing anyway? I thought being a med doctor was your thing?'

'No, I'm doing architecture, remember? Artists don't get regular payslips. You need a Plan B, as Mum keeps saying.'

'True. I … just don't know why you still call her "Mum".'

'Look, you only ever smoke when something's up. Who's annoyed you this time? It's been your second smoke this month already.'

She's right, but how can she tell I've been smoking? Oh right, the smell and probably my eyes too. Even though she's my sister, I'd fucking hate to be Molly's boyfriend – that would be a pain.

'Moz, why don't you just go back upstairs and chill, OK? I'm fine, honestly.'

Molly gives me a real concerned look, analysing me like a science test subject for a few seconds, perhaps wondering whether I am actually her brother or not. What an impostor I must be to her now. She then disappears into the darkness in the corridor, a shadow of the only person in my life that seems right and just. I tidy up the remnants of my munchies-induced behaviour in the kitchen and make myself a ham and cheese sandwich while pondering on my sister's words.

5

Detective Chief Inspector Frank Walker, Saturday, 16th December, 7:12am

Frank found that the excruciating thing about crying was the soothing relief he usually got from letting go and making himself vulnerable once in a while. *You don't want anyone to see you do it, unless you're a super-rich, spoilt young athlete*, he thought to himself. He woke up in his office and glanced at the bottle of Scotch whisky that was left on his table. Although it was unopened, he knew he'd be walking on a tightrope here. He ripped up the label and put it back on the bottle upside down. It was still early – 7.15am, his watch said. His stomach was churning even more from whatever in the world he'd eaten the previous night.

He then rushed to the toilets to throw up – anything to get the morning grogginess out of him – and washed his mouth, seeing bits of tuna and sweet corn in the sink. He reluctantly glanced at the mirror: tired, aged and defeated. That was the ironic thing about mirrors, no matter how much you tried to hide whatever you could about yourself, the flaws and defects would always be there. He then went back to his office and made himself a cup of coffee. Black. Perhaps that might wake him up.

After sending the report to McIntlock, Frank found that the bright side in all this was seeing the bottle of Scotch unopened, its plastic cap firmly in place – it just lay there on his desk with its label ripped. *It's been months now. Ten gold stars for you, Frank. Well done*. His neck was throbbing though, as a consequence of his sleeping position, but it was time to complete his diary that he'd religiously kept over the years.

DCI Frank Walker   *Diary Entry: DR520-1*
Day: Saturday 16th December   *Time: 7:25am*

I have my investigation board open at home where I keep track of unsolved work involving the Romanenko crime family, who are widely suspected of the distribution of the Kraken product. The most intriguing thing about this is how fast they were at going incognito. I have written below all that I have found out so far about the Romanenko family and its operations.

Earlier this year there was an anonymous tip sent through about a factory producing the product in Shooters Hill, South London – coincidently where this new drug was known to be most prevalent. Plenty of suspects were apprehended, all in possession of Kraken. This is, allegedly, known to be the mother of all forms of crack cocaine of contemporary times.

I have successfully managed to pull a few strings in the evidence room with careful planning. Finding a way to get the product could have got me easily compromised in my position. The last thing I'd want is Romanenko knowing that he has people onto him, as if stealing the evidence from the lock-up wasn't bad enough. Drax operatives are always required to do what is necessary to achieve the goal.

The product itself comes in a small 5cm x 5cm envelope with a strange squid-like silhouette on the front symbolising the legendary monster, the Kraken.

After numerous temptations and punctilious observation, I decided not to try out the product. This is the type of thing that could be smuggled into nightclubs for easy targets – i.e. students and young adults who just want to escape from the tedium of sitting in lectures and other such pursuits. From what I have found, it could have been detrimental to me due to my own past bouts with anxiety and depression. I might've been open to it a decade ago, but no longer. If consumed incorrectly, it can lead to unpleasant side effects – there was a young lady who overdosed from the drug this summer in Marbella. That was the first death linked to the drug, followed by another in Newcastle.

The swiftness of the Kraken deaths is what drew me to pursuing this case and has led my enthusiasm. Despite DSU McIntlock displaying an uncooperative attitude towards me, I feel concerning myself with his opinions is unnecessary. It's as if these deaths meant nothing to anyone except the victim's next of kin. Sarah Hewings, a former student of Berkenshire University, graduated with a first degree in psychology. You would think someone who had their head on straight wouldn't be likely to get involved with drugs. She and her group of friends, who were interviewed, did not appear to possess any of the drug, but the nightclub where she tripped out was shut down indefinitely because of the death. The second victim was in Newcastle – a Romanian migrant – but, since he arrived in Newcastle illegally, I would expect that might be swept under the carpet pretty swiftly, but it still doesn't justify a life being taken.

Either way, what my investigation shows is that both were easy targets for such a substance. The Romanenkos clearly know their market well. They target the young, impetuous, and vulnerable. Slip the drug to the correct market, let the quality of the product do the talking for you, and before you know it, everyone wants a piece of the action.

My prime candidate for this is none other than Andrei Romanenko, a former Russian mercenary whose career was based on taking classified government contracts and went wayward after the debacle between Russia and Ukraine. I have adequate intel on my board that he was rumoured to have been in Venezuela and India, possibly where Kraken is produced? I shall continue to investigate. In my opinion, this is excruciatingly cunning; cheap labour and sourcing of material – expensive risk and a high probability of failure, but if worked correctly, could reward tenfold. Clearly fortune has worked in his favour so far.

We initially responded when the two deaths were reported a week apart from each other. Kraken activity has been little to nothing this year, and as much as I have emphasised my concerns to DSU McIntlock and my department, I only ever get the same response: 'It'll come around', 'Something will come up', 'We might as well push this aside'. It's as if no one cares, but they will care when I'm done with it.

Never say die

*

Even though he knew that he'd directly taken a stab at McIntlock for not taking him seriously in his report, and even in his diary, he still knew that persevering on such a case WAS the right thing to do. Sometimes it's about sending out the correct message, thought Frank.

A headache overcame him all of a sudden, with Frank realising that he was thinking too much again.

Usually when he felt this way, he would take his Paroxetine tablets to calm down 'shaky time' a little bit. That was another thing his recently estranged partner Leanne wasn't too impressed about. The last he'd heard of her was that she was visiting her family in Ghana. The loneliness contributed to shaky time, and it always used to arrive at the most inconvenient moments – his first date and his driving test, for example. Frank had always found it a struggle dealing with the underlying pressures of society, but maybe being dismissed by McIntlock yesterday may have given him a lifeline to fight those inner demons.

*

Young Frank very much liked to keep to himself, and he was used to it; reading crime novels and autobiographies of the world's most famous gangsters – Charlie 'Lucky' Luciano, Frank Lucas, Al Capone, Nicky Barnes, Meyer Lansky, the Kray twins, (to name just a few) – as well as noir comics was what he liked to do during his downtime. Things like that would keep him distracted from the tortuous nature of his parents' negligence to him – particularly when the doctors prescribed him as a frequent anxiety sufferer. You would think that parents would be more attentive to their children with such a condition, and they tried, but creating a calm environment for a sensitive, emotional child like Frank would prove to be too big a burden for some.

Bullying was something that was always overlooked by his teachers and supervisors as well. '*He'll come to his senses one day and man up soon,*' his father would always reiterate to his mother and teachers during PTA meetings. All of this simply made young Frank fall deeper and deeper into a shell. Shaky time was something that the kids in secondary school made up, simply because, back then, he knew he needed his Ritalin medicine whenever his hands would shake slightly.

There was always a fire that burned within him though, a deep passion, an overwhelming hatred for authority, the bullies he encountered in primary school and the tough guys in secondary school. But a taste of his caged animal was released during an early hot summer day when studying for his A levels in college.

George Sanderson was his name. Both Frank and George were studying sociology together and developed a friendship of some sort, which much to Frank's bemusement would only ever mean George contacting him if he needed to get some help for his essay work. Frank tried to socialise with him during break times, but this would result in George trying to veer him away from his other friends. '*Not now, Frank, we'll talk in class.*'

The end of the line came that day when George got an A-star for his essay on his take on 'Racial Inequality and Difference', something that Frank wrote! Frank refused to talk to him afterwards, with bitter feelings engulfing him every time he witnessed George do well while he received mediocre results – the consequence of not spending as much time on his own work. He couldn't endure this anymore; the only way he was going to achieve better was to work better. He went to the library during break time to get some extra research done, with his heart pumping a little faster as usual. This meant he was due for his afternoon dose of Ritalin to keep him focused. By then, Frank had been able to control shaky time a little better, knowing when to take the medication and slowly controlling his nervousness towards other people. He had grown used to his inadequacy with his peers.

Class had finished for the day, but Frank, as usual, wanted to stay behind and commit himself to more work. He reached into his bag and checked behind the books for the box of meds. Not there. He riffled through the front pocket of the bag. No sign of the Ritalin. Maybe he'd left it in the library? He'd spent his lunchtime there after all; it may have slipped out there. No, it can't have been. He wouldn't have taken his medicine in the middle of the college library like that. He looked up at the teacher's desk and witnessed the horror of seeing his medicinal box already opened with a yellow post-it note displaying: 'SOMEFIN U R NT TELLIN US, FRANSIS?' Frank knew that George wasn't good at spelling, his handwriting making it obvious that it was him. How could he? George had a habit of writing in text message slang. They weren't very good friends anyway, not even classmates. Frank finally realised. *He's been using me.*

It was the end of the college day and he *needed* his dose. His heart was pumping and racing faster than usual, his palms sweating, eyes blinking at a quicker pace. Frank's loneliness and depression deepened. Class had only finished fifteen minutes ago, so George couldn't have gone too far. Frank then found himself running as fast as he could, needing to unleash his sadness and pain in whatever way possible, fast. Running out of the college building, he noticed George by the bus stop sharing a laugh with his underlings; probably joking at how funny it was to take someone's medication and keep it from him – *ha ha ha ha ha ha ha, very funny.* As Frank ran towards George, his smug grin quickly turned from cocky-confident to terrified in a matter of seconds. Frank launched blows to his eyes, stomach and nose – this animal, this thing, crying out in pain with each kick to the stomach – it all happened so fast.

His petrified friend gave him his medication. It was all so oddly satisfying to Frank, power being exemplified in its most base form.

Inflicting violence on another human being seemed to be a much stronger anaesthetic than Ritalin ever was.

Even though he knew he was in deep trouble when the police arrived, Frank had never felt more alive, more human. The officer in the passenger seat of the police vehicle spoke with a certain calmness, like he was used to dealing with angry adolescent men.

'You gave that young man quite a beating back there,' he said with almost no emotion, no judgement.

'Good,' Frank said.

'Good? Do you not realise how much you hurt that boy?'

'He deserved it.'

'He deserved it,' the policeman parroted.

'You don't understand. People like him need to be shown that they aren't tough. He betrayed me, never wanted me around, just like everybody else. I'm not a bad person ... I ...'

'It's OK. We'll talk when we get to the station. I've just spoken to your parents. They'll meet us over there.'

'Did you speak to my mum or my dad?'

'Your mum. If you have to know, she sounded very neutral about it. Couldn't tell if she was angry or not. Has this type of thing happened before?'

'Not really.'

'Not really as in ...?'

'Not really as in I haven't physically hurt anyone before. George isn't a good person. He thought he was strong and tough so I had to prove him wrong. He might have been jealous because I helped him with the coursework.'

'By hurting him?'

'He had my medicine!' Frank exclaimed.

'OK.'

The rage about George Sanderson still engulfed him. What made him quiet and solemn, though, was the sight of his knuckles covered with blood. He really had hurt another human being. What was he going to explain to his parents anyway? That he was being punished for fighting back against someone who was troubling him? They might as well not be there.

During that twenty-minute ride to the station, he kept thinking about what had happened. Then came the familiar loneliness, the sadness, the early mornings waking up reading crime noir novels and late nights watching crime dramas and gangster movies, the girls that kept walking away from him, the boys who kept sniggering at him.

He found himself sleeping twice on the way to the station, slightly muttering sentences that didn't make sense – the adrenaline clearly wearing off. This police officer, whoever he was, seemed to possess the uncanny ability of reaching out to someone with as few words as possible. Approaching the station's car park, Frank believed that he could trust this man, which later he would learn was a psychological tactic: everyone has emotional layers. Break them down bit by bit and you can probably get them to do your bidding. Frank was vulnerable and needed someone who could put an arm around him and open up a little. Generating some rapport, some sympathy, can be much better than listening and being sympathetic to someone else. Frank knew deep down though that shaky time needed to be tamed and fought against, and after all these years he had finally found out the consequences of what would happen if it wasn't controlled.

Sitting in the station's interrogation room, his mother sitting on the other side of the soundproof glass, Frank sat patiently waiting for the officer's return.

'I'll be with you in couple of minutes. Feel free to have some water,' he said, while gesturing at the jug of water and glass cup.

Frank was impatient now, clicking his knuckles, and Sanderson's blood was dry from the earlier onslaught. The rusty steel door in front of Frank swung open, a squeak echoing around the room.

'Apologies for making you wait. It's a been a busy day,' the officer said, smiling, a whiff of coffee under his breath.

'OK,' said Frank, waiting to hear the consequences of his actions. *Two years, five years in jail maybe*?

'I'd like to talk to you about the Drax initiative.'

'What's that?'

'Sorry, I don't believe I've introduced myself to you properly, Frank. My name's Matthew Paul McIntlock III, but you can just call me McIntlock.'

6

Monday morning

As you already know, I believe in looking after myself. Shit gets serious on weekday mornings. My alarm wakes me at 6am, interrupting my slumber with my phone vibrating along with its classic alarm bell ringtone. I usually tend to spend about ten minutes stretching, but both of my hamstrings feel incredibly stiff this morning so I spend an extra minute or so touching my toes, which feels much better.

Early morning workouts are the key to mental and physical sharpness for the day. While everyone else is waking up looking and feeling rough, my endorphins make me feel like the captain of my ship. I tend to time myself on how many ab crunches I can do in five minutes – I can do two hundred, but soon I hope to make it to two-fifty. I like to listen to Brian Tyler and Steve Jablonsky while enduring the pain, especially going through my daily sets. The majority of the music that I listen to is usually of the epic, cinematic tone – the hero finally embarking on his quest to save the damsel in distress from trouble – that type of music. You'd be surprised at how much motivation this music brings to a workout.

After my sit-ups, I do three sets of thirty push-ups; much harder than it sounds, believe me. My chest and arms could do with a little extra toning up, so this is great. Fortunately, there's plenty of space in my room to use my skipping rope; I have a sound-insulated floor in here, so no one can complain about the noise, if any.

After my short but intense cardio set, arguably the most pleasurable part of the morning is the shower. If you didn't believe that the post-workout feeling is great, wait until the lukewarm water touches your skin and subtly reminds you of the blissfulness of life. I use an Amazon-jungle-scented shampoo then leave the shower room smelling like the Garden of Eden.

Moisturising, too, is a serious business, never to be taken likely. The standard Vaseline and shea/cocoa butter could do a job, but I find that Tolle's for Men energises my face to a premium, that extra sheen needed, taking a year or two off my face. Add that to the razor-sharp trim Fabrica gave me with Wayne's hair conditioner and gel, and I believe the fire marshal is going to have to be in attendance for when I arrive in the office today.

An espresso usually does the job before leaving the house – wondering whether the caffeine energy jolt makes me forget about my father's growling snore, or the mystery of whether the incense candles are still burning in my sister's room. Molly has always had trouble with sleeping, especially when Dad went crazy for a bit. She used to always just hide herself with her notebook, to get away from the dysfunction, and Dad was just putting the blame on me. I would then light up my sister's candles at night – usually the scented ones that would help her catch her Z's, but now she's got into the habit of doing that for herself.

*

Immersing myself in the crowd of gorilla-breathed zombies on the Central line train en route to work is always a humorous experience. Most of the time I don't even notice myself nodding to my '*Beast Mode*' playlist, filling myself with fuel to take over and win the day.

The cramped space of the London Underground train, whichever one you're in, can be excruciatingly painful, particularly if you're in the middle of it. Watching the odd couple kiss each other goodbye on the Oxford Circus stop is cute, but by the time the train reaches there, the majority of people in the carriage have left and there's more space to breathe.

We reach Bond Street, and in a democratic way I tell the zombies *'Sorry'*, *'Excuse me'* and *'Thank you'*, along with a trademark fake wry smile as I depart my carriage. Today, this is seen as appropriate behaviour, particularly when you deep down want to push every zombie-corporate, white collar slave out of the way. I very briefly enjoy the warm effervescence of the London Underground station before the crisp winter air slaps me out of my comfort zone and reminds me that it is Monday morning and NOT Friday afternoon.

I like to get to work early. To be honest, it has nothing to do with impressing anyone, but just so that I can settle in quickly and rummage through the tedious task of reading emails I probably won't respond to. Another advantage of coming into the office early is that everyone says good morning to *you*, rather than the other way around. I may still be a junior at this place, but I can have that authority at least.

Approaching my desk and seeing it containing a load of paperwork already fills me with annoyance because this is something that a work experience kid should be doing. *Hello, I have a degree (can anyone hear me)*? They're a set of the architect's drawings that need organising before the meeting this morning for Cliveden Place. Kelly, the receptionist, who I'm sure has a mad crush on me, greets me with a 'Good morning'. Today, her hair is tied in a bun and she's wearing a pair of glasses that basically tell you to piss off, in a weak attempt to hide her good looks. I'm sure she's had her fair share of male visitors make a move on her today already.

'Good weekend, Luke?'

'It was OK, yours?'

'Good. JT – I mean Mr Turnbull – asked me to remind you about the design meeting this morning and kindly asked if you could provide the refreshments as well as take down the meeting minutes,' she says.

'Which JT was it?' I ask.

'Jimmy.'

'Hmmm, OK then. He could have easily told me that himself.'

It's an early indication that Jim is clearly doing what he can to exert his influence on this office as early as possible before his old man retires.

'A smile usually looks good on people,' Kelly says condescendingly. Please. Walk away from me.

'It's Monday, Kelly,' I say.

'I know, but you're here for a reason, right? My boyfriend and I were talking about some article that was online about a generation of people out there who come out of uni and get into jobs they don't like. You should read it.'

'I don't hate my job though,' I lie, giving her no indication I want out of here yet.

'You look like you do. Maybe it's your game face. I'm sorry, it's just that I'm kinda excited,' Kelly says, grinning.

'What about?' Finally. Something possibly interesting.

'No, it's … it's nothing'

'Are you sure, Kelly?'

'I'm leaving early today. Got a casting with a model agency.'

'Oh, that's nice. Good luck with that.'

'Thanks, Luke! I knew I could tell you anything.'

Kelly can't become a model, but good luck to her anyway. I'm sure she'll tell me how she got rejected tomorrow, or she probably won't mention it again.

If there was anyone in the office today I'd expect to notice my haircut, it would've been her. So, no fire marshal unfortunately, but I would like to burn this place to the ground. Why Jimmy couldn't have asked me to do this is beyond me, but the fact that I'm the one doing the minutes in the meeting today aswell gives me mixed feelings. A number of people walk in now and a series of *Good mornings* and *How are yous* follow, with no one again noticing my haircut.

In the conference room, the drawings are all set up and ready now, all up to date for the big meeting. Design change after change after change, sometimes you wonder why the big dogs get paid so much money. Seems more like everyone's paid just to make noise and not do anything about it; big proposals, innovative design ideas and intentions that go all up in smoke because Johnny has the last say. Why? Because he's Johnny bloody Turnbull, that's why.

'Mawnin' Lukey Wukey,' Jimmy says behind me while I neatly set today's agenda in the boardroom.

'All right, mate,' I reply.

'All good in the hood?'

'All good in the hood,' I say.

'Cheers for sorting this out for us. This meeting is critical. After this, all the design work is going to be frozen, no more changes, no nothing. It's basically the bitch's last shot at provin' to the old man that they're the right people for Cliveden. What's that?'

Jim's chirpy mood this morning already pisses me off. I force a smile to match his, but it takes more effort than expected. Is he the one and only zombie to highlight my haircut?

'Erm … what's what?' I ask. Usually I like to accomplish my office tasks in peace, no interruption from anybody, but, coincidentally, this is the boss's son and my mate too.

'What moisturiser are you using today? Your face looks brighter,' Jimmy asks.

'It's a secret,' I say.

'Fuck off, I tell you everything I use – condoms, protein shakes, hair gel, everything. Even that bird I was seeing.'

'Why don't you get your notebook ready for this meeting? I'm sure daddy's waiting,' I say in a tease.

'Prick. How's your missus?'

'Susie, you mean.'

'Yeah, her. Surprised you haven't asked for her hand in marriage yet.'

'It's been three years, mate. Things like that take time. Gotta develop the loyalty, you know. Ever heard of that? Loyalty?' I ask.

'Ha ha, whatever you say, mate.' *Three bloody years.*

'What's the plan for Friday?' I ask while arranging the drawings, which I know now are all up to date, already wishing and hoping that Friday was here. Kelly printed these drawings so they should be right. She doesn't usually get these kinds of things wrong.

'You know the plan. It hasn't changed. It's Monday, anyway, bro-ski, bit early to worry about those things.'

'Yeah, you're right.'

'Course I'm right. Oh yeah, I don't think we'll be needing you for this morning now. It's cool.'

'You sure? I wouldn't mind just sitting in at least?'

'It's OK, mate. I know you wouldn't want to be in that meeting as much as anyone, eh?'

'All right.'

'Good maaan. Could you chase up Teymor Plumbing for the quote on that flat? It's been nearly two weeks now. I think Alexander Pierce is coming down for my dad's charity ball on Christmas Eve. Gotta get things ready for him.'

'All right, I'll get on it.'

'Cheers.'

Is there any need to patronise me in such an environment? Jimmy can just as easily get on the phone and sort this out himself. It's his flat after all. *I think I WILL burn this place to the ground.* This is the thing about working that I hate: the strings that are pulled behind one's back. You don't know what the other's planning, so you ask someone to do things that you don't want to do. You try so hard to do the correct thing (whatever that is), but you still see the hypocrisy, contradictions and predilection of one's power. It's all just one big game of snakes and ladders but with very few ladders – the unwritten laws of power that aren't taught to you anywhere.

After the hubbub of the design meeting is all done and dusted, the only thing that I was actually looking forward to all day was to meet up with Susie after work for a hot drink. Usually it would be dinner or the cinema but it simply isn't the time for it. It was my suggestion, and she kept banging on about how bored she was in the hotel. Her so-called best mate Tamera had been away trying to sort things out with her boyfriend Louis, which made me think perhaps Tamera should get a job herself, right?

I've already bought us tickets for Winter Wonderland at Hyde Park, so that's something to look forward to at least. Nope, Susie isn't the type of lady to just do things on her accord. It would normally take everyone in our circle to convince her to do things that would be beneficial to her. Our old friend Sarah used to be the one who would instigate things like Winter Wonderland, or any other theme park – her energy and engaging childish innocence could convince you to do pretty much anything, but since she isn't around anymore, motivation is at an all-time low with Susie.

Today, however, I feel we need to clear things up. She's been more unresponsive to me than usual, not that I'm suspecting anything, but I just want to see a familiar face that I genuinely like seeing. All I want to do is talk. We go to the nearest coffee shop after work and both have hot chocolates – large and perfect for this winter snuggle-time weather.

'I'll be moving back home next week,' she says.

'When next week?'

'After Pill's birthday. Are you going?'

'I'll come, but I want you to come too. We haven't had a proper night out for a while now'

'Yeah, it's all right. Tam's been a real help.'

'She's your mate. She should be.'

'Yeah, but she could've easily walked away, especially now that she's working full-time and that.' So Tamera IS working after all.

'Yeah, true. How's your old man?' I ask.

'He's still stressing about how expensive the loft conversion was for the house. I don't even know why he's complaining though, it was his idea.'

'You sure it wasn't your mum's?'

'Not everyone's like *your* mum, Luke.'

'I didn't mean it like that … She isn't my mum anyway, you know she isn't.'

I take a sip from my mug. You just can't beat a winter hot chocolate. Some marshmallows would be superb right now, but I know I'll regret it at Reece's Gym. Susie always had a way of making everything someone else's problem. I honestly didn't believe the loft conversion was Susie's dad's idea, but I guess this is what I get for putting out my honest feelings and opinions.

'Anyway, what have you got planned for the rest of the week, Suus? You need to be doing something with yourself.'

'I want to start season four of *24* tomorrow and then start watching all of season five. I heard it's amazing.'

'How are you going to do that?'

'Erm, I'm going to watch it?'

'Each episode is about an hour long, and there're twenty-four episodes, which means it'll take you a whole day to watch a whole season.'

'Oh, I never saw it like that.'

As banal as this conversion is, it's just good talking to her again. It feels like we have that quirky spark we had when we first met back on campus. Not exactly how it was like back then, but slightly better than recently. I don't even feel the need to explain my hatred of my job to her. She'd more than likely respond to that with some bullshit of how she nearly cried when she had no choice but to drink instant coffee at the hotel. Can't live with them, can't live without them, I suppose.

Pill's Birthday (Last Friday before Xmas)

Tonight should be interesting. The beauty of nights out like these is the mystery of what *might* happen. We'll definitely be drinking, but we don't know how much. There *will* be girls and loud music, but we don't know if they'll be good-looking or if the music will be any good.

In my case, what is definite is how good I'm going to be looking tonight. Skinny navy chinos, a pair of brown leather Marks and Spencer brogues, a white smart shirt with a navy slim-fit blazer to match the chinos. My costume is at the helm. I undergo my stretches and workout routine (minus the cardio) to get me pumped up for tonight. I then checkout how my biceps flex in the mirror every time I move my right arm. Bloody beautiful, mate. I take a shower and stay in there a little longer than usual for two reasons:

1.   I'm always the first one to these events, which means I'll more than likely be the one to wait for everyone to turn up at the meet.
2.   I fucking love the shower.

I now smell so much like Eden, Eve herself would've wanted a new spouse. I'm freshly energised and ready for the night. If you're wondering, this new-found ambivalence is from the power nap I took straight after work, plus the loud music I have on. I spend roughly ten minutes double-checking my posture in the mirror. Before this I hear some shouting downstairs, which I assume is Molly.

'Can you turn the noise down?'

It's not noise, it's hip-hop. I don't verbally reply. I just turn the music down. Anyways, lately I've been working on my posture because *Alpha Digest* suggests that keeping your back straight improves your height by at least half an inch. I think. Or something along those lines. I'm not the tallest lad in the group, and certainly not the shortest, but I know I can work it when necessary. I finally finish dressing and head downstairs to see Julia giving me that 'proud son' look on her face. *I'm not your son.*

Dad just sits there in his chair watching the TV again, presumably the sports news, which confuses me because the football transfer deadline day isn't until next month in January, so it's all just gossip and bullshit. Very inventive, Papa Bear. *Proud of you, old man.*

'Have fun out there, and look after Susie. I'm sure a lady like her is going to need some closure,' Julia says.

'OK.'

'Have you got your keys, Lukey? You sure you won't be cold without a jacket?'

'Yep, and no I don't need a jacket,' I respond, shaking my blazer pocket to the jingling sound of keys.

'I got it. You're a *man* I guess,' Julia says in a deep condescending voice. 'All right then, have fun! Don't do anything Susie wouldn't want you doing, handsome!'.

I didn't even know what that meant, but I'm going to start heading off now. Dad starts to mumble a few words, but I'm already perplexed by the icy frost by the front door, so I couldn't really care now. Good thing I'm out of that cauldron. I close up the first two buttons of my shirt and give a telepathic goodbye to our snowman with its carrot nose looking crooked, then I head down to Loughton station.

*

I fucking knew this would happen. Being the first one down here doesn't pose many benefits standing out in the cold, other than your nipples hardening, which in any case isn't a benefit. I'm standing outside Bank station now, hands in pockets, awaiting a message from Phil or Jim Turnbull telling me that they'll be here any minute. However, come to think of it, the sight of St Paul's Cathedral is a sight to behold, though, together with the ambience of the minimal traffic on the roads, the echoing cackles of men and women making their way to the clubs only to get themselves intoxicated tonight and depressed tomorrow morning. *Why am I not one of them*? This is how it should be for me. We should all be a group heading to this thing. It was like that in uni – why not now?

So here I am outside this station wondering why the hell I bothered to come all the way out here if I'm just going to be waiting out here like a plonker. My phone begins to vibrate. It's a message from Susie telling me they'll be at Bank station in about ten minutes and asking if I can meet both her and Tamera here. *Yeah. Sure. Boyfriend duties*. Fantastic, not only have the guys not been replying to me, but my girlfriend and her compadre are going to find me in the winter cold all by myself. It makes sense to head back inside the station and meet them there. It's warmer and it's a common-sense solution to a common problem I have with these people.

I don't even know why it never came to mind in the first place. While walking back into the station, I see a homeless dude, bearded with a placard saying: *Nowhere to stay or eat. Please spare some change*. I believe he truly has no place to stay, considering the glacier-like atmosphere around here tonight and the helplessness in his eyes. I reach into my blazer pocket and take out all the change I have – about two pounds fifty – and then give it to him. He has a real grateful look and says, 'Thank you so much. God bless you. Your prayers will be answered!'

'That's OK,' I say, as I walk back into the station.

I walk back towards the ticket office area, where after about fifteen minutes waiting a few other folks go past, and all of a sudden I hear some female cackling that sound way too familiar. I quickly dash outside through the exit closest to St Paul's Cathedral – oddly, my homeless friend has vanished. *Your prayers will be answered.*

The laughter I'm hearing now, though, could only come from one mouth.

'Hey, babe.' Susie arrives and greets me with a hug, diligently avoiding smearing her make-up on my Ralph Lauren shirt. She knows better. *That's my girl.* Tamera's dark, femme-fatale presence signals that she's here to supervise Susie, which is sweet, but I can tell this'll be annoying for me tonight.

'Hey,' I reply.

'How long have you been waiting?'

'Mmmmm, about ten minutes,' I lie.

'Who were you waiting for?' Tamera asks. As if it isn't in my best interests to wait for someone out in the cold. Bitch.

'Pill and Jim. Then you two. I thought we were all going to Eros together?'

'That's weird. Pill and Jimbo are walking up to the club now,' says Susie. *Jimbo? That's new.*

'Really?' I say. 'I was never told about it. Probably bad network.'

'Probably.'

'At least you have us as company, right?' Susie gestures to Tamera, who tries to force a smile, a quiet *'Please don't force me into this'* type of smile. I can smell the Martini lemonade under Susie's breath – a subtle reminder of Marbella. That trip changed us all in different ways.

'You look smart tonight,' Tamera says sluggishly. Perhaps rum was influencing her chain of thought there, but, nevertheless, *thank you.*

'We warmed ourselves up to bashment earlier,' Susie says, her low-cut dress just asking for uninvited attention.

'Really? Who were you listening to?' I ask.

'Ludacris, some Nelly, just some old CDs I found while moving my stuff back home.' Tamera pulls out a cigarette, grinning, passes one over to Susie, both of them totally oblivious of the biting cold out here.

'That's not bashment,' I say.

'What?' she mumbles, while she struggles to put the lighter to her cigarette, hands shaking, finally noticing the cold now.

'Never mind.'

The silver lining from this is that I'm the one coming into the club with two girls. No issues from the bouncer, that's for sure.

It takes us roughly ten minutes for us to walk to Eros. There are a couple of honks and whistles from bright Lamborghinis, Aston Martins, Bugattis, Ferraris – presumably from Arab sheiks and European aristocrats vying to get these girls' attention. I look over to Tamera, expecting that she would've liked this type of attention, but no. She walks on with us, stoically. Nights like these make me bloody glad I'm not a woman. All these unattractive uber-wealthy men doing whatever they can for female attention is a preposterous sight to see.

From what I remember the last time I went to this club, Eros has two floors: ground floor for the commercial noise pollution – all the latest claptrap from the despondent recesses of MTV and VH1 – and the first floor for the more urban scene, hip-hop, house and dancehall. In that order.

As we approach the establishment, there's no trouble from the bouncers, as expected, and the club looks to already be in full swing. Bottles of sparkling champagne are everywhere and there's a crowd at the bar. As much as I'd love to be upstairs, we are already surrounded by an array of birthday balloons, fake smoke … and here he is, the birthday boy himself. With the darkness of the club being lit up by flashing green, blue and pink lights, I can just about work out what Halloween costume our mate Phillip has decided to grace us with. A cream blazer, a smart black shirt, cream chinos with loafers. Not bad at all, Pill. *You win this round.* He comes over to us, a bottle of Moët & Chandon in his hand, and greets the girls. Eros couldn't have asked for a cheesier smile for their webpage. Both Susie and Tamera head over to a table that I hope is Pill's.

'Here he is, Essex's next top model,' Pill says.

'Cheers, mate. Happy birthday,' I say.

'Cheers, what you drinking?'

'The usual, Phillip. Where's Jimmy?'

'He's over by the bar with Lance and all his mates.'

'But he can just come over to the table, we got more than enough right?' I say.

'Doesn't matter, mate, we're here. Susie looks great tonight, though. Better keep an eye her. Saying that, I got plenty to choose from in here already. Keep an eye out for Susie though. You don't want her wandering off again like last time,' says Pill.

'What!' I scream out, raising my voice away from the noise vying to know what the hell he meant by Susie wandering off again, but he's in too much of a birthday mood, smiling pathetically at every girl that walks past. It's his night, and he's acutely aware of it. He then looks at me, remembering that I still exist, and I say, 'Ha, Susie's cool, mate. She's with her mate, I'm with mine, let's fucking get to it, son!' I raise my voice a little louder because the music livens up a bit more.

After nodding incessantly to various tracks, I drift towards our table and see Tamera's already occupying herself with vodka and lemonade. She doesn't waste time. Pill is over by the bar with Jimmy. I figure there's no point going over to see him if he can't be bothered to tell me that he's here. That's what he gets for keeping me waiting like a prick at Bank station.

'Hey you!'

I look over and notice Tamera's actually trying to commence a conversation with me.

'Susie went off to the loo,' she says.

'OK. You all right?' I ask rhetorically; her eyes are already intoxicated with fatigue and alcohol. Tamera was never the one for late nights and loud noise as much as Susie and Sarah were.

'Yeah, music's not bad in here tonight. I was expecting some cheesy off the chart shit,' she says.

'It is,' I say. She does that cute suggestive smile that she does, her teeth expertly arranged to showcase a damaged innocence.

'You look good tonight, Lukey. Pill should be glad we all came out for him.'

'Yup, he's a happy lad, he is.' *Susie come and save me. Please stop talking to me, woman.* She does that smile again. Twice in one go. That's rare from her.

'Goodness only knows how much this table cost. Did you chip in for it?'

'Yeah, Jim and I split the cost, but I don't remember all these drinks being part of the bill though.'

'Why do you hang out with these people, Luke? They clearly don't appreciate you. I don't remember Jimmy doing any of this for *your* birthday.' She's kinda right. I say *kinda* because she shouldn't be talking to me, and she knows precisely why.

'Susie and I went out for a meal on my birthday and I was happy enough with that.'

'I'm sure you were.' I try my best to distract myself with the music playing, but she keeps going. 'Susie doesn't know what she's got. You're one of the good boys.'

'Why are you saying all this stuff?'

'I … I don't know. I guess there's no point in me holding anything back anymore.' She says this holding my lap, her face coming in a little closer than it should. I've only had a couple of sips of rum and Coke and I don't know whether that's making me feel woozy right now. I subtly remove her hand from my lap. *It's for her own good.* 'Aren't you still together with Louis … isn't he supposed to be here?' I ask, desperately trying to defuse the situation.

'I broke up with that prick last month, Luke. Didn't Susie tell you?'

'What an arsehole. No, she never told me. I never liked that guy anyway.'

She laughs slightly, me thinking of a way, any way, of politely walking away from this conversation. How Tamera found the confidence to sit on her own and say all this bullshit to me, I don't know.

Susie suddenly appears at the table, her red dress standing out from the crowd, that fruity smell that she takes pride in giving me no indication of any deception or manipulation, only the embodiment of a young woman who's hungry for a good night. She looks deep into my eyes, caring and compassionate, ocean-blue. I can still make out the blue even in the darkness of the club.

'Jimmy's asking about you, Lukey. You're not angry he didn't meet you at the station, are you?'

'What? No, course not. I'm happier that you made it out tonight.' She holds my face then kisses me, her soft luscious lips touching mine, eventually then her tongue wrestling with mine, a slight taste of vodka. Even though I can't see it, I can *feel* Tamera's gaze upon us. That's my Susie, always picking the right moment to say the right thing, like it was all choreographed and staged. It's as if Tamera's earlier inquisition has been made obsolete.

'There's a hotel down the road from here if you like?' Jimmy's raised voice makes itself known to us at the table. I couldn't help but sense some bitterness.

'We're just enjoying the party, Jimbo,' Susie says. *Jimbo* again. *Where the hell did 'Jimbo' come from*?

'All right, mate. I thought you hated Lance?' I ask.

'Nah, he's all right, mate. His dad's thinking of buying into Cliveden Place.' Keeping your enemies close. Smart move. *Fucking Jimbo*.

'Where's Tamera?'

'Probably out on the floor somewhere,' Susie says defensively, like she's protecting her mate from him.

'Oooh, I feel sorry for any of the fellas out here tonight then.'

'Why does everyone say that?' Susie asks, sounding like a child whose mother just took their teddy bear.

'Seeing her earlier, she looks like she's begging for a new boyfriend and a shag. Spoilt bitch.' Jimmy smiles in my direction, as if expecting me to join in his warped idea of a joke. Usually I would join in, but I simply can't right now.

Susie walks off in disgust. If she has a problem with something, it's the whole world's job to fix it. As I motion to go after her, Jimmy stops me, hand on my chest. I see Birthday Boy Pill dancing extravagantly in the background and then he disappears into the crowd again.

'Don't bother, mate. I don't get why she's emotional. You're wasting time with her anyway, believe me.' *Why*? *What has she done*?

Jimmy is dispassionate and what he said was unnecessary, his abhorrent behaviour once again reminding me that, in his world, some people are dispensable – even if it is your best mate's girlfriend. I try to keep my eye on her within the lights and smoke, her and her dress dissolving in and out into the crowd. 'They all seem nice in the beginning, don't they?' he says. I walk away from him and once again catch Pill giving his best shot at dancing, otherwise known as 'shuffling', to house music – every indication for me to leave anyway.

I head outside Club Eros towards the smoking section, expecting to see both Tamera and Susie out here, but they're nowhere to be found, just the icy breeze welcoming me again. I check the nearest bus stop, nearly slipping on ice, with the noise of the club now faint and in the background. I call Susie on her phone. Then Tamera. No answer. Tamera calls back.

'Hey, where are ya?' I ask.

'In a cab going back home.'

'Susie's not picking up her phone.'

'She's … she's had a tough time recently, Luke. We'll talk soon, OK?'

'Wait—'

She hangs up, leaving me in suspense. Everything seemed to be working OK up until then. I call up the nearest cab office, falsely hoping the ride home can drive out my loneliness.

The London metropolis has a multitude of stories. Some are happy, mostly sad, but few can possibly have as much elusiveness as my current predicament. Jimmy's venomous words and Pill's obtuse dull-wittedness contrasts with the beauty this city's architecture. Top that with the current solemn innocence of the winter snow, and you see true beauty even at this time of night.

7

In the past, Drax was used as a disciplinary programme for troubled teens to put them in their place, an anaesthetic to their hormonal primal rage, but in many ways this was, of course, not the case. This was a programme where young men and women found 'healthy' outlets to vent their social frustrations. Orphans, runaways, the abandoned, and especially the 'indigo' children, are grouped together to help express themselves fully, depending on their natural talents and inclinations. Young Frank's natural interest was criminology, so after that fateful day in college where he first met McIntlock, his parents concluded it was best they weren't involved in his life anymore. This at first seemed harsh and cold but turned out to be a blessing in disguise – anything for Frank to get away from his already elusive father and mother.

Drax's origins, sketchy as it may be, goes as far back as the nineteenth century, shortly after the end of the transatlantic slave trade. Rumours speculated that it was an escaped runaway slave that had started the organisation somehow, firstly committing to community service for members of the public and then to eventually working to solve crimes and injustice in London for other former slaves as well as solving murders, including the Whitechapel Ripper. It then established itself as a shadow intelligence/counterterrorism agency, thus creating an effective spy network, even playing a hand in exposing Hitler's propaganda campaign and providing field support to soldiers during World War II.

In contemporary times, offices were set up in Whitehall, Westminster, now currently backed and funded by a variety of shadow investors, including the Ministry of Defence. However, after the tragedy of the July 7th terrorist attack, a more insidious approach needed to be taken. Superiors at Drax felt it would be an effective strategy to have Drax operatives used as sleeper agents for whenever a potential threat endangered Britain. This would prove useful for its agents as some would be able to work in its headquarters for intelligence gathering while others would be able to live normal lives until their services were required.

'Liberate the minds of men and ultimately you'll liberate the bodies of men,' McIntlock said once to young Frank, while he was still under his training and guidance.

'Who said that?' Frank asked.

'I just said that.'

'No you didn't. I meant, who did you quote that from?'

'What makes you think that, Frank?'

'You're a smart man, Mr McIntlock. You say the right things to the right people to get what you want. You even used that quote to convince me to leave my parents for a while, so a quote like that obviously sounds like it's worked before.'

McIntlock smiled wryly.

'It's the whole Drax philosophy for both men and women, creed and colour, but, OK, you got me, young man. Now, where did I get that quote from?'

'Marcus Garvey. Easy. Edgar Hoover was obsessed with locking him and John Dillinger up; I came across that quote plenty of times. I don't believe Hoover would've been able to catch Dillinger without finding the resolve to sabotage someone like Garvey first. Plus, I know Drax had strong connections with Garvey too.'

'Very impressive.'

'Thanks, sir.'

After multiple counselling sessions, young Frank eventually didn't feel any need to take the Ritalin medicine anymore; he was just highly focused on becoming a crime detective like Melvin Purvis, or even someone fictional like Sherlock Homes. So much so that shaky time didn't seem to exist anymore. He even met his first love Leanne in the programme. Her quiet, gentle nature proved to be a calm enough stimulus for him. Falling in love with both Leanne and his upcoming career was enough happiness for him.

8

Nights like these make me question why I drink alcohol at all. I do indeed feel drowsy and sleepy after Club Eros but it certainly hasn't helped me obtain any peaceful slumber. Rum and Coke do that to you. While lying on my bed, as hard as it is for me to resist picking up my phone to check any notifications from Susie, Tamera and hopefully not Pill, I once again begin to reminisce about our time in Marbella. My mind tends to switch off whenever I start to think about what happened in the summer, and lord knows I need some sleep if I'm going to establish some ground with Susie later on. So here it goes.

THAT Holiday in the Summer

Despite the prank we played on poor old Phillip, the rest of the holiday relied on alcohol consumption and the last time I would ever condone any form of illegal narcotics. It was our third night in this paradise, and Jim came into the penthouse suite in his usual laddish manner. Phil was still in the hospital after his 'accident', so it's only Jim and me there. *The original dynamic duo.*

Susie and the girls were getting their nails done at their spa so we thought we might as well let them have their fun. Jimmy's missus at the time was former Miss England Olivia May, so having her around the hotel certainly kept me on my toes. I was just so bloody glad Phil wasn't there.

'If Phillip was here, do you think he'd be able to get it up around these girls?' I asked quietly, making sure Olivia wasn't around when I said this. She wasn't. *Phew.*

'What would be the point? He'd be shooting blanks anyway,' Jimmy said, both of us sharing a collective snigger.

'What the hell was Pill thinking?' I asked.

'Who's Pill?'

'Phil, I mean.'

'No, that's a good one. Just call him that for bants – see how he takes it,' Jim suggested.

'Ha ha, OK then, let's see how that sounds to him.'

'Fuck it, just call him Pill from now on.' And this is how Phillip was named Pill in the end. No permission. No questions asked.

I was in a pretty fresh mood after spending the night with Susie, so I was up for whatever adventure the day had in store for us. I wanted to go on quad bikes, maybe even go snorkelling, but instead Jim wanted to stay with Olivia and go snorkelling with her, which meant I would be the third wheel. Well, not in this lifetime, so I then decided it was just the girls and me.

The day was pretty lazy, with Sarah being the last one to get ready after the spa, which was irritating because she was usually the one to wake up first among the three of them. All of that waiting around in the girls' hotel lobby consisted of Susie repeatedly telling me to be patient, greeted with a tired irritated smile from me. I guess I slightly wished Pill were there? No. Never that.

'I'm happy you're here, Lukey,' Susie said to me before we jetted off.

'I am too, Suus,' I lied. Lying became a habit after this holiday, with obvious signs that this whole trip wasn't going to go well, but we were there, the sun was out and that was all that mattered back then. There was, however, an unnecessary rift between Tamera and Sarah. Some bullshit about bra sizes and a rumour about Tamera having a boob job, I think. In my opinion, I thought Tamera looked after herself the best out of all three of the girls, but hey, I know better than to get in the middle of a heated female conversation. Having a male presence among them, I think, made the girls a little more self-conscious. A guy like me being around them represented the threat of humiliation and judgement on my part, especially if they made a slip of the tongue.

The best part of being with them that day in particular though was the beach. I had several beach lads giving me a thumbs-up. I couldn't help but wonder whether they were giving me a nod to my ego because they thought I was some sort of pimp or whether I was a gay best friend – *more than likely a gay best friend*.

I headed down to the beach bar, which was very reminiscent of that Tom Cruise movie *Cocktail*. In fact, so reminiscent that I believe that this bar was intended to be some sort of throwback to the eighties in some way. I ordered two pina colada cocktails (Sarah and Tamera), One Malibu and lemonade (Susie), and of course a JD and Coke for me. *Man drink*. Susie came over, all relaxed, joyous and free because she's in the comfort of her friends and lover.

'What was up with Tamera earlier?' I asked.

'She's a little lairy about Sarah.'

'Why's that?' I asked smugly.

Susie laughed to herself, understanding full well how pathetic the argument was. 'Aww, that's sweet, Lukey.'

I always thought Tamera had a great figure, all three of them did actually, but Tamera was more of a doer than any of the other girls. She was the kind of girl who would take her diets and her workouts seriously. Why she couldn't maintain a relationship with Louis is a mystery to me. No wonder it was only an on and off thing – he's an ugly vain bastard anyway. Sarah and Susie, on the other hand, were the type of women who would be naturally hated by everyone – both natural textbook mainstream California cheerleader beauties – blonde with perfect smiles.

'I'm really glad we've spent time together,' Susie said, clearly enjoying her drink. Everything always seems to taste better when it's free. As I held her by her waist, I picked up the rest of the drinks and Susie called the other girls over, clearly happy about having the safety blanket of her boyfriend for the day. *He's my man.* Where's *yours*?

'Thanks, Lukey,' Sarah said, panting, catching her breath from swimming, water still dripping from her hair. Tamera smiled, quietly sipping her drink, telepathically thanking me with a wink.

'Who's up for tonight then?' Sarah said, always smiling, always up for a good time. Bless her.

'Club Nino's. Jim's sorted us out with a table over there.'

'What about Phil?' Sarah asked. I caught Susie wince slightly at Sarah's question. She's the only one I told about the whole Pill incident. I found myself smirking before I replied to Sarah. 'Err, he's a little busy tonight. Sorting things out with Maria,' I said in a poor attempt to excuse poor Phil.

'I thought they broke up?' Tamera asked in an investigative tone, her piercing gaze seeing through my deception straight away.

'It's complicated.' *Great answer, Luke.* Sarah finished her pina colada through her straw like a kid eager to finish their drink at a McDonalds before playing with her happy meal toy.

'I never liked her anyway. She tried making a move on Declan back at campus. Do you remember that, Tam?' Sarah asked.

'Yeah, she thought she could play the sweet girl. All because … you know Phil couldn't finish apparently,' Tamera said quietly, and in came an awkward silence over all four of us. I didn't even realise how hot the temperature was on this island, the double whisky already doing a number on me a little bit. Me, Sarah and Susie started laughing right on cue, like it was choreographed. The humour of this wasn't the fact that Pill couldn't finish, we all knew that, but the tone of Tamera's statement – whispering those last few words. It was unnecessary and ignorant to say that, but coming out of her mouth, it wasn't surprising.

'You can't fault him for trying, can you?' I said in Pill's defence, though slightly amused and pleased that they could see how much of a lowlife he is.

'Yeah, but he's the same age as us, right? You aren't supposed to have problems with your dick until later, right?' Tamera continued.

'Right, I want to head to the sea quickly, before we head to Nino's. You both know what you're wearing?' Susie said.

'Course, babe,' Sarah replied.

'Sure thing, Suus,' Tamera said.

As if the conversation was getting too vulgar for her liking, Susie gave me a quick kiss and I noticed a whiff of lemonade on her breath. All three of them made for the beach, making the most of their bikini bodies before the light dresses and high heels appeared later, and Susie, as always, re-affirmed herself as the queen bee.

Even when the sun set that day in Marbella, the sheer humidity reminded me of where I was. This was in no way a complaint about the weather, but it seemed as if the sun was draining to an extent that some of us were getting a little tired of pretending, you know, about that mask you put on as to who you think you should be. For the rest of that day I just wanted to be lazy and simply chill, but the thought of making an effort to head out to Nino's back then felt more of a chore than anything else.

Sadly, that day reminded me of where I was with these people, the wolves in sheep's clothing, the ugly dark side that's usually repressed when you're with other people. Ironically, I found out in the end that following what everyone else does force you to be just that. *You are who you really are when no one's watching.*

Club Nino was the club that we'd been hotly anticipating ever since we'd landed, but before we did all of that we also wanted to cover all the holiday essentials on the list: swimming, snorkelling, jet-skiing, visiting the water park, the list went on, but somehow getting wasted at a nightclub was one of the priorities.

You're probably still wondering why I don't like Tamera. Hang tight, folks, you'll find out soon enough. Back at the penthouse suite it was just the jukebox and me having LL Cool J's *Mama Said Knock You Out* at full blast on repeat.

The girls were all getting ready for the night in the hotel next to us. They usually take their time for things like this. Sarah was no doubt pretending to get her freak-a-leek on, using those pole dancing lessons to good effect – just subtle entertainment for Susie and Tamera.

It was only me in the penthouse suite for now, so I took a quick shower and slapped my favourite cocoa butter on while the bass was bumping in the background. I found myself jumping into my bedroom, Afro hairbrush in hand, miming the lyrics. The energy and innocent aggression of this song was something to behold. I pressed the skip button to hear '*Appetite 4 Destruction*' by N.W.A.

By now I had my outfit all ready: white Ralph Lauren long-sleeve shirt, brown Abercrombie three-quarter-length shorts and Timberland boat shoes. Outfit done. While I nodded my head violently to the music, all of a sudden I heard female laughter followed by a male voice. It could only be Jimmy and Olivia. I quickly lowered the volume all the way to zero, knowing they wouldn't want to listen to this 'music'. So I quickly put my Abercrombie shorts on and checked out my hair in the bathroom mirror to show Olivia that I was more than just a third wheel there, which was stupid because I had my own girlfriend, but, of course, not a girlfriend who'd been in a beauty competition. Yet.

'You all right, mate. Bloody hell, how many sit-ups did you just do?' Jimmy said with a wry grin on his face. Yup, he was jealous.

'None, just getting ready for Nino's. Oh, hey, Olivia.'

'Hi, you getting into that pre-rave mood then, are you?' she said while quickly glancing at my abdominals.

'Oh yes, it's the only way to warm up really.'

'Phil sends his regards.'

'It's Pill, remember?'

'Oh yeah,' Jim said.

'Who's Pill?' Olivia asked, as if she was itching to get into the inner circle with us.

'It's the guy we just met, but it's a personal joke anyway, Liv,' Jim said, smiling.

'How's he doing?' I asked.

'He should be out by tomorrow. Doctors say the swelling should be gone by the afternoon.'

I expected Olivia to pull a face of disgust but she was busy staring at her phone, then she walked over to the lounge. *Help yourself, why don't you.*

'That's good. Thank fuck for insurance.'

'He looked well comfy, busy watching telly while the nurse keeps checking his dick. I bet he's itching for a wank.'

Nice. I guess I was supposed to be disappointed in Jimmy spending his time and effort in seeing Pill that day. In actual fact I didn't really give a shit. We were going to destroy Club Nino's and announce our arrival to Marbella.

Olivia was already fully dressed and raring to go. Her loose-fitting white crop top complemented her bronze-tanned skin. Miss England indeed. Jimmy, who clearly took a page out of my book, changed into a white Ralph Lauren T-shirt, skinny brown chinos and a pink blazer with loafers, which shut me down in every department except footwear, because I HATE loafers. The girls were meeting us by the strip, and since it was taking Jimmy too bloody long to get ready, I asked Susie to find the best place for pre drinks.

Even though the girls were meeting me, Jimmy and Olivia, I didn't want to keep them waiting – especially Susie, as I also hate being late. However, the time it was taking Jim that night, who was already fully dressed and ready a half-hour before, was infuriating. My impatience made me go to Jimmy's room to find him with some small plastic bags, several of them with white powder in them.

'You ready?' he asked, sniffing in whatever he had on him.

'Yeah, what's that?' I asked. Jimmy put something in his blazer breast pocket.

'I was gonna show you later on. It's this new thing called Kraken. Makes you go fucking mental, mate.' Jimmy said in animated fashion.

'Kraken? Isn't that in a movie or something?' I asked.

'Yeah, some sea monster, I think. I don't know. Listen, me and Liv are gonna have some when we go for pre drinks. Care to join?'

'I don't—'

'Jiiiiiim, taxi's here!' Olivia shouted out.

Jim sported a really devilish grin. This was a look I hadn't seen in a while, like he was ready to commit mass murder and enjoy every second of it.

'You didn't give any to Pill, did you?' Totally ignoring Olivia's call, I felt my eyebrows arch when I asked this. Jim simply smiled and walked out of the room, a strong smell of Château de Fleur Masculin whisking away from his bedroom.

Jim was always capable of doing crazy things. Things that you could look back on and perhaps laugh at. Yeah, stink bombs in lecture rooms, usually on coursework deadline days, giving him an excuse to do something nasty as a kind of twisted revenge of some sort, but, you know, harmless. In fact, if I remember correctly, pretty much every problem that he went through – not revising enough or completing the essay on time – he somehow got over it. Which led me to the assumption that his dad probably played a hand in him graduating somehow. I even remember the fire alarm going off three times during our last exam period before graduation. Coincidence? From that moment in the apartment, I knew something was up. I should've seen it coming.

We decided to meet the girls at the strip, a long line of bars and nightclubs. The repeated head-banging disturbance on the strip left you with an anticipation of what was in store for you in the club.

When we approached Homer's Tavern for pre drinks, I found myself to be the first to leave the cab, walking at a faster pace than usual. I'd never been late to see Susie. Never. I didn't intend to start now, plus, seeing what I saw in the apartment froze me a little.

'Your missus will be fine, Lukey,' Jimmy said.

'Awww, let him go, Jim.' Olivia joined in with the condescension. An uncommon rage then befell me. *I want to fit in but they don't understand me.* I slowed down as I drew closer to the bar as I assumed Susie would be pissed off with me anyway. There had been countless times where I'd had to wait for her, so I guessed she could wait.

I turned around to find Jimmy dancing to the background noise, clearly warming himself up for Club Nino's, his hair flopping as he did so. Had the effects of that Kraken stuff already taken effect? Olivia watched in slight bemusement, but once again, instead of looking disgusted and complacent, as she probably should, she just smiled and then continued to stare at her phone, like she was supposed to indulge all of this – the good weather and energy of the night clearly not good enough for her.

As I walked up and approached Homer's Tavern, I just about spotted good ol' Sarah giving her seventies disco moves a shot while ABBA's *'Dancing Queen'* was playing. Susie and Tamera were looking like two parents being astounded by their child.

'Hey, Lukey, Oi Oi,' shouted Sarah.

Susie and Tamera greeted me with pleasantries, with me hoping that Susie didn't notice my tardiness – she had a wry smile on her face, which might have been because of my tardiness or of the sight of Olivia a couple of paces behind me, so that was cool.

'Aww, you're wearing my favourite shirt, babe.'

'Thanks, Sue. Remember, I picked it out myself?' I found myself clearing my throat, as if challenging her opinion was a cardinal sin.

'Did I get that for your birthday?'

'No, I got it myself through those Christmas vouchers you got me, remember?'

'It's a nice shirt anyway. What did I get you for your birthday?' *Fuck all.* I looked across to Tamera who was looking in my direction.

'Hey, Tam, aren't you gonna join the dancing queen over there?' I asked. Tamera was still looking in my direction, but I didn't think she heard what I asked her, so I guessed that counted as me drawing a blank with her. Why was Jimmy taking so long to get to us?

'Heeey, here we are, how you doing?' Jim said with his arms out.

'Heeey!' all three of the girls said in unison – Sarah catching her breath from her disco endeavours.

'Let's get some drinks in then … the usual?' Without an answer, Jimmy headed over to the bar without the courtesy of introducing Olivia to the group.

Liv greeted the girls reluctantly, like they were in her way. I could already tell Susie couldn't stand her. She had that fake look of hers: big wide smile, lips together, like it's all *forced* from her. A person with a perfect smile like Susie would always want to show it off, so why shouldn't she? Yup, she never liked Olivia at all.

'Drink up, guys,' Jimmy said, while bringing over a fish bowl that was coloured yellow and pink. What fabricated concoction is this? 'Sex on the beach, vodka, rum, blah, blah …' The rest of what he said was a blur to me. Mixing drinks on a night out is always a risky business.

After everyone had their share of alcohol in their system, we all went back to our mutual groups. Jimmy and Olivia started talking on the side while looking at their smartphones – unconscious arousal I liked to call it – while Sarah, Tamera and Susie started chatting away admiring each other's tanned bodies, and rightly so, they looked great. It's funny, though, looking at people who tan, sometimes I think some folk just wish they were simply brown with the amount of time and money they spend at tanning salons. Not like I need one anytime soon – *The gift of melanin.*

Anyway, there's me, the middle man, and my girlfriend's on one side and my best friend's on the other. While we drink and allow the alcohol to insidiously demean and cloud our judgement for the next couple of hours, I know I'll get fully heckled by Jim later, but I go over to Susie anyway. *Boyfriend duties.*

'How's Pill?' Tamera asked, giving me the assumption that Susie had told the rest about Pill's demise. Just as I was about to respond, Jimmy steps in and stops whatever conversation he had with Olivia to reply as if he's his PR officer.

'He'll be back on his feet tomorrow. May his cock rest in peace.'

'Amen,' I say. We all laugh and raise our glasses to dear old Phillip. The only thing missing was a twenty-one gun salute, but not to worry. Club Nino was ours for the taking.

Susie couldn't have looked any hotter than she did that night in a red maxi dress that complemented that slender figure of hers. For some odd reason her sandy hair smelled more fruity than it usually did. Two lads and four girls.

Club Nino was packed from front to back. We had our own VIP table with champagne, whisky, vodka – you name it, we had it. Some vodka shots and drunk kisses later, I decided to catch my breath a little. It was about 3am and the club was still busy, like everyone had a piece of Jimmy's Kraken. I was on my lonesome at the table before Tamera came over to me, her brunette hair and hazel eyes morphing under different neon lights every few seconds. She mumbled a few words, which I couldn't really understand, so I asked her to feel my biceps for few seconds and then she maniacally started laughing. *Why?* Even now I don't know why.

Sadly, rum hits me hard. The mix of Coke in this drink didn't really do its job effectively, so I pulled a sour face in response to the beverage entering my system. The night itself epitomised what nightclubs back home didn't have. The beach was only a little way away – no doubt already suffering its fair share of British tourist vandalism.

This fateful night, though, Club Nino's was in full flow. Even though I was still in shock over the Tamera's laughter, the DJ of the night certainly knew how to fuse the old-school with the new-school tracks. At that point I was glad I was at least sober enough to realise that old-school garage and funky house always found a way to suit everyone's taste.

After roughly an hour of dancing and shuffling, I needed a breather. I went over to our table again to find Susie looking melancholy. Despite the neo-noir atmospheric lighting of the place, as I approached her, she couldn't have looked any more like a distraught damsel, a beacon of loneliness and despair. At the time her father wasn't present much, and what I saw that night was a little girl who just needed some attention.

'You all right?' I asked, my arm already around her.

'Have you seen Sarah?' she asked.

'I thought she was by the bar?'

'Yeah, I thought she was too.'

'Look, I'm really glad we're all out here, having fun. We've all graduated now. I was thinking we should do this again next year. Just the two of us. Less distractions.'

'Yeah, that's nice, Lukey.' She looked over to the crowd like she was in a trance, almost possessed. I thought she might've been looking for Tamera.

'Luke, we need to look for Sarah. I think I made a big mistake. Y-you know what she's like. I think I saw her with Jim.'

'Yeah, she could be anywhere.'

Sarah was always very much a wanderer. Typically, every student night out, we went back to our campus on a mission to look for Sarah. It ended up becoming routine. This time, it was a little different. We were in a (not so) foreign land, with an open space, an ocean, where pretty much anyone can get lost. We had to find our Sarah, and fast. Olivia and Jimmy were nowhere to be found either, but Susie and I couldn't have cared less about them at that moment in time.

Tamera eventually joined us when we headed out of Nino's. The worried look on her face told me she knew the drill and she was already privy about the situation.

'She might be out on the beach. Remember, she kept banging on about making snow angels in the sand the next time we were out here,' Tamera said, looking like she'd had more than enough fun – her mascara was slowly running down her cheeks. She looked oddly attractive that way actually.

'How the hell can you make snow angels in the sand?' I asked.

'It's true. For fuck's sake, why does she always do this!' Susie ran her hand along her forehead like a worried mother. 'I should've kept an eye on her.'

'Don't blame yourself Su—'

'Ahh, fuck off, Luke. You wouldn't have come if Jim weren't here.'

'What the hell, I'm trying to help.'

'Just stop helping then.' The dagger hit hard. It was a low blow from her. As we were walking across the strip, I felt an unsuspecting hand around my back – warm, slim and soft too. It was Tamera. I was tempted to repay the favour, but it was stupid because I didn't have any feelings for her, which was odd.

The cold, haunting atmosphere of the situation overcame the warm humidity that engulfed us that night outside the club. Sarah's venom towards me hadn't been called for and, to be honest, I didn't really want to be there anymore.

'She may have decided to go back to that bar we were in. Maybe she forgot something there,' I suggested, and without further ado we walked back past Club Nino. Finally, someone among the three of us had something worthwhile to say until ...

'Where's Phillip?' Susie asked suddenly.

'In hospital. I told you.'

'OK, well, where's Jimmy and that Liv girl?'

'Why do you want to know where they are?'

'Because they should be here with us looking for Sarah.' Do you see what I mean about Susie? Tamera continued walking silently, not filling the ambivalent air with stupid questions. I could still tell she was worried though, like the rest of us.

We'd walked roughly a mile away from Club Nino's when we saw the blue lights flashing. If my Spanish served me correctly (which it did), I saw an ambulance that had Médecins Sans Frontières', which meant Doctors Without Borders, which was odd because those are the type of vans you see when some freak accident happens to someone or something. You usually hear stories about backpackers going missing or being incarcerated for some ignorant shit on holiday, but tonight it was something so frightening it would haunt us all. As we were slowly approaching the lights, with every step we made we got more and more worried about what we were going to find. I decided to push on ahead of the girls, walking a little faster, thinking that I might as well find out first what was about to affect us all.

Initially, all I saw was a strand of blonde hair. A male paramedic with a thick Spanish accent, but who's English was good enough to understand, put a hand out asking me to stop.

'Excuse me, sir, do you know this woman?'

I was in shock. Sarah's virtuous eyes were wide open. She was a guiltless girl, always carefree, always bouncing, making the most out of life, and here she was lifeless. Gone. Dead. I felt tears trickling down my cheeks before I could answer the question. I think my crying gave the paramedic the answer he needed.

'W-what happened?!' I asked.

'I've spoken to the policeman over there – he's investigating – but it looks like a drug overdose, we—'

Before the paramedic could finish his sentence, a massive screech enveloped the whole crime scene, inviting more bar hoppers and general pedestrians over to the scene.

Susie's panic and sadness was too much for any of us to bear. From that point on, it all happened too fast, and looking back now, it was a blur – the commiserations and then the eventual questions:

'Why did Sarah always have a reason to drift off on nights out?'

'Did any of you know that she was sensitive to bright lights?'

'It's extremely dangerous for an attractive young woman to be walking out in the dark by herself. Do any of you know if she was supposed to be meeting someone else?'

None of us were able to give any definitive answers, but surely they must have expected that. I guess none of us knew Sarah as much as we thought. Tamera was distraught, her silent, hushed sense of self crushed by this scene, but it hurt Susie the most. I wanted to go with her to the police, along with the body. Boyfriend duties or not, it was the correct thing to do.

'Someone has to tell her dad, Lukey. Just look after Tamera,' Susie said.

As much as we all wanted to go, the authorities emphasised that only one of us was allowed to go to the hospital, which didn't seem fair at the time, but looking back now, I can imagine the hospital having a whole plethora of people at that time of night – alcohol poisoning and whatnot.

Before we knew it, all the vans were gone and the small crowd had dispersed into the night. It was just Tamera and me left, two lone survivors from the battlefield. Pill was gone, Jimmy and Olivia had disappeared, Susie departed, and the only other true kindred spirit to us all was deceased. I looked at Tamera and the mascara was running down her face. I embraced her, foolishly hoping my hug would stop the tears from coming.

'I'm so sorry. It's not your fault. We should go back,' I said. Tamera nodded, her arms holding me tighter. It made sense instead of allowing her to go back by herself. Both of us needed closure and company. In the cab back to the villa we embraced each other a little more closely, and before I knew it my lips touched hers. Jimmy still wasn't around, which was a relief to both of us I think. Tamera had come out of a bad relationship and I was still pissed off at Susie, but either way we all tragically lost a mutual friend that night.

I always thought Tamera was cold-blooded, an ice queen, but her skin was soft and warm. I even smelled that Château de Fleur Feminine scent. My favourite.

When we got back to the hotel I lay on the bed first, glad that it was soothing, inviting, perfect for the both of us. I pulled Tamera over to me and we made out. She took her clothes off the slow and more difficult way, the way you always see in the movies. We were two hurt, damaged people fornicating on holiday in Marbella; it was only the next morning that we realised what we had actually done.

*

The morning sun woke me up to a text message from Jimmy telling me he'd heard what had happened and that he was on his way. Even though I'd established myself that day as a cheat, a dog, a Casanova, a rake – whatever you want to call it – I couldn't afford anyone else having knowledge of my transgression, especially Jimmy. As beautiful and peaceful as Tamera looked while she was sleeping, she couldn't be here much longer, but she was only half-asleep.

'Rise and shine, Jim's on his way.'

'Ahh, shit,' she spewed out.

It was difficult to disturb a sleeping beauty from her slumber, but for both our sakes I had to. Tamera got up wearily, fully naked, understanding the critical nature of the situation. She'd be seen as a slut, promiscuous, a whore, and I'll just be the player, the lad who got what he wanted while on holiday. It's the labels that will be the consequences, our punishment. Morbid to say the least.

Outside, we embraced each other one last time before she skipped over to her hotel. *When we get back home, let's talk.*

I turned to see Jimmy already watching from a distance. How long had he been standing there? Instead of a cheeky 'I know what you did last night' look, all I saw was an emotionless face, his clothes from the night before creased and out of place. He looked suspiciously guilty.

'I'm … I'm sorry about last night,' Jim said. 'They took her over to the same hospital as Phil.'

'Did you find out what killed her?' I asked.

'I don't know. I saw Susie there though. Why weren't you there? She spoke to Sarah's parents on the phone. Didn't sound pleasant … fucking … aahhh, fuck. That's what you get for not controlling yourself.'

'What are you on about?' I said, and some saliva spewed out of my mouth, construing my hatred towards Jimmy for his cowardly blaming of the victim. I looked at this excuse of a man, blaming our friend Sarah for her own death. We stood in silence briefly, the sweat already breaking out on my forehead, looking at Jimmy in disbelief. I wasn't sure at the time whether he was still in shock or surprised that I actually showed him some resistance.

'It's best we all go back home. I'm gonna have to speak to my old man, tell him what happened. It's a bloody disaster. Where were you last night anyway?' I asked as I caught Jimmy daydreaming, his eyes transfixed on my chest. Now wasn't the time to start comparing our pectorals.

'Jimmy!'

'Have a word with Tam and Susie. I'll pick up Pill at the hospital,' Jim said.

'If Susie's still at the hospital you're probably best to bring her back too.'

'Do I look like her boyfriend?' Jimmy retaliated.

'OK.'

'Liv's staying an extra couple of nights with her mates.'

'OK then. Best head inside and get something to eat,' I said. Then came that arrogant smirk of his.

'Didn't you have breakfast with Tamera?'

'What?'

'HA HA, you think I couldn't tell? That girl's been on you since you made it official with Susie.'

Even though my cover was blown, I really didn't need to hear this shit, but there was nothing I could've done about it anyway. At this point, however, I decided I might as well act dumb. If Tamera had always had a thing for me and I hadn't noticed, then it shouldn't be too hard. I eventually came to the possibility that Sarah's death could have been a ruse for her to get into bed with me? She was indeed patient, lurking in the shadows for an opportunity. Could she have? No, it couldn't be. It's because of all these questions that after that holiday I always despised and detested her presence. Even today my mind is opening up a web of riddles every time I see her – one question, one assumption, leads to another, and another.

It took a while for us all to adjust when we got back home. It doesn't take much for a woman like Susie to feel lonely, so out of genuine courtesy and empathy, but most of all guilt, I paid frequent visits to Susie's house. There wasn't much sex, just warm cuddles, hot chocolate and biscuits, just some genuine comfort that a boyfriend would give, despite the skeletons lurking in the closet. *We needed to talk*. Despite my conscience telling me that that would've been the smart thing to do with Tamera. Even a text message would have helped, but no, there was always the risk of Susie going through either of our phones and finding out, so we kept it at that. No third-party correspondence, just a mutual silence and the writing on the wall.

9

Frank woke up on his couch, stiff and groggy but oddly refreshed from the sleep. *What time did I go to bed?* The last thing he remembered was putting together the board showing the Kraken suspects, Romanenko's possible location, and the victims of the drug. Then came the odd reminiscing about his first meeting with McIntlock many years ago and his early days in the Drax programme. A lot had happened since then.

He checked his watch. It was 10am, meaning Frank had had roughly ten hours sleep. As extravagant as this sleep time was, it felt as if he was making up for the late nights he'd lost working in the office. He washed up, ate breakfast, and then decided his apartment needed a good scrub up. Time to get to work. Firstly, the documents in the living room needed to be sorted and filed appropriately, the dirty dishes by the kitchen area were crying out to be washed, and the mouldy pizza from last week needed clearing out. Even though all of this seemed tedious at best, there was a slight sense of euphoria that came with this activity – the one-bedroom apartment was finally starting to look like a decent living space.

Even though Frank had quit drinking for months now, there were still bottles of vodka and rum sitting in his kitchen cupboard and fridge. This was the difficult part. Following the ending of his relationship with Leanne, his drinking became even more excessive, simply another outlet to quell the pain of her walking away. He opened the bottles of rum and vodka and poured them down the kitchen sink, the smell filling the room with guilt and tragedy. Frank rinsed the sink and then quickly applied some bleach as if to erase the memory of his former girlfriend's tears. This apartment was all he could afford, and the only thing that was getting him going was working for the force as a covert Drax operative.

After he poured the last bottle of whisky down the sink, he stared at the investigation board. What on earth was it about this drug that drew users? Marijuana was a much more obvious choice for a temporary high. Just looking at the board gave Frank a sense of relief that he wasn't in the office or had to worry about going in for a while. His phone began buzzing in his pocket – who could be trying to contact him now? McIntlock. A missed call and a brief voicemail checking up on him – Seeing this filled Frank with a slight joy, but who else could it be? His parents had been estranged after he joined the Drax programme all those years ago.

Despite this thought, Frank now felt slightly revitalised, his mind directed towards thoughts of solving the Romanenko case, and this gave him a sense of purpose and direction. The late-night reminiscing must have reminded him of why he took the role in the first place. Frank was expecting some correspondence today from Winston, his informant.

Winston was currently an enforcer and a long-time friend of the notorious McAllister family. The McAllister's were into illegal gambling, historically loan-sharking their way to the top of the crime spectrum from the mid-eighties to the present day. Narcotics and organ trafficking was never really their forte. It was always a risky field to fall into, but not for Winston. Some months back, Frank had been keeping an eye on the McAllister family and caught Winston in possession of a stuffed fox with cocaine inside it. Frank managed to strike a deal with him, enabling a very unlikely alliance between the two men. Winston would inform Frank of McAllister's activities in exchange for his freedom.

Cocaine wasn't supposed to be as popular today as it was back in the eighties and nineties, but with Kraken as a purer alternative and growing more and more popular, Winston was almost the perfect ally to have on his side – keeping his ear out on the streets and knowing what to expect. With the two recent deaths from the Kraken drug, bringing down the McAllister's would have to be postponed for now. Besides, if Winston wanted to betray Frank, he would have done it by now.

Admiring his spring-cleaned apartment, he heard was a knocking on the door. It was very odd for someone, anyone, to be knocking on his door. Mum? Leanne?

Winston.

'Morning?' Frank said, surprised at his informant's appearance at the door.

'Morning,' replied Winston.

'How'd you know where I live?'

'Remember that night you took me in? Wow, it's bloody freezing today.'

'Come inside, mate.'

Winston came in. He was slightly taller than Frank. With his hands in his bomber jacket pockets, face red, courteously wiped the snow off of his boots on the doormat.

'Come on mate, you of all people should that *everyone* is being watched,' Winston said.

Frank felt disgusted. How could he have been so easily compromised? A gang member had entered his home and he had no recollection of anything being out of place.

'Besides, do you think I would've survived this long with Ian if I didn't show *some* bollocks? After you let me free I followed you home just to be sure, and by the looks of things you've finally done some homework,' Winston said, observing and admiring Frank's newly cleaned apartment.

'You've been into my home?'

'A couple of times, yeah. After you got me nicked, Ian got paranoid. We weren't making that much from the poker games, and guess who he thought was working with the coppers?' Winston said, gesturing to himself amusingly.

'All right, all right, I understand, it's been a hard life for you,' Frank said. Frank always had a way of saying sniping comments at people, especially criminals who extorted money for profit. Frank certainly knew how intimidating Winston could be – someone who you'd rather go to war with, never against. Frank and Winston, over the past couple of months, had got on well and formed a sort of partnership, but Frank always suspected Winston had the upper hand, a member of a crime gang knowing the location of a law enforcer's home, but Frank felt slightly relieved with the information that he had been followed, oddly enough.

'Look, I had to have a reason whether to trust you or not,' Winston said.

'I'm not really a copper, you know that?' Frank affirmed.

'You aren't the first person to say that, Franky boy.'

'Aaah, shit, where are my manners … tea?'

Winston gestured to reject Frank's offer. 'How are you getting on with our good friend Kraken?'

'Not well, mate.' Frank went over to the kitchen area and started boiling the kettle. He was never confident in having to explain himself to other people, especially to local gangsters. 'I'm still lost on this Romanenko fella. The weird thing about this is that every time I try and link the product to him, I find plenty of reasons why he wouldn't be involved. Borders are a lot tighter than before.'

'What makes you so sure that it's him? If you're desperate, there's always a way to make things happen.'

'Well, there's a reason why Romanenko would want to stay incognito,' Frank suggested, while pouring the hot water into his teacup. His morning fix sorted. Shaky time would usually give him every reason to avoid consuming any caffeine, but controlling his consumption wouldn't affect him much.

'See, that's your problem. You say you aren't a copper, but you think a lot like one, basing your theories on assumptions.'

'Well that's why you're here. I go by the information that's given to me, Winston, and if I really was a copper, you wouldn't be standing here.'

'It's been months now since I've started to rat against my best mate. If I was loyal to Ian, it wouldn't be a shock to me if you woke up on Christmas Day with your head blown off and your body in the trunk.' A subtle silence between the two men hung in the air in Frank's apartment. Frank always got a little grumpy anytime someone assumed he was in the police force. To counter that, Winston was always happy to bite back at any threat to him with authentic venom.

'Look, Frank, I'm not here to make enemies. I've done that way too many times before. You know about my situation. I want to be away from Ian. He isn't the same as he used to be, ever since his father died and started taking over the business, things have changed, Maybe you can get me on that Dra—'

'It's all right,' Frank said reassuringly. *I heard you the first time.*

'Well, anyway, there's gonna be a little set-up tonight over at some kid's house party in Chelsea. Might be a perfect opportunity to distribute more of that product out there – thought you'd like to check it out.'

Frank listened sceptically while drinking his tea. Earl Grey. His favourite.

'And how do you know all this?' Frank asked. Winston raised his eyebrow as if insulted by his question.

'OK, I see,' Frank said, noticing Winston's annoyance.

'That was pretty much what I came here for, mate. Keep your eyes open.'

'You could've used one of these things called mobile phones, you know. They've been around for quite a while now,' Frank said, raising his phone.

'I don't trust none of that shit,' Winston replied vehemently.

'Not even a disposable?'

'None. You know how important all this is to me.'

Frank knew full well how important this was to Winston. Ian McAllister was the type of man, much like his predecessor, who would use whatever was necessary to get you to do his bidding. He would demand trust, loyalty and respect as a bare minimum. If there was even the slightest suspicion of betrayal, you would disappear without a whisper, justifying Winston's necessity to cover his tracks. The underlying plan was to bring down Romanenko and then eventually gather enough dirt on McAllister. *'Help me find Kraken and I'll do what I can to help get you back to your family'* Frank had once said to Winston. If McAllister ever knew about Winston's wife and daughter then that could be used as leverage against him. Winston needed to cut his ties with the McAllisters.

'I'll let you know what happens,' said Frank, readily understanding the situation.

'Ian may have guys at the party. He's had a couple of new young bucks come through. Just don't do anything stupid, Franky boy.'

At least Winston had something to lose. His family. This made Frank slightly envious – a wife to come home to, a child that calls him daddy, something to look forward to, children play dates, changing nappies, PTA meetings and summer barbecues. But no, the reality was a one-bedroom apartment, overdue rent and solving a crime case while on leave. Frank didn't have shaky time to blame anymore. It was just him. If this was all he had, then this was all that was going for him.

He was pretty much used to being alone. Watching Winston walk out of his apartment ironically exempliefied what Frank felt everyone else did in their lives. His parents, Leanne, and even though McIntlock offered a new direction with the Drax initiative all those years back, life with a normal family wasn't a negative prospect to aspire to. Frank did have something to fight for then, something to lose, and like Winston, this was a chance to put the demons behind him.

10

After all that painful reminiscing about our trip, I wake up on this late Saturday morning on my double memory foam mattress feeling oddly solemn. I suppose revisiting my nightmare brought a silver lining of sorts. Sadly, thoughts of Club Eros churn up now. I didn't drink as much as I would've liked but it doesn't matter. I can recall last night's events at Eros with more clarity and sense than I can the Marbella horror show. Jimmy's unnecessary attitude, Pill's shitty dancing (nothing new), Tamera's mind game with me, and Susie … well, just being Susie. Just another regular night out in London, although judging by the way it ended, I expect some clarification from the girls at some point today. I sluggishly go over to my side and look at my phone and notice a message from Pill:

> **You get home all right?**
> **Thank you so much for coming xx**

No real man would ever put kisses at the end of a message. Does he think I'm some sort of retard to think that this message was for me personally? I reply back saying:

No worries, mate. It was good fun, just save your dance moves for Vegas! Ha ha ;)

Even though I can still feel the alcohol wrenching itself in my stomach, or perhaps my liver, I continue to persevere with my daily stretches. It's the only way I can ever really wake up effectively. While touching my toes to stretch my hamstrings, I hear my phone buzzing and I see Pill's reply:

Who's this?

My point exactly. It's official then, I must be a retard. An ice-cold pint of water sets everything straight and I feel a little bit more like myself. It's late morning and I assume that Tamera and Susie shared the same bed last night. I ring up Susie, and I once again receive no answer. It's concerning because she's usually awake at this time of day. I swipe my phone to Tamera's name and deliberate whether I dare contact her. Forget it. Too risky. No point raising suspicions once again.

Molly knocks and comes into my room, leisurely dressed for a Saturday, which makes me turn straight into big brother mode.

'How was last night?' she asks.

'It was all right. Pill was a happy boy. Just a usual night out really, nothing exciting.'

'Right. So what was the deal with Susie then?'

'What?' How did she know so fast? It was only a couple of hours ago.

'Friend of mine saw you at Eros last night and said some pretty blonde girl stormed off away from you. I've always liked Susie, but I've never understood her, Luke.'

'Jimmy said something nasty to her and she wasn't too happy so—'

'So you did go chasing after her – aww, poor thing.' We both chuckle.

That's one of the best things about my sister – always making light of a big situation.

'Look, Moz, I think I'm gonna need an hour or two extra hours' kip. My stomach still feels odd and I can feel my eye bags without touching them.'

'Yeah, you look like shit.' My sister couldn't be any more right, and that's why I have to cut the conversation short. She always says the right thing – even if it hurts. She probably got that from our real mother because I can't see any of *his* traits in either of us. I spend roughly ten minutes in the shower to see if I can get the grogginess out of my system. Some more sleep is definitely required.

The chilling thing after the warm shower is a message I get from Susie:

We need to talk. Are you free later on? xx

Why is it that every time I hear or read someone saying '*we need to talk*' it feels like something bad is going to happen? I dress and head to Molly's room down the hallway. I suppose that couple of hours of extra kip isn't going to be needed.

Whenever things don't make sense, Molly somehow has a way of piecing things together. When I told her about what happened with Tamera, she said she always knew she would make her move – even reminding me before the trip to Marbella that the temptation would be there for her. *Sharks always smell blood in water.* The new riddle to decipher is what in the world is up with my girlfriend.

'Susie's probably pregnant, Luke. I don't know. I can't read her mind, but she's an attention whore, so it could be anything. Her dog's probably got diarrhoea or something.'

'Come on, Moz, you know everything, you're the genius of the family.'

'And you're the first one who got a degree in the family,' she says.

'Along with being twenty grand in debt from student loans.'

Molly's room is filled with her sketches of portraits, flowers, grand landscapes, all around her bedroom wall. The room just reeks of hairspray, nail varnish and Luciano coffee.

'Are you sure you want my opinion, Luke? I'll just tell you the same thing that I've always been telling you.'

'And what's that? Oh, right, break up with the bitch?'

'Otherwise she'll do it to you first and you'll feel tarnished by it.'

She's right, Susie will be the 'victim' in all this and I will be the bad guy. Susie will claim victory. Best break up with her now to quell the pain of guilt.

'What would you be missing from her anyway? Sex? You said Tamera was the best you ever had,' Molly says, which makes me wince back to last night's nightmare again.

'Only because of the whole thing with Sarah. We weren't ever going to speak about that again. Besides, aren't you seeing someone?' I say in desperation, to shift the conversation away from my sexual transgression.

'You always do that.'

'Do what?'

'Change the subject whenever things get awkward for you.'

'Listen, I'm going to reply to this message asking her to meet at that Luciano's me and you used to always go to. I'll sort things out with her then.'

'Whatever you say, *Lukey Wukey*, ha ha,' Molly says in an insulting attempt to imitate my sporadic girlfriend humorously.

So replying to her message is precisely what I do, and Susie agrees. Her favourite coffee store is a Luciano's not far off Shoreditch High Street and Liverpool Street. It's also where we had our first date. Time to grab the bull by its horns. I take the next few hours lying on my bed figuring out how I can spill the truth to my girlfriend before I doze off.

Luciano's

Many memories were spent at good old Luciano's coffee shop. Over the years, Molly and I spent many winter nights together here, mainly consisting of me helping her out with her homework. I was never much of a linguist or a mathematician, but I think being there for my baby sister helped, especially when the old man occasionally went off the rails at home.

When I finally grew myself a pair bollocks to ask Susie out, I took her here. Where else? I couldn't think of anywhere else I could take her that I was able to afford for a girl like her. I've had nothing but good, heart-warming memories here, and that's why it makes sense to use this place, this good luck charm, to break the news to her. More importantly, I need to listen to what she had to say.

As much as I want this relationship to work out, I can't keep my guilt together anymore. This is the time to come clean about Tamera. In my defence, she used my emotional frailty against me, and even though we all lost a good friend that night in Marbella, Susie took the loss the hardest. As you already know, I was there for her, gave her no sense of abandonment. I filled an emotional hole, the antiseptic to a wound – a naïve wound though, as this was something that could've been prevented had we kept a closer eye on our friend. But no, the Hewings' family lost their child that night and we all suffered, *so it was always possible anything with anyone was bound to happen as a result.*

So that's about it. That's the excuse I will use to tell my girlfriend the reason why I cheated on her – our friend's death. How fitting, blaming the dead for your own inadequacy.

As I walk up to the shop I feel the snow start falling on my face. I see the window table where Molly and I always used to sit. She'd bring out her maths book and then ask me: 'So how was your day?' Even at her young age she was already showing empathy for her big brother as she continued to do in the coming years. So let the therapy begin.

Susie walks in wearing a leopard-print jacket that I bought from Vincenzo's for her birthday. It matches her wedge shoes, complementing that perfect figure of hers. As she sits down, I smell that soothing aroma of Château de Fleur Feminine, the perfume I also bought for her birthday. I feel myself smile at her, and once again, for a millionth, gazillionth, time, I get lost in her eyes, nearly not noticing her half-awkward, half 'I'm-not-sure-if-I-should-smile-or-not' face.

'How you doing?' I ask.

'Fine.'

'Good. I've just ordered a hot chocolate with cream, and some marshmallows are on the way too.'

'You didn't have to, Lukey.'

'No. I wanted to.'

'I want this to be as quick as possible. It hurts me to say this but—'

'You sounded concerned on your text earlier today. Are you OK? If it's about Jimmy last night, don't worry about it. You know what he's like.'

'This isn't about last night. Listen, Luke, you've been good to me. I—'

'Oh, here's your drink. Thank you,' I tell the waitress. Susie does look great tonight, but because it's the evening and she's dressed so elegantly, I have to ask, 'So what's the plan for tonight?'

'There is no plan, Lukey. I wanted to tell you that this isn't working out. I've given this plenty of thought about how I wanted to put it, but you are the sweetest, kindest guy ever. I know how special you are, but I just want to move on now.'

Ladies and gentlemen start your engines. The meltdown commences in three, two, one …

'Lukey? Luke? Can you hear me? Luke!' *WAKE UP*! Back to Planet Earth.

'Errr, yeah.'

She kisses me on the cheek and leaves the store, with the marshmallows untouched. She must have continued talking while I was in shock. I'm staring down at her untouched hot chocolate mug in a whirlpool of thoughts. My baby sister's prophecy was right once again – *she'll do it to you first and you'll feel tarnished by it*. I'm supposed to feel freedom at present though, right? Not 'tarnished' Usually, when other guys say they're out of a relationship, the shackles are usually off, you can go off fornicating without guilt, but right now there's no catharsis, no relief and sadly no Winter Wonderland. Ironic that this happens in the same spot where we had our first date – just pure nothingness, an oblivion where nothing matters, no good, no evil, only existence. It's pretty dark outside so I check my phone to see if I've missed anything. Just a couple of notifications, a sales message asking if I've been wrongly sold PPI, and a message from Jimmy five minutes ago asking if I'm near the Cock and Bull pub. I'm not too far from there, but I've heard all sorts of rumours and stories of what goes on there. Apparently some gangster used to own it.

DRAX

Either way, anywhere besides Luciano's would be great now.

Part 2

Awakening

11

Young Frank's natural, gregarious behaviour got him into the habit and discipline of research in Drax. Any bit of information that didn't fit right with him, he had to commit to his own independent method of sleuthing to connect the dots. This was a much more satisfying task than relying on someone from Drax's small research and development division. They were usually too slow in getting the information, and when they did it was never totally sufficient, for reasons unbeknown to him.

Either way, Frank's entrepreneurial, independent spirit impressed McIntlock and the governing bodies of the Drax programme. They found that his rigorous work ethic had begun to have an effect on his colleagues. His fellow upstarts were beginning to look up to Frank as a role model of sorts. By the time Frank began his first assignment, he had already begun a fruitful relationship with Leanne – eventually the both of them sharing rent on an apartment above The Huntington Boxing Club.

He eventually worked shoulder to shoulder with McIntlock and was involved on a number of assignments, also being part of the Drax response unit who undertook services during the fateful July 7th bombings in London. A truly challenging moment for Frank, which prompted McIntlock to force a leave of absence until further notice – much to both McIntlock and Frank's dismay. Although he had more time to spend with Leanne in their new flat, Frank grew restless one day. The video games and television DVD box sets provided only a menial, banal distraction to his boredom. Was shaky time coming back for an encore? He'd thought it'd be best to take some meds just to be safe.

Being idle wasn't one of Frank's strongest fortes, and he hadn't have taken the medication for an awfully long time at that point. He'd hesitantly glanced at the bottle of Ritalin inside his bathroom cabinet and curiously examined the warning label on the side of the bottle:

Ritalin (Methylphenidate) – Do not use if:
- *You have glaucoma*
- *You have family or personal history of severe anxiety or agitation, as this could make the symptoms worse*

Frank was unsure exactly what he was looking at. He always thought Ritalin was just a normal medicinal drug that the local general practice simply prescribed to calm him down. His mother would simply give him his medicine in the mornings (on school days in particular) and all of sudden, as if by magic, he would seem less active and more calm in school.

This prompted Frank to do some extra research, as if he had come across another case. No one in his family history had ever had severe anxiety – not to his knowledge anyway – he was the first. It was also one of the reasons why he thought his father always looked at him with some scorn. If he wasn't supposed to be taking any ADHD medicine for his anxiety, why was he then prescribed it?

Methylphenidate was a popular psychostimulant drug used to increase brain activity. Frank assumed the only reason why Ritalin was prescribed to him at such a young age would've been to keep him behaving in class. He knew that he found it strenuous to sit still for seven hours a day. It certainly didn't improve his SATS mock results in school, which led to him being sent to special education classes. As much as he hated being seen as one of the slow children, he used to take solace in knowing that he was going to go home to his crime novels anyway.

The newly revamped Drax database told him that methylphenidate was classified as a Class B drug in the UK, with it being a Schedule 2 drug in the United States: the same category of drugs as codeine, amphetamine, opium and cocaine! In a burst of rage, he went straight to the patronising medicinal cupboard in the bathroom and threw everything out. Paracetamol tablets, vitamin tablets, ibuprofen, cough syrup. *WHY DOESN'T ANYTHING MAKE SENSE*? Were Frank's parents to blame? He hadn't been in contact with them for years, now fully estranged. He never got back in contact as he felt they would've been 'bad for his mental state in the field' as McIntlock suggested once.

Frank sat on the bathroom floor. There were tears all over his face and the medication was scattered, cough syrup spilt all over the floor and the bathroom reeking of codeine vapour. He was a lost figure alone with pharmaceuticals, pills that were supposedly used to help people with their problems. They were all nothing but smoke screens to his inherent sadness. Despite his recent accolades within the Drax programme, he was a fallen champion. *What would they think if they saw me now?* Frank thought. He wept and lamented until he noticed a crimson box – Early Pregnancy Test. At a rush, he opened up the box and saw the stick with the two bright red lines in the screen and next to it in bold letters – **Pregnant**.

*

Detective Chief Inspector Frank Walker, Saturday 23rd December, 9:22pm

Frank's meeting with Winston earlier in the day not only gave him new energy, but it also gave him every reason to proceed with the investigation board. Winston hadn't noticed this when he came in earlier in the day, because the evidence board was somewhat personal to Frank; no one would understand his method of thinking more than he would. *What people don't know won't hurt them.*

After all, his favourite detectives in the books he used to read always somehow operated in the dark despite the chaos around them. This was his chance to redeem himself, not only to ensure that the young lady who passed away in Marbella wouldn't have died in vain but to also prove to himself that he was still the right man for this line of work, as well as proving that the Drax initiative was still as relevant today as it ever had been.

Staring at the investigation board in front of him, Frank made himself yet another Earl Grey tea, this time black, remembering that black tea tended to be more nutritious than the traditional builder's tea. Feeling the caffeine shoot up into his system, he looked at his evidence board enthusiastically. How can an Eastern European drug baron manage to distribute Kraken overseas? It would be easy to lose track of how such a product is distributed. Anything that is easily accessible, cheap and gives a quick thrill like that would induce continuous consumption, which would make it popular with youthful consumers and, in particular, the economy. Frank groaned to himself when his phone vibrated with another private call.

'You ready for tonight, Treacle? I have an update for you.' It was Winston.

'I'm listening.'

'One of Ian's young dogs is going to be at the party. He could give you more information about this whole Kraken business, maybe even some insight to this Romanenko guy too.'

'OK, do you have a name? Something that I can identify him by?'

'Other than him being an annoying little shit? No. I've seen him a few times. Ian's been bringing him up himself, feels that he's got potential, a rough-looking kid.'

'Why do I get a sense that you just don't like this guy?'

'Kids are given too much these days, Frank. You have to walk before you run. You should spot him when you get there. I'll leave you to your detective instincts.'

'So I'll just look for the annoying little shit. Cheers, mate.'

Frank wanted to end the conversation before Winston got into another condescending lecture about how society had failed him in his youth and all of that. Now that he had an almost solid lead to go by, Frank returned to his evidence board, grateful for Winston's call, and placed Ian McAllister into the mix. Suddenly the case had got a lot more interesting.

12

Bemused and dejected, I make my way to the Cock and Bull pub, reeling and stomping my way through the icy December cold in confusion. Once again I'm placing my reliance and sense of sanity on Jimmy Turnbull, my boss's son – Turnbull and Partners' poster boy. I've just lost my girlfriend, my only bastion of hope on Planet Earth and now I'm going to drown my sorrows with a borderline misanthrope, a guy who can have pretty much have anything he wants at the snap of his fingers, and has had that privilege since childhood. A new car, watch, video game, the latest gadget, you name it, he can have it. I would even pose a question about him buying the popularity he had in Berkenshire Uni too. Losing a woman like Susie would probably mean nothing to him, but how would he know if he hasn't been through that yet?

People think and assume that cheap pleasures like alcohol and drugs solve their problems – you're in a deep sense of flightiness, everything suddenly moves differently and your defences are down, albeit temporarily. Then the depressant kicks in, and it's hard to confuse this atmosphere with reality because everyone wants to live in this fantasy world that you've so vehemently created. A land of the living dead, a world that simply doesn't exist deep within yourself – so much so that you deceive your mind into thinking it's real.

In this realm, everyone is perfect and happy, right and just. Your bills are paid, mortgages don't exist and diseases are no more. Wouldn't that be a great world to live in, or does it sound stupid to you? Of course it bloody does. The world would be in absolute anarchy if there were no chaos to feed from. Someone or something always profits and benefits from misery and suffering. Businesses don't make much money unless consumers aren't satisfied with themselves. This is what you're not taught in school: the laws of human nature that coincide with increasing one's wealth on this stinking planet – how to profit from your fellow humans' insecurities and sadness.

So tonight I'm going to pay my share to the Cock and Bull pub. It's rumoured to be a residence of the McAllisters. There have always been whispers and talk about what goes on in there, but quite frankly I don't give a shit anymore. Things can't get worse than they already are. Jimmy said he wanted to meet me for a chat and that's precisely what we're going to do.

The Cock and Bull Pub

The pub itself just looks like any normal pub on a Saturday night in East London – so much for all the big fuss about the supposed criminal gang affiliation. It's fairly busy tonight, and it has that traditional fusion of smells in a public place, topped up with the laughter of men and women socialising along with the background sounds from a jukebox playing remixed Christmas carols. I enter with my forehead aching a little bit from all the frowning I've done since I left Luciano's. I order a Malibu with lemonade and drink it down faster than usual. Just as I'm about to order another one, I realise that this is the same bloody drink I used to always get for Susie. It was simply routine for me to get her one. I then order a Jack

Daniels straight double whiskey with ice. A traditional drink for your grandfather, who'll more than likely sit by the fireplace at home and reminisce about how things used to be. Well, it feels like that'll be me soon enough. I can already feel the liquid traversing its way into me, the depressant kicking into my system now. *That hits the spot.*

My phone vibrates repeatedly in my pocket. It's a message from Jimmy telling me he's in the pub. I turn around and look at the entrance door repeatedly to try and scope him out. I then turn to my left and witness the familiar blonde, slick-haired, smug-faced son of a bitch already ordering a drink. *Thanks for the courtesy drink, mate.* His condescending, pathetic presence already pisses me off. Is Uncle Jack Daniels helping me to see reason? As soon as he finishes ordering his drink, more than likely a Disaronno and Coke (because he's too much of a pussy to handle a grandaddy drink like mine), he glances at me and makes his way over.

'You all right, mate?' he says with that smug grin on his face.

'Yeah.'

'Thanks for coming out, last free Saturday night before Christmas. I fucking had to have a sit down with my dad about the future of T and P earlier.'

'Why's that?'

'He doesn't want it to be Turnbull and Partners anymore. He's trying to cut some of the other investors out of the board. He's thinking Turnbull and Son or Turnbull and Pierce. Looks like the amazing Alexander Pierce isn't coming to Dad's charity ball tomorrow.'

'How fascinating. Looks like you might have to answer to someone else other than your dad now,' I say.

'I know, right?'

'Are you going to the ball?' I ask.

'I'm gonna have to. I need to show the old man I can handle responsibility and all that shit,' Jimmy says languidly before he begins the consumption of his drink.

'Who's gonna be there?'

'Usual people – Dad's friends in high places, some important people and that.'

'How glamorous.'

'Indeed,' Jim replies.

'I thought you were the only child in the family?' I ask.

'I think so. He might have some lost bastard child out in LA or Paris somewhere,' Jim says jokingly. 'I didn't say this to him but I couldn't help but think he's doing this to encourage me to settle down and shit.'

'The notorious Jimmy Turnbull, settling down, till death do you part.'

'Yeah, right, *Lukey Wukey*. I thought you were out with Susie tonight?' Jim says, seeming almost startled by the audacious nature of me biting back at him for a change.

'Why do you do that?' I ask.

'Do what?'

'Change the subject like that all the time? Besides, what Susie and I do hasn't got anything to do with you anyway.'

'All right all right, keep your hair on. It's Christmas, bloody hell,' says Jimmy, smiling. I don't think I've spoken to Jimmy like that before. Maybe it's the pain from Susie earlier or Uncle Jack doing his magic once again, but whatever it is, it feels good.

I order a round of drinks and the pub looks to have gotten a little busier since I got here. If I'm going to drown my sorrows tonight, let me at least start swimming in my whirlpool of self-pity and decadence.

'You said your dad wanted to change the company to Turnbull and Sons or maybe Pierce, why's that?'

'Because he's not going to retire anytime soon. He wants me to get more experience in the field first. Thing is, I'm the one who entertains the clients. You saw them at Eros last night. I keep telling him I'm ready.'

'Yeah, what you said to Susie wasn't cool, mate. You know I went chasing after her?'

'Did you find her?'

'No.'

'Good. Have I ever told you how much of an attention-seeker your ex-girlfriend is?' Jimmy asks, to my shock. How did he find out so fast?

'Ex-girlfriend? What do you mean?'

'Come on, Luke, mate, I'm sorry, but it's a cold game.' I continue to stare at the transparent whisky glass ahead of me – a despondent symbol of my shame and guilt. 'That's why I asked if you were supposed to see her tonight. It's all right, Lukey Wukey. If it helps, just know that you can always do better than her anyway. Like Tamera.' *Is that supposed to make me feel better*?

'Why did you choose to come to this place, out of all the places you could've asked to meet?' I ask, as if I'm trying to blame the failure of my relationship on him.

'Now you're doing it.'

'Doing what?'

'Changing the subject and that.'

'Fuck off, I lost my girlfriend.'

'All right, fucking hell. Listen, that's the reason I thought we should meet here. As soon as I found out, I thought it'd make sense to meet. Anyway, there's this poker thing that's happening tonight.'

'You know I don't play poker much, Jim.'

'So what? Play some more. Fancy another drink? I'll get this round.'

'Sure.' *I thought you'd never ask.* 'What about you?'

'What about me?'

'Aren't you going to play too?' I ask.

I tried listening to Jimmy's response, but it wasn't clear as a group of friends behind where we were sitting roared with laughter, which felt very much like laughter at my current predicament. I guess playing a bit of poker wouldn't hurt. It's not like I have anything to lose. I've already lost my prize and have definitely drunk a little too much. I might as well keep on going while I'm out of my cage.

'You seem a little tense, Lukey boy,' Jimmy says, condescendingly.

'What?'

'Are you ready for the game? You won't be taken in if you're all fucked out of your face.'

'I'm OK.'

'Are you sure? This isn't like last night at Eros. You can't just walk out and leave everybody behind like your mum did.'

Right now I feel the urge to smash my whisky glass across this parasite's face, but instead I find myself staring at him, and all I see now is a coy smile from him, a look of slight desperation, but for what? The impetuous Jimmy Turnbull, intimidated just by me looking at him. He knows he's gone too far with that comment about my real mother.

'Pub's gonna be a little more busier because of the ... errr "festive season". Just make sure you stick around, that's how they'll know you've entered the game. You can be my proxy,' Jimmy says.

I really want Jimmy to fuck off now, to just let me sit here in this pub and watch everyone's pitiful faces before I get in this poker game. *I just want to go home and cry.*

'And Lukey, don't forget you're a proper legend for this, a real lad.'

'All right, mate.'

Jimmy disappears to the loo, I think, but I'm unsure. Sadly, Auntie Malibu – I mean Uncle Jack – is having an effect on me. I order a glass of water, and then finally I notice that the Cock and Bull pub is suddenly more busy and Jimmy is nowhere to be found – my dear old friend clearly playing his infamous disappearing act again. *My wish is granted then.* I see only a few fellas left in the pub. The mood seems solemn and the jukebox is off, which gives me an indication that I need to be in alert mode. I go off to the toilets for a quick leak and possibly to find Jim. Nope. Nowhere to be found. My head's spinning a little less now, after my brief daydream earlier. I was hoping we would both play this game together, but he's actually disappeared. I walk back to the main bar area to maybe find him sat down with another drink, but no, he has actually left me here to rot. I call him on his phone and hear his patronising voice message:

'Hello? ... Hello? Ha ha, just messing with ya. Leave ya message after the tone ...' – BEEP.

Moments afterwards, a man in a bomber jacket – quite tall, who looks threatening but in a kind of 'don't you dare touch my daughter' kind of way – motions myself and a couple of other guys over behind the counter and down a flight of stairs that leads into a luxurious lounge area that feels like it's for gentlemen only. As soon as I get a feel for it, I look for and motion towards the door we just walked through, but then I'm stopped by Mr Bomber Jacket.

'Where are you going?' he asks me with a scowl on his face.

'Just having a look.'

'Well have a look over there. I saw you earlier with Jimmy. I take it you're his proxy?'

'He asked me to come and play, yeah.'

'That kid doesn't know when to stop,' he says, nodding to himself.

'What?'

'Nothing, just make yourself comfortable. The game starts soon. Grab a drink or something.'

'I'm good, thank you. Do you know where he went? Maybe he might come back.'

'No, I saw him leave the pub about twenty minutes ago.'

As much as I would love to fly kick this bastard, after sizing him up a little, it looks like once again the odds are against me here, so starting a fight with this dude right now doesn't seem feasible. *I've made my bed, now I'm lying in it.*

The lounge looks real classy: leather chairs, pool table, dart board – it certainly has that old-school gentlemen feel to the place. It's complemented by the smell of cigar smoke and whisky. *I don't think I should be here.* It's clearly a social event as much as a gambling one. I can already smell the mutual arrogance from these men, one of them commenting on divorcing his wife for a younger woman, another boasting about cheating on his wife a number of times – this seems to be a scene for men to fully express themselves without the so-called political correctness of society governing them.

While I wait patiently for our poker game to proceed, in comes this younger guy who's looks just about my age, with a tall, athletic frame, looking like he just came out of an Afro edition of *Alpha Digest*. He glances at me briefly when he orders a drink, which looks to be a bourbon whiskey, maybe even an old fashioned cocktail looking at the glass or even an apple juice, I don't know. I readjust myself. *Seems like this place isn't just for older people.* Mr Bomber Jacket approaches him while he's enjoying his drink.

'You're late again, Jacob,' Bomber Jacket says.

'And a very Merry Christmas to you too, Winston. So, how's my favourite organ harvester?' the young man called Jacob says, grinning. I hoped he was joking about the organ harvesting. 'Come on, you know what I'm like, don't you?'

'Yeah. Never on schedule but always on time.'

'Precisely, my good man. How's Darth Vader?'

'Well, Ian isn't too happy with tardiness, especially when money's involved. Looks like good old Johnny T's kid flunked it tonight and has brought himself a proxy to take the fall,' I overhear Bomber Jacket Winston say as they both take a quick glance over in my direction.

'My oh my, you worry too much, Winston.' I catch myself smiling at the contrast between this Jacob character's devil-may-care, witty behaviour and Bomber's juggernaut presence.

We are all then escorted to a room with the table set up perfectly. Six men, one poker table. Who dares wins.

'All right, boys. You know the drill, hand them over.' Mr Bomber Jacket, who I now know to be called Winston, brings out a tray to me first.

'What do you mean?' I ask.

'Your phone,' he says impatiently.

'Why's that?'

'Because we don't want you checking your Facebook status during the game.'

'Why would I want to do that?' Already I get the impression that this Winston character doesn't like me. Impatient and clearly not one to invite for a Sunday roast, I really wish this guy would just smoke a joint or something. I put my phone onto the tray and so do the other fellas. I catch Jacob sitting leisurely, all of a sudden with a lollipop, like this is a normal routine for him to hang out in the underground basement of an alleged local gangster's pub.

Throughout the game, tall, dark and charming Jacob just sits there in front of me giving people advice, banal chatter, joking around. I definitely don't feel like I should be here, but I was doing Jimbo a favour I suppose. I'm not very good at poker, and it clearly shows, but looking at the folks I'm up against, neither is anyone else. Everyone seems to warm to Jacob a lot, and I notice a certain gentle open presence that I've rarely seen from anyone else before.

I come to my senses as soon as I put down my cards to fold from the game. Winston comes towards me at the table, almost out of nowhere, and asks me to leave the room.

'You need to come with me, and for God's sake, don't ask any questions,' Winston says, as if pleading with me to not say anything. We go round the snooker table, past the bar, into a darkly lit corridor. Winston escorts me into an office of some sort that's similar in design to the lounge we were in. A beige carpet, a stuffed, full-sized bear by a desk – I was beginning to think that this might be the big boss's room.

'You made a big mistake trusting your "friend". Take a seat.'

'Would it be a stupid question if I asked why?'

'Yes it would.'

'OK, I'm sorry.'

'Don't be. Your friend should be. Jimmy owes my boss a lot money. I suppose he brought you here to hopefully win his money back.'

'I didn't know he owed anyone any money. He's rich anyway. I'm sure he could pay you back at some point.'

'Just remember, no more stupid questions.'

With my heart racing and my mind pounding with all sorts of 'stupid' questions, I conclude that any question I ask now will be pretty stupid so I might as well not say anything and maybe I'll learn something. If I had my phone, I could call Jimmy up and tell him to come down and sort this mess out. Why the hell would he put me in this predicament?

The chair I'm sitting on feels comfortable enough though. Leather. Looks similar to the chair that's used for those shrink offices in the movies, where the patient sits in front of the desk and the doctor holds up pictures of black splodges, checking on whether they're insane or not. I think our late friend Sarah called it a Rorschach test or something. I was never able to pronounce the damn word anyway.

Winston stands next to where I'm sitting and I have an urge to ask why his boss has a full-sized stuffed bear in his office, but I'll leave the stupid questions until afterwards. I hear some laughing and conversation outside the door, which probably means the poker game in the other room is over. No doubt that Jacob character is sharing a drink with them all or something. I wonder what he would do in a situation like this.

'Remember what I told you,' Winston says to me, giving me an indication that perhaps this middle-aged man isn't that bad after all, seeing that he's trying to help me. The door opens and in comes a man who could do with a shave but could probably get away with it, in his forties maybe, who looks at me like he's trying to judge whether I'm someone to trust or not.

'Ian, this is one of Jimmy's mates. Looks like he's pulled another fast one, mate.'

'Why's he *here* then?'

'Because I thought you wanted to settle the debt with the Turnbull boy.'

'Yeah, I know that, Winston, but why the fuck is he here then?'

'Well, you know the Russkies are increasing their scope. This Romanenko geezer's obviously here to stay – best sort this out quick and be done with it,' Winston says, playing the pragmatist. I get it now. Winston's the good cop, the other guy Ian must be the bad cop – well, not cops though.

'Maybe you can both agree to a deal or something? Listen, if we're going to get out of this whole thing then I suggest you think of a way to get your money fast,' Winston suggests.

'I didn't bloody ask for your suggestion.'

I haven't said a word yet, and it seems I'm not the only one who's prone to making silly judgements. I presume the McAllister rumours are true then, seeing as Winston has just called this man Ian and he continues to evaluate me.

'What's your name?'

'Err … L-Luke.'

'Errr … are you sure?' Ian says, mocking my stammer.

'Of course I'm sure.'

'Then why did you hesitate when I asked for your name? You know, the one word that was given to you from birth,' Ian asks.

'Bloody hell, Ian, not now, it's Christmas,' Winston intervenes. Ian looks up at Winston with disdain and my armpits trickle with sweat and anxiety. I guess I failed that Rorschach test. I'm insane.

'Your mate Turnbull has been a very bad boy, Luke. Coming here every Saturday night gambling away big daddy's money. What's the point of having all that power and money if you can't abuse it, eh?' I catch myself nodding, still resisting the urge to want to ask a question. My mind is riddled with them now, although, on first analysis, I can't really think of anything to describe Ian. As much as I would like to say he's a reasonable man because I'm still alive, I'm still unsure on how this is going to end.

'I'm not an evil man, Luke. I just want a simple life. How can I go out there and make myself an honest living when there's no economy out there? Follow in my daddy's footsteps, of course. This is my uncle's pub. He went to the grave never knowing what his nephew was getting up to in his old wine cellar. This massive, huge old place used to be a World War Two bunker. Winston and I were making a living selling wines and spirits back in the day. But the funny thing about the past, young Luke, is how it can be used to determine the present. Enlightened yet?' he asks rhetorically.

Ian glances up at Winston, presumably to tell him that he's going to tell me something that he's not supposed to.

'I'm close to retirement and it looks like your cuntflap of a friend Jimmy Turnbull is holding me back from a tasty pay-off.' I glance up at Winston to see if I'm on cue to finally ask a question. Here it goes.

'How much does he owe you?' I ask, looking at Winston, his stone-cold eyes not giving anything away.

'Ten grand. Does that sound like a lot to you? It shouldn't seem like a lot to you boys, right? You're all sitting comfortably behind mum and dad. I'm even sure Mummy's got the kettle on ready for ya with your eggnog,' Ian says condescendingly. *You don't know anything old man.*

'What do you want me to do then?' I ask.

'Ahh, you're smarter than you look, Lukey boy.'

'Thank you.'

'That wasn't a compliment.'

'Oh.'

'Where do you work?'

'How would you know if I work or not?' I ask. Both Winston and Ian stare at me in a cold silence. 'Turnbull and Partners,' I say, sighing.

'So you work for the kid's dad? Perfect. Johnny T is a very wealthy man. Even funded part of the prime minister's election campaign,' Winston stepped in to say. 'Ideally, getting to him somehow would be the best route.'

'No, it's not. Rumour has it that his company's claiming bankruptcy in the new year,' says Ian, playing the sceptic, sounding a little remorseful that Winston came up with the idea. Seems as if my future prospects at T and P are less important.

'Luke, you seem like a good kid, so I'll be fair and open with you. There have been a lot of men who've come down here and never made it out. Tomorrow is Christmas Eve. I'm gonna need the money by this time tomorrow. Now, I don't care how you do it. Speak to Jim, rob a bank, donate your organs … fuck, Winston can help you out with that – I don't know, don't care, just bring it to me.'

Winston takes my number and hands me back my phone. Something's telling me he wishes Ian would just let me go, and so do I. Winston then gestures for me to leave the office and go back into the lounge area, which is now empty and solemn, though the smell of lager, Scotch and cigarettes remains.

I'm now in a predicament that doesn't make sense. I make my way out of the lounge, walking up the stairs into the main pub area. My mind is once again riddled with thoughts. *There have been a lot of men who've been down there and never made it out*. Riddled with the consequences of what will happen if I don't find this ten grand. So what could it be? Fed to pigs, castration, starvation, drowned – take your pick, Luke. Either way, it isn't going to end well.

On my way out of the pub, there are still a few folks hanging around, probably on their last drink and I notice a figure by the Christmas tree wearing a red leather jacket, which isn't too shabby for my taste. Don't think I could pinpoint the designer for you though. It looks as if Jacob has been waiting for me all this time. With a lollipop in his mouth, he has a cheeky grin, like one of those male models you see on the high-street billboards.

'Hello, Prince Charming,' he says. Even though today is now officially the worst day of my life, this Jacob fella just appearing out of nowhere makes me wonder if it's going to get worse.

'What do you want? Do I owe you money too?' I ask.

'Whoa, easy there, old sport.' He smiles as he says this.

'Has anyone taught you how to play poker before?'

'I've only played it once or twice. Thought I'd, you know, try to do what I've seen on TV.' He laughs and, thinking about it, I can't blame him. Among the stupid things I've done so far tonight, trying to copy something I've seen on television is a pretty ridiculous thing to do.

'This is going to be fun. Anyway, walls have ears, mate. Let's go outside.'

13

As soon as we exit the pub, a strong gust of icy wind re-announces the arrival of winter tonight – and it looks like it's here to stay. I also notice a small group of people outside the Cock and Bull whom I recognise from television; usually I'd want to pop over and say '*Hi, nice to meet you*', but *they're* the ones with the money and fame, so I'd expect them to greet me, it's the least they can do. Seeing these people is a regular occurrence for us in this part of town, so it's not like they're anything special. Their presence on the big screen is enough respect that these people should ever get. When we walk past them, they nod to Jacob like he already knows them. He then formally introduces himself to me with a business card:

Jacob Brown

Entrepreneur

'Your friendly neighbourhood connoisseur at your service'

I flip to the other side of the card to see a black-silhouetted image of a bird, a falcon I think, with its wings flapping. I'm unsure what it symbolises, but it seems like it's something significant.

'You're an interesting guy, Luke,' Jacob says.

'And you're by far the most interesting person I've met so far. How do you know my name?' I ask him.

'Who doesn't? You are officially the worst poker player in the history of the Cock and Bull pub. What in the world made you want to play tonight?'

'My mate Jimmy.'

'Did you want to play?'

'I was doing him a favour.'

'Of course you were,' he says, smiling.

I don't usually hang around this area because of what apparently goes on in this part of town, but as we walk along Shoreditch High Street we go into the same coffee shop where my nightmare tonight commenced: Luciano's. The bright side of all this is that Christmas Eve isn't too far away. As we enter, I allow myself to go first, before Jacob, to avoid him choosing the spot where Susie dumped me as a place to sit. In fact, I choose the table where Molly and I used to always sit – that way, at least I won't have to think of what happened earlier.

'You been here before?' Jacob asks, clearly sensing my anxiety.

'A couple of times, yeah.'

We take our seats and Jacob orders two herbal teas.

'How would you know if I like lemon and ginger tea or not?' I ask.

'I don't, but you're going to need it. I know what the crack is between you and Ian. Anyone who gets pulled out of a poker game, gets himself sent to Ian's office and comes out of it alive is usually a lucky man.'

'What usually happens?'

'It's a mystery to me. You remember that other bloke with the bomber jacket? His name's Winston, He does all the nasty work for Ian. They've been together for years.'

'Like bum chums, I get it. How do you know all of this? Do you work for him too?'

'You're asking the wrong questions,' Jacob says. *Well at least it isn't stupid.* Jacob has a real piercing look into my eyes, as if he can read my thoughts.

'Do you know how I can get Ian's money back?' I ask.

He smiles and then says, 'Bingo. Now that's what I'm talking about. Always set your price high – you'll be surprised what you get.'

After a few sips of the tea, I can already tell what Jacob means by that. If I'd set my own price high, I might not be in this predicament.

We both get acquainted. Usually I find it difficult to open up to people, but somehow everything seems a little more relaxed with this guy, so I end up telling him everything about me, and he just listens.

Even though Jacob hasn't so far mentioned any tangible plan about getting Ian's money back, I can tell why everyone likes him in the Cock and Bull, but today couldn't have gotten any worse. 'Everything made sense until now. I don't even know if I deserve all of this,' I say pitifully.

'Round pegs in square holes, mate,' Jacob says, like he's slightly annoyed at my self-pity.

'What?'

'Falcons don't fly with pigeons, do they? You need to understand something. Over the years, not much has actually changed. Centuries ago, there were no self-help books, corny motivational tapes or YouTube videos. People only had each other. Everything that you might have thought was real … all these "things" that you've probably been chasing? It's an illusion. All of it, like fairy dust. So now you're sitting here sobbing about what's happened to you like it's a bloody curse,' Jacob says, while I continue to look at him, intrigued. 'People talk to themselves so much they create their own little world, unaware of the deception that's actually being played on them. Your girlfriend didn't leave you because you were an arsehole, I can see that. She left you because she was filling a void that you were more than capable of filling yourself. Believe me there's a lot more going on out there than worrying about a snowbunny you fell for, my friend. Besides, this sounds like a perfect opportunity to put things to bed..'

'So there's a chance I can get out of this whole thing alive?'

'You're still breathing, aren't you?'

'Well, just about,' I say. 'I'd much rather not be in this situation, to be honest. I feel like shit.'

'Why's that? You've already set off a chain of events that's going to happen regardless of your feelings, old sport,' Jacob says.

'I bloody hate that.'

'Well that's a strong word.'

'I'm not supposed to be going through this. I'm supposed to be at home, nice and warm.'

'Sounds like bollocks, mate,' Jacob says, confirming to me that he's tired of my moaning and whining.

It is only through pain and adversity that our strength and resolve can really be tested. I could listen to Jacob for days, yet he only seems to want to listen to what I have to say. I guess that's why all those people in the pub warmed to him easily.

'A nation is only as strong as its weakest component. What separates the slave from the conqueror is a fine line, believe me,' Jacob says, sipping his tea, which I'm grateful for accepting now because I already feel a little more refreshed than before. Jacob continues looking at me intently. 'There was a time when we actually stood for something, something to fight for, a purpose, a means to an end. Now we get our knickers in a twist at pretty much anything, jumping from one place to the next in the blind hope that some messiah will come down and save us. Climate change, police brutality, systemic racism, nuclear bombs, terrorism, none of that scares me. What *concerns* me are insurance policies, loans, Viagra, Ritalin, mortgages, credit unions, TV series box sets, lifestyle/celebrity blogs and magazines – that stuff concerns the crap out of me.'

'Why's that?' I ask, finishing off my tea.

'Why's what?'

'Why are you scared of all those things?'

'They don't scare me, they just concern me, that's all. I say we stop trying to live up to this smoky, made-up ideology in *trying* to be perfect and just ... be.'

'That's deep, mate. Do you think I'm going to die if I don't get the money back to Ian in time?' I ask.

'Seems to me you were already dead before you got here.'

There certainly was a time I thought I did everything correctly in this world. My parents always tried to push me to get an education, get a good job, meet a nice girl, but here I am in massive debt with student loans, in deep with a gangster now, as well as hating my job, and the woman I thought I loved is gone.

'Cheer up, lad. I know someone who could help us out, owes me a favour. There's this Christmas house party in Chelsea that we can go to tonight, and you look like you're in need of one.' Jacob gives me a steely gaze while paying the waitress before we leave.

'Why are you helping me?' I ask. Arguably the smartest thing I've asked today, what with the half-drunken filth I more than likely said to Jimmy earlier before he tricked me into his gambling debt.

'You remind me of someone I used to know,' Jacob says.

14

After the revelation about the psychiatric drugs that he was taking during those troubled times as a teenager, Leanne found that young Frank was a lot more mellow than usual. He had just commenced taking boxing lessons from his landlord Richard Reid, who was also tutoring other young men and women on the art of the sport. Frank had made a deal with Richard – pay off the rest of the rent to the end of the year and he'd receive free private boxing lessons in the evening.

From then on, Frank learned to discipline his mind to endure the physical fitness regime that boxing requires of its athletes, once again proving that it was only the supreme focus on a goal that benefitted the troubled young man. Neither Frank nor Leanne had spoken about the impending arrival of their baby. This was surely something that Frank expected his long-time girlfriend to mention at some point, but oddly there was no discussion about it.

McIntlock had then decided it was time to bring Frank back into the field, so he paid a visit to him and Leanne at their apartment one day.

'HQ hasn't been the same without you, Frank. The new set of lads and ladies could really use you both to set an example,' McIntlock said.

'Are you sure, Chief? I have to admit, I've grown a little used to this ... "retired" lifestyle,' Frank said with a cheeky grin, wondering why it had taken them this long to realise he was ready for the field again.

'I'm not going back out to work unless you're ready,' Leanne said reassuringly to Frank.'What work would he be doing? We could really do with a new profiler over at our department,' Leanne continued, seeming gravely concerned that they'd send him in the deep end before he was ready. Frank put his hand out to her as a sign of reassurance.

'I'll be fine, Lea, trust me.'

'I've always admired your enthusiasm, Frank, but I understand her concern. We'll restart you slowly, then gradually put you back to where you belong in mud and muck – how does that sound?'

'Sounds like bullshit to me,' Frank said, annoyed at both Leanne's and McIntlock's lack of confidence in him.

'What do you mean, Frank?'

'Like everything else you did ever since that day in college. Care to explain why you never told me about the Ritalin?'

'Now listen here, Frank ...'

'What about my parents? Was the whole "*not wanting anything to do with me*" part of the plan too?'

'Frank, please, do this for me,' Leanne said calmly, for she was the only one at that moment capable of taming Frank's frustration. He believed that she had to tell him about the pregnancy at some point – the subtle weight gain hadn't come from nowhere.

'There have been a few changes over at HQ. The department heads in Westminster are thinking of pulling the plug on recruitment. More and more kids these days are getting more focused on these new gadgets. You can say it's a bad thing, but in actual fact it's keeping them off the streets. I'm not supposed to be saying this, but you need to understand that it's all to do with funding. I'm asking you to come back because you're the only man I know who can hold their own in the field,' McIntlock explained. 'We'll brief you on your new assignment bright and breezy in the morning if you like. It'll be good to have you back.'

'I'll see you there,' Frank replied, once again taken in by McIntlock's cool stoic approach to him.

'Good. Thank you, Leanne.'

As soon as McIntlock exited the apartment, Frank had a feeling of uncertainty. It had been months since he'd been in the field, some time to spend with Leanne, to detox his mind away from the chaos, but it seemed as if he was in more trouble when he wasn't working. He wasn't settled.

'I'm sorry about that, Frank. I called him because you were acting stranger than usual. You haven't done much since you left.'

'That's fine, Lea. It's just … it's the medicine I told you about. I thought he could've told me about that. When I first met him, he seemed to have the answers to everything. I just feel *lied* to, that's all. It's not the first time he's done things like that, but the boxing's helping at least.' They both embraced in a display of their trust and love for each other.

'Frank, I have to show you something.' Then, much to his and her relief, Leanne showed Frank the pregnancy test, to which he then feigned his astonishment at the news.

'How many months?'

'Two and a half months. I was trying to find the best way to tell you but as you seemed really agitated about things recently, I wasn't sure how you were going to take it.'

'Of course I'm fine with it!' *I'm going to be a daddy!*

Frank had completed a number of successful Drax counterterrorism assignments, increasing his reputation with each successful mission, travelling all over Europe to prevent incoming threats to national security before his time off. Frank simply loved the thrill of fighting for a cause, but this time he had the knowledge and anticipation being a father one day – a son or daughter that would look up to him. Become the parent his predecessors never were.

Indeed, he might very soon have to give up the travelling and the hunt. Up to seven months into the pregnancy, Leanne had a number of premature cramps in her lower abdomen. It looked like Frank's time as an on-site Drax operative might have to be cut short once again.

Frank and Leanne quarrelled many times, separating from each other for months on end after the miscarriage, with Leanne moving in briefly with her friend. Then came Frank's excessive drinking to quell the pain of his loneliness – it was only his Drax assignments that kept his sanity. McIntlock, very much aware of Frank's personal problems, offered him a job working with the Serious Organised Crime Agency as a detective chief inspector. He would work mainly at a desk but solve crimes much like his favourite childhood detectives, and this would of course be in real-life situations, away from the hue and cry of counterterrorism. He could stop organised crime, but as a covert Drax operative, meaning that the initiative would receive more funding from Westminster whenever Frank successfully apprehended a suspect. It was a gamble on McIntlock's part, but one that proved to be successful. Frank moved out of the apartment above The Huntington Club but failed to patch things up with Leanne. Drax, however, despite it being a shadow organisation, was finally getting the recognition it deserved.

*

Detective Chief Inspector Frank Walker, Saturday, December 23rd, 10:20pm

While Frank was driving on his way to the place pinpointed by the proposed lead, he groaned when he remembered he was making his way to the Royal Borough of Kensington and Chelsea. Places like these always provided a stark contrast to the environment where he grew up. As he was wrestling through the traffic of the evening, he witnessed plenty of the nightlife, young and old, enjoying the scenery with their friends.

A part of him wished he were among them, drinking a champagne end to the New Year, catching up with friends at five star restaurants, setting out New Year resolutions and more than likely not keeping them. *They can keep the champagne*, Frank thought to himself, for he knew there was always greater solace in being comfortable in your own company.

He checked his phone: 10:26pm. He wanted to contact Winston to find out more information, if possible to find out any more about the supposed '*annoying little shit*' to find at this location. However, the way that Winston and even Ian himself operated was that *they* would always find *you*, hence the private untraceable phone calls. Frustrating as that may be, as always, Frank would simply have to rely on his instincts, and that had proven to be useful more often than not in the past.

15

Liverpool Street station isn't as busy as I thought it would be on a Saturday night, but that doesn't concern me because I'm more intrigued to know what type of friends Jacob likes to hang around with and what kind of help we might get from his apparently close friend Cleo. They've been friends for a while, he says, but I get the impression that there's more to it than that. A noticeable thing about Mr tall-dark-and-red-leather-custom-jacket-handsome Jacob is that he somehow knows how to grab a crowd without saying anything. He walks across the station with me imbued with so much magnetism and optimism that I wouldn't have been surprised to see someone come out of the blue and ask for his autograph, but this isn't to be. It feels great to be in the presence of someone who appreciates life like he does, but my heart drops once again at the thought of Jimmy putting me in the shit tonight for some bloody gambling debt. It's not like I have a rich benefactor for a father or anything. *Pathetic*. I've continuously tried calling this bastard since leaving the pub, but to no avail.

Seeing as it's the 'Eve' before Christmas Eve, I would have expected to see groups of so-called social rebels heading into streets of Hackney. Anti-zeitgeists like these taking to the streets on Saturday nights are always prevalent in a vibrant East London, particularly in this part of town, where it isn't only the city bankers, investment dragons and property juggernauts all wanting a piece of the city's wealth. Needless to say, you can argue that they are part of the problem. It's kind of the reason why some of the so-called cool parts of London always end up becoming less cool – rich socialites try to become more cool by hanging out in the cool areas on Saturday nights, which makes these places less cool. Spots like these always carry a history with them, a past that not many places in the world could ever dream of having. Not what you'd normally read in your average Key Stage One primary school history book, but the type of history that *you* and *only you* can remember through your own experiences. Me coming out of this situation would be history, for example, but only to me, not one for the history books. *My destruction is my evolution.*

Now I'm sitting on the London Underground Central line train on the way to Mile-End station with a quietly enigmatic companion, and I'm still rather drowsy from all the drinking done previously, but the herbal tea taken earlier is sorting that out for now. The carriage we're in is fairly empty, with only a few drunk and lonely zombies, which makes me wonder whether that would've been me if Jacob hadn't come into my life tonight. *Distant, depressed and good for nothing Luke.* As we switch trains to the District line on the way to Fulham Broadway, a drunk couple come into the train with us, kissing real slow and sloppy, then sadly they decide to sit in the same carriage as us, making me grateful I was a couple of seats away from them. I can smell the lager from here – what a sight.

'My friend Cleo isn't too friendly with strangers, but it's late at night and the party should be warmed up by now so hopefully she'll be a little more open. She always knows how to throw one, believe me,' Jacob says.

'How do you two know each other?'

121

'Long story ... let's just say we haven't acquainted ourselves for a while,' Jacob says with a cheeky half-smile.

'How do you think Cleo will be able to help me out?' I ask.

'I didn't say she can help you out. That comes tomorrow. You're thinking too much, Luke. Let's just get there first. Besides, it's way too late in the day to sort your mess out right now'. As much as I would've liked for us to sort this whole thing out tonight, and despite my poor luck in getting hold of Jimmy, heading to this party didn't seem like a bad idea. Looking back in the direction of the drunk smooching couple made me briefly think about Susie again. Marbella must have been where it all went wrong for us; Sarah's tragedy planted a seed of anguish and loss, thus making our love for each other nothing more than a phantom, fading away into the memory bank.

How alone can we really be in this circus called life? I can barely remember my real mother. She's nowhere to be found, and I can't stand to be in the same room as my father. He is the image I try my utmost to avoid. Damaged, snappy and, worst of all, *aged. I have to be better than him.* Julia has done what she can and I very much appreciate her efforts towards Molly and me, but the mystery of the woman whose womb my sister and I came out of will be a question that will always continue to haunt me.

As the train approaches Victoria and some other passengers disembark, Jacob locks eyes with me, as if he needs to inform me of something important. *Please mind the gap between the train and the platform.*

'I'm going to need you to do me a big favour when we get there,' Jacob says. 'Just mingle, try to enjoy yourself and ... come to think of it, you look like you could do with a party.' He more than likely notices my self-pity and is clearly geeing me up for what's in store.

It clearly works. 'Jacob?'

'Yes, mate?'

'Have you ever listened to *Doggystyle*?'

'One of the greatest albums of all time. I think I have it on vinyl. You should hear it – much better than all that digital stuff,' Jacob says in response to my excitement. At last someone who's finally on the same plane with me on the hip-hop.

'OK, just get what you need from Cleo and we'll be on our way then,' I say with my heart sinking at the thought of going to a party and not knowing anyone. 'It'll be embarrassing enough as it is just hanging around in a house party all by myself. Who does that anyway?' I ask inquisitively.

'A guy whose penis will be fed to pigs if he doesn't pay back his gambling debt to the McAllister crime family,' Jacob replies bluntly.

'Touché'

'Indeed.'

*

Fulham Broadway station is brimming with the Christmas buzz. Christmas lights around lampposts, carollers singing outside a makeshift nativity barn, it looks like it all came straight out of a Hallmark photo card – but in Chelsea. I suppose we're killing two birds with one stone. I'm one step closer to sorting out this mess and I can at least try and have a good time doing it.

Entering a side road, each house has its predictable set of decorations outside on the windows. Red and white silhouettes of Santa Claus and reindeer were emblazoned along the whole road. As we turn down another side road, it's clear that Jacob knows his way to his lady friend's place very well.

'Don't worry, I've made this trip frequently before in the past,' he says. As we approach the house, we can hear the loud music from where we are already 'Just as I said, Cleo always knows how to throw one,' Jacob says, grinning.

It's a semi-detached house, typical for a place with a stiff upper lip like Chelsea, but not as nice as mine, certainly not as festive as mine at the moment. There's a slight whiff of marijuana in the air, but everyone looks to be having a reasonably good time. Jacob is instantly greeted by two blokes and he asks where Cleo is. I guess he just has one of those faces.

'Did she invite you here?' one of the guys asks, clearly high. I could definitely do with a couple of puffs of that skunk right now too.

'I'm always invited,' Jacob replies, right before three girls come and greet him like it's a reunion of some kind – this is certainly Jacob's scene. Rightly thinking it's best to let Jacob get acquainted, I head into a room that I presume is the lounge because the main dining table is filled with different vodkas, whiskies and rum. Looking for a plastic cup to indulge myself, I catch myself nodding while pouring Coke into my cup of vodka to Craig Mack's '*Flava in Ya Ear*', to which the majority of the party crowd acknowledge with a 'Whooooah'. It's definitely the remix, because I hear The Notorious B.I.G. verse.

Maybe this situation isn't that bad after all. After a couple sips of my drink, I know this isn't my *usual* crowd. People like Jimmy and Pill would definitely stick out like two pale sore thumbs here. The thought of the both of them being here amuses me – until a familiar dark brunette femme-fatale figure appears.

'Oh my God, Luke?'

'Shit, Tamera?' *Shit*. Despite the history and my current misgivings at today's events, Tamera looks … beautiful, but not in your face beautiful. She's wearing much less make-up than she wore to Eros last night for Pill's birthday, and she looks laid-back, like nothing in the world is troubling her. I assume she knows about Susie and me.

'What are you doing here?' she asks, giving me a smile I've never seen from her before. A smile I wish I could've seen more often.

'I'm here with a friend. What about you?' I say.

'I've been friends with Cleo for a while. Her parents travel to Barbados every Christmas, so while they're away she does this party every year. It's kind of a tradition now. So where's your friend?'

'That's good,' I say, still wondering what the hell she's doing here.

'He's around here somewhere – just sorting some shit out.'

'Oh, so *Lukey Wukey* has another friend other than Jim and the gang. This certainly wouldn't be his scene. Anyway, it's good to see a familiar face, but you don't have to lie to me, Lukey,' she says, laughing, which makes me wonder whether she's either high or just being patronising to me. Maybe if I take a couple more sips of this vodka and Coke she might be less annoying.

'What do you mean?'

'You came here by yourself, didn't you?' She's lucky that her laughter's infectious, otherwise I would've been tempted to just find Jacob and get this thing sorted out.

The DJ in here was clearly sent from heaven because I hear some old-school garage music fresh from the chambers of the early noughties. It's fitting that I hear these anthems that I haven't heard in years suddenly, and it breeds a churning feeling of nostalgia. Craig David graces the airwaves now and everyone in the main living room are reciting the lyrics to *Fill me in* like an ancient biblical scripture. While I continue to enjoy the atmosphere of the party, the mood suddenly grows mellow as the music turns to classic RnB, which kind of seems fitting considering I'm with Tamera in a way.

Looking back into the crowd, I see Jacob slow dancing with a woman, also beautiful, naturally kinky-haired, and who's roughly on the same level of pretty as Tamera tonight, if not prettier. I notice them straight away because they stand apart from everyone else, like the stage was set for them and only them. I can only assume that this lady is Cleo.

'I take it you heard about me and Susie then?'

'What? Why?' she asks, interrupting our admiration of the couple on the dance floor.

'We broke up earlier. Sorry, it's just that I saw Jimmy earlier and he seemed to know,' I say.

'Ahh, shit. I'm so sorry, Lukey.'

'Didn't she tell you earlier? That's what she would've done before.'

'No, it's just ... she's been acting a little weird recently. I'm sure you've noticed.'

'Well ... erm ...'

'There's no point defending her now, Luke,' Tamera says, returning to her deep, hushed tone.

'What is it then? Is she pregnant?' I ask, fearing the worst.

'No, of course not,' Tamera says while sipping on her drink. 'Don't you think it's strange that Jimmy knew about you and Susie as soon as you broke up with her earlier? She didn't even tell *me*.' Tamera seems as if she feels slightly betrayed. I gesture towards the main table containing drink while I attempt to fathom Tam's question.

As a courtesy, I get Tamera another drink while getting my refill. While pouring the rum and Coke for her, trying to process all the bullshit coming out of her mouth, I notice Cleo and Jacob sitting very close together. They've certainly had a history – I can tell. I suppose a re-acquainting was necessary for both of them.

'Thanks, Luke.'

'Well, either way, Jimmy's put me in the shit tonight,' I say.

'How's that?' she asks.

'Long story, but I need to sort this out fast Tam. Jim's got a gambling debt with the McAllisters.'

'I thought they weren't real.'

'They're very real. I've got to pay it before tomorrow night.'

'Just before Christmas Day? How fitting. Have you tried calling him?'

'Yeah, several times. All I get is the same annoying voicemail he's had since uni. That's why Jacob and I are here. I think your friend Cleo knows a thing or two which might help us.'

'Well it doesn't shock me that you're in this mess, Luke. Jimmy's always taken you for granted. You've just never seen it until now.'

'Yeah, well, such is life,' I say. That was probably the most intelligent thing I've heard Tamera come out with. Ever. The ghosts of Marbella are still poking their ugly heads at me. That was why I was always fickle about Tam's presence, and why I felt awkward around her last night – guilt of what we did together – but tonight shows a different side to her, a side of her I'd much prefer to be around.

'Tam, what did we do in Marbella?'

She grins while sipping on her rum and Coke, and it quickly turns to a grimace. 'A lot happened. You know that – why?'

'I'm just confused about a lot of shit, you know? A lot of things have happened in the past few hours.'

She giggles to herself, something that I've rarely seen her do.

'What's so funny?'

'You are. You lost your girlfriend – my friend – and you're in trouble with some gangster, so the first thing you do is come to a house party in Chelsea. That's pretty ballsy to me, and funny too.'

126

I catch myself laughing at that as well. Despite all that's happened so far, it is a pretty insane thing to do. I don't particularly remember sharing a moment like this with Susie actually. The conversation would somehow just drift back to her and her problems, which got tiring after a while.

We share a joke or two more by some steps, with another refill of our drinks as the crowd grows. A couple more guests arrive with Santa Claus hats and fake white beards. Everyone seems pretty drunk, or is about to be drunk. I just pity whoever's going to clean all this up. I end up forgetting about Susie, Jimmy and the money while talking to Tamera. I head back into the living room to get another refill when I spot Jacob signalling to me that we have to go.

'Hey, Tam, I need to go.'

'Duty calls?'

'Duty calls,' I say.

'How about you call me?'

'I can certainly do that.'

'Well, whatever happens … just be careful, OK?'

'I will.'

'TAM?'

Just as I'm about to walk away, yet another familiar figure (but not so friendly) appears before me: five foot eight, slight stubble, stocky. I could say he's been putting in the work in the gym, but not frequently enough. He's not as tall as I am and definitely not as nice-looking – Tamera's 'ex' Louis.

'Tam, I thought you were staying at home tonight?' He says this like she owes him a lifetime of apologies. I haven't seen this guy since uni last year and he looks just as degenerate as he did the last time I saw him.

'Not now, Louis – sorry, Luke.'

The courteous thing that Louis could do is to acknowledge my existence, but he's still fixated on Tamera. His face turns red and I swear I can see his eyes water a little. Just seeing his sorry self with his mates sniggering in the background makes me glad that I'm not as pathetic with Susie as he clearly is with Tamera, but either way, I really wish this guy would just fuck off so that me and Jacob can be on our way.

'Are all your ex-boyfriends such pricks?' I ask Tamera, the glisten in her eyes replaced by despair and annoyance. I look deeply back at Louis and suddenly...

WHACK!

I feel a sudden sting on my cheekbones after saying this. There's certainly an ache on the left side of my jaw now. After I readjust myself, I send one back to him on his ear and we scuffle ourselves to the kitchen. I've never taken any boxing classes but I can certainly get used to this. *This feels good.* I hear a number of wails from Tamera while I beat his face a couple more times. I'm lifted off the floor by another guy, probably one of Louis' mates, I think, then he holds me by my arms and I'm hit in the stomach by another bastard. This all happens pretty quickly, and then people start dispersing from the kitchen, the music turns off, and all of a sudden Louis gets back to his feet. I notice the wails of police sirens and a flashing blue as I look across to the front door past the corridor.

It's only now that I realise that Tamera's disappeared – perhaps with Cleo and Jacob? Louis shouts some expletives at me as I walk towards the front door along the corridor and trip over a bottle.

As I desperately attempt to escape the house with the rest of crowd, still wondering where the hell Jacob is, an older man suddenly appears, presumably in his mid-thirties, probably older, black, gives me a real concerned look and asks, 'Rough night? You need to come with me. Let's have a chat, young man.'

'It wasn't my fault, I swear,' I say.

'Keep on walking, chap.'

My mouth tastes of sweat and blood now. The casual nature of this man's sentence makes me laugh ironically, which I regret because of the excruciating pain around my body and my mouth in particular. Hopefully knowing the identity of this fella may well shed some light on what exactly is happening.

'Can you tell me who you are at least?' I ask, desperately wanting a breather from the sudden adrenaline rush.

'You need to breathe. Calm down and tell me everything you know. I'm DCI Frank Walker.'

16

Frank escorted the young miscreant who he assumed was the potential upstart from Ian's crew to his car. This was supposed to be the young lad who would point him in the correct direction to getting deeper into the Kraken operation. The road where this party was taking place, albeit a small road, was swamped by police vehicles. This was in response to a neighbour reporting 'loud music and disruptive behaviour' and causing the party to shut down.

The 'anonymous tip' was from Frank of course. Being a Drax sleeper agent, he had to find a way to cause some sort of disruption to the party, thus allowing him to carry out his own objective. He was still suspended by McIntlock, and he had to be incredibly discreet about finding the young man. He traced his memory of Winston's description – *Just look for the annoying little shit*. Well, he'd seen the kid just coming out of a fight and stumbling out of the house, and from the young man's haircut and appearance, he seemed to fit that vague description, and by the way he was adjusting himself, making sure there wasn't any blood or any creases on his clothes, he was maybe a little vain too.

'I think you've had enough for tonight, mate,' Frank said.

'I'm sorry. P-please don't tell my parents.'

'What's your name?' Frank asked the young man, his adrenaline clearly taking flight now.

'Luke. Luke Edwards.'

'Just calm down. What happened in there, Luke?'

'My friend's ex-boyfriend came out of nowhere and started harassing her, so I tried to stop them and then he and his mates rushed me.'

'Rushed?'

'They all came together and got at me.'

'All right. Well you and I need to talk. Our mutual friend tells me you're the man I need to find.'

'What?'

Frank decided to drive away from the scene and let the authorities clear the mess up and ask everyone to leave the area and go home. It was when he drove Luke away from the scene that it reminded him of that fateful day in college and his first meeting with McIntlock. To Frank, it could easily have been interpreted as history repeating itself, but the pragmatist in him saw that this was an opportunity he could take advantage of. He gave the young man some plasters, and tissues that he always conveniently kept in his car, to tend to the wounds on his face, to which Luke refused. All Frank saw in the boy's face was a fading innocence, an ingenuous naiveté that all young men go through in their lives, but with Luke he also saw a very troubled boy. Something, somewhere, was troubling him – perhaps his presumed affiliation with Ian McAllister may have played a part in it.

'How long have you worked for Ian?' Frank asked.

'Huh?'

'McAllister, the Cock and Bull pub.'

'I didn't know he existed until earlier tonight,' Luke said, sounding down, unaware of the events that were about to engulf him.

'He's a very smart man. He wouldn't have lasted all these years without learning how to cover his tracks. Listen, I'm not like other cops. I can help you get out of this – just help me help you.'

'What do you mean? I don't work for Ian. I work at Turnbull and Partners.'

Frank grimaced at Luke's words. His apparent failure to find the 'annoying little shit' filled his heart with dread and frustration. *What good will this kid be to me then*? Maybe Frank could approach this from another angle. Critical thinking was always a primary part of the curriculum that Drax recruits had to study. Thinking fast about how to use the circumstance in his favour, Frank continued probing.

'So how did you meet Ian tonight then?' he asked. Luke explained the night's events, from his meeting at the Cock and Bull, Jimmy's manipulation, meeting Ian then Jacob to now.

'I'm impressed,' Frank said with a wry grin.

'Impressed about what?' Luke asked.

'You've committed two criminal offences within the space of two and a half hours – illegal gambling and GBH. Sounds like you've had a pretty rough night, but I think I can find a way to fix this to serve both of us.' Frank knew that anyone, when put in adverse circumstances, would always find a way out when pushed. The young man looked astonished that he wasn't being taken to the police station yet.

'And how's that?' Luke asked.

'Just do what you need to do for Ian and I'll make sure none of this ever happened.'

'What does that mean?'

'It means I already have a case on McAllister, and you can help me put him away,' Frank said enthusiastically.

'I guess it'll be a stupid thing to ask if I have a choice in this?' Luke said.

'Well, you don't fancy a trip to the station now, do you?'

The moral is to the physical as three to one. Napoleon Bonaparte came to mind to Frank, meaning that, in this case, Luke, being in the desperate position he was in, could pay good dividends towards achieving Frank's goal, as well as Luke saving his own life. Of course, morally he wouldn't allow McAllister to hurt Luke, but using his new-found sense of purpose would eventually prove useful for bringing down McAllister while he persevered with his work on Kraken.

'You need to find your friend, this Jacob character. He seems to know where he's going with this. Any idea where he might be now?'

'Probably still at the party. He seemed pretty close to the host. She lives back at the house,' Luke said, now touching the wounds on his face, clearly still in pain.

'All right, Luke, I'll be in touch. Everything will be OK. Just keep your phone on, and please don't try anything stupid.'

When the young man who Frank now knew as Luke Edwards left his car, he knew at once that this investigation had taken another turn. He knew that, as soon he got back home, he would add another name to the investigation board. Johnny Turnbull.

17

Walking back to Cleo's house while enduring the pain racking my body, I'm still trying to fathom what actually happened back there. With the snow now settling on the ground, there's a slight menace to the winter air – and there's been yet another twist to my torrid tale. An individual comes out of nowhere to the house, takes me to his car and asks me a bunch of random questions. He was police – at least I think he was – but he didn't seem like those normal ones you see on television, which is pissing me off now because I realise that I don't remember seeing his badge. *I'm not like other cops. I can help you get out of this. Just help me help you.* What was his goal, and why me? He must've missed Louis and his lot when he came in. In fact, I'm pretty sure he would have wanted to see Louis and NOT me. Now everything has got that much worse.

Right now, finding Jacob is the priority. It seems that paying Ian back will in turn help Detective Frank out. He sounded like he was law enforcement, but not entirely – no uniform, no badge, just a little bit off as an officer. Jacob will know what to do in this situation. Even though the party was real busy, I don't know why he didn't help me out against Louis. *Tall, dark and fearless Jacob.* He's probably still with that Cleo girl.

Approaching Cleo's street, I see a police vehicle still situated outside the house, and some groups of people still hanging around wondering what to do with their sorry lives. I see police trying to control the situation, just in case irate neighbours show their displeasure at intoxicated millennials disturbing their peace.

I receive a text message from Tamera:

Hope you're not in too much trouble, Luke. Thank you for helping me with Louis. Call me when you can, and be careful xxx

By the way this text message is worded, I assume that Tamera has made her own way back home and that she'd like to see me another time, which is sweet and at the same time annoying because women in general like to communicate in a cryptic language for some reason. That's why you always have to pay close attention to what they're saying – *read between the lines, that's the trick.*

Thank goodness I still pretty much remember my way from where Frank drove me. It must have been the adrenaline keeping me up the whole time, but I could really do with a couple of hours sleep now, with almost everywhere in my body aching for a warm bath with bubbles. Lord knows how my face looks.

While approaching Cleo's front doors, a policeman tries to stop me from entering.

'Party's over, mate,' he says.

'My friends are in there,' I mention before he lets me in.

The house doors are wide open, with a couple of guests either too drunk to leave or just about to leave. With the music off, the house is now looking more like a normal place to live. The DJ was packing his equipment away and most of the lounge lights were on. I notice the girl who I assumed to be Cleo and a couple of her friends reluctantly tidying up the place.

'Hi, are you Cleo?' I ask, my jaw giving me a pinch of pain every time I speak. Best keep the questions to the minimum.

'Yeah, you're not the dickhead who called the police, are you? I saw you talking to Tamera – is she OK? A lot of people said you got arrested,' Cleo says.

'No, he's the fool who got his arse kicked in the kitchen earlier.' Jacob appears holding a black bag, presumably helping the girls out with the tidying up. As annoyed as I am, it's a relief hearing his voice though.

'I wasn't arrested. I just had a … err … a slap on the wrist. Tamera's my girlfr— my ex's close mate.'

'How did you meet this guy, Jay?' Cleo asks, already deciphering my bullshit.

'He's the guy I was telling you about. He's in trouble with good ol' Ian.'

'Well Ian must be desperate if he's getting little boys to do his dirty work now,' Cleo says.

'No, I told you what happened. His so-called friend put him in this mess,' Jacob replies in my defence.

'Do what you got to do, Jay. Just make sure Mia gets paid tomorrow.'

'Your sister's been a real help with the store, Cleo. You should be proud of her.'

'I think she's there just to piss me off sometimes, you know especially with all that's going on at her uni, leaving me to go off with her friends and that, but … thank you.'

'Well she's safe with me, and you know you don't have to thank me either,' Jacob says warmly with a slight grin.

'I know. I just … feel I have to after all of this,' Cleo says, clearly disheartened by my fight with fuckface Louis. I turn away from them both, looking around the living room like I've got something to do, but I clearly don't. Looking back at them both, I see them embrace like they haven't seen each other for while, giving me every indication that I probably shouldn't be here anymore. I sit on the main couch, which again seems awkward while everyone else who's here is either about to leave the house or helping tidy up the place.

I then notice Mademoiselle Cleo, clearly disinterested in my possible castration tomorrow night, walk off to carry on with the spring clean.

'I told you she doesn't take strangers lightly, especially ones who trash parties,' Jacob says in an 'I told you so' fashion.

'You don't understand what happened,' I say, to which Jacob puts an index finger to his lips and points outside. *Walls have ears*.

*

Walking back along the main road, I explain to Jacob about my encounter with the black Lone Ranger. I reluctantly ask if I can crash at his place for the night, which he has no problem with. 'Just don't talk in your sleep,' he says. I simply don't have the energy to explain my rough appearance to my family, so it makes sense. I send a text to my sister, letting her know that I'm staying over at a friend's place tonight – she'll probably assume it's Susie.

We get on a night bus back down to Fulham Broadway station, which feels like a temporary safe haven while the menacing cold is making its presence known this late at night. The Chelsea streets are now very quiet and eerie, giving me every indication that I should be back home in Loughton drinking a hot mug of cocoa before reading *Alpha Digest* until I fall asleep. Sadly I'm a long way from there, plus it would look suspicious going home with my face in the state that it is. For someone like Jacob, I presume, home is a sanctuary of hope – the grateful realisation that you've gotten home safely to fight another day is enough of a Christmas present for him.

'Do you have any family?' I ask.

'No. Orphan. You live with your parents?'

I reply with a silent nod, and an odd sense of guilt sadly. I have something exponential that he doesn't have.

'Lucky sod,' Jacob says sadly, smiling to himself.

In some ways, I don't want to go to sleep, because I know my face is going to swell up and I'll have to kiss those *Alpha Digest* cover model dreams goodbye. My jaw still pains me, clicking every time I move my mouth sideways now.

'Does it hurt?' Jacob asks with little sympathy, to which I give another pitiful nod.

'Do you want to know what *real* pain is?' Jacob asks rhetorically. 'A single mother with anxiety issues gets wrongly accused of child neglect and her son is sent to an orphanage. The child grows up with abandonment issues, not trusting anyone, suffers from a lot of bullying in school and, to make matters worse, he eventually finds out from the social worker that his mother committed suicide from not seeing her child anymore. OD'd on the prescriptive pills – the anxiety was too much for her to bear apparently.'

'That's a shit story,' I say immediately. The last thing I want to hear tonight is a sad story. Ahh, Shit. 'Sorry, was that *your* mum?' I ask.

'Listen. Pain is temporary, suffering is optional,' Jacob says.

Getting off the night bus, Jacob looks melancholy and deep in thought, hopefully about a plan to get me out of this mess, but whatever it is, I can only imagine what kind of past he had. I guess we never really know the beauty of anything unless we experience the ugly side. Is it down to my emotion-led decisions that have brought me to where I am tonight? I never wanted any of this – Susie walking away, Jimmy's deception, Ian's threat, fighting Louis and getting interrogated by a pseudo police detective – all in the space of a couple of hours. The fortuitousness of today's events have helped me shake some steam off though. They were indeed unexpected, but oddly, instead of running away, I got through today's trials, and with that has come a certain feeling of saintliness. Not the type of saintliness you get in church though; sometimes, I think people just go there out of sheer guilt. Which then makes me wonder what God must think of us when we go through our own trials. If our parents, mentors and teachers are our models, our 'God' if you like, and you realise that what was taught to you by them was a fabrication, then what does that say to you about God? *Pain is temporary. Suffering is optional. Smart. Forceful. Wise Jacob.* The sanctified feeling that I have now after surviving today's events certainly feels better than any workout circuits I ever did at Reece's Gym, but what tomorrow holds is a mystery, and whatever happens, it's been a ride so far.

18

Detective Chief Inspector Frank Walker, December 24th, 8:05am

Frank woke up on Christmas Eve morning with an extra spring in his step. He knew that yesterday's events, as tumultuous as they may have been, had taken a turn for the better, the right direction. *Everything might just work out.* The flat was looking more like a conscientious human being was living in it, the lounge area even having a whiff of lemon too, all thanks to the air freshener that Frank had bought yesterday.

It was Christmas Eve and he knew that today was the day that people spent their time buying their last few presents before tomorrow – embarrassed dads buying their Santa Claus costumes and mums contemplating whether to be the good parent and buy the latest technological distraction for the kids or be the bad parent and buy them what they really need, if anything. Either way, today would be the perfect opportunity to make a breakthrough on the Kraken case. Police units would be dispersed throughout the capital to contain the festive celebrations, and seeing as tomorrow was a bank holiday, the public festivities would be at a premium tonight.

As grateful as he was to see the number of messages sent to him wishing him Happy Holidays, Frank, secretly hoping he would've received one from Leanne, was more sharply focused on the evidence board in front of him. Last night's events in Chelsea were an interesting addition. Even though he had failed to find Winston's contact, his encounter with a supposed young scoundrel would seem to be beneficial, as through him he could now build a case on McAllister. Coincidence? Maybe, but this opportunity wasn't one to be taken lightly for Frank.

With the McAllister's illegal gambling/loan-sharking trade and Romanenko's alleged distribution of the Kraken drug, linking the two together didn't make much sense. From the intelligence that Winston had given to Frank, Ian was currently looking to get out of the game altogether and retire. The Romanenko's arriving on the scene the way they did would interrupt proceedings though – instead of people heading to Ian to take a gamble for a possible extra wad of cash, consumers could simply get a temporary high off of Kraken and forget about life altogether. From those recent cases, it seemed as if the trend in drug taking was on the rise once again – and that would be bad business for Ian.

On his board, he placed photographs of property magnate Johnny Turnbull and Ian McAllister to try and distinguish a link between the two. Why would Johnny's son Jimmy Turnbull, a young man whose father earns millions of pounds from his property asset portfolio, all of a sudden decide to gamble his father's money away? There must be a distant relationship between the two men. *Daddy issues*. Frank knew what it was like living with absent parents, but they certainly weren't as high profile as Johnny Turnbull.

Frank then began a search on the Turnbull and Partners' website – perhaps there might be something that might have added value for him:

St Augustine's Drive – 3 bedroom luxury house turned grand hall/art gallery £4,500,000
Magella Square – 2 penthouse apartments £25,000,000

22 Buckley Street – 1 luxury apartment £6,000,000
10 Coleman Place – 3-bedroom luxury apartment £10,000,000

Despite it being an impressive portfolio, Frank also came across an article that detailed Cliveden Place, an area in Bethnal Green, East London, for which Turnbull and Partners had recently obtained planning permission. Its estimated worth wasn't given on the piece, but, compared to previous projects, Cliveden Place was looking to be the most profitable project for T and P. It involved the refurbishment of almost an entire community, '*enhancing the lives of the locals and improving the direction of the entire housing sector*' it detailed in the small article.

The only link Frank could get from this was that if McAllister knew Luke had a connection with the Turnbull family, then that would possibly be his way in to get a piece of the pie – ideal for a low-key gangster's retirement plan. McAllister knew that the resurgence of the drug trade would affect business, so the only way for him to get out would be to take a big financial cut and walk away without a trace – by any means necessary.

So that was Ian's motivation figured out. Having Luke to pay the gambling debt to Ian tonight would be beneficial to Frank; perhaps he could somehow catch him in the act. Which then brought him to Luke. Was there something more to this boy than what he'd seen last night? Frank signed himself onto the Drax database on his laptop, secretly hoping McIntlock hadn't blocked him out of the servers. He signed in with his password – his birthday.

Frank breathed a sigh of relief when he saw the '*Welcome back, Mr Walker*' message when he signed on to the database. *Good to be back.* Drax person profile databases were able to run a background check on any individual that an operative had been in contact with. Good thing Luke had mentioned that he's an employee of Turnbull and Partners, that way he could narrow the search to the individuals currently employed by Turnbull – this included social media profiles, financial transactions, statements, letters, and personal information about an individual that rival shadow organisations would kill to receive.

Frank eventually found the familiar, insecure, misguided face of the young adult he'd met last night. Luke Edwards. Twenty-three years old, lives with his father, stepmother and sister. Biological mother disappeared, no trace or any point of contact. Currently works in the project department of T and P as a trainee, so he should have at least some foresight on the Cliveden Place development, perhaps even being actively involved in the planning process of what's to be built there. Frank very quickly connected the dots to Luke's friendships and social media pages and found that he was one of the group of friends who was with Sarah Hewings in Marbella, the first victim of the Kraken drug, who died last summer. Frank's natural empathy made him wonder how such an event could mentally and emotionally wound an individual. 'Poor boy,' Frank heard himself say out loud.

Despite the pity that Frank felt for Luke, he realised that he might just be more useful to him than originally thought – he may possibly know more about the Kraken drug. It all went back to last summer during that trip to Marbella. *Sun's out, guns out*, as the kids would say today. Perhaps there was something suspicious about one of his peers. The database reports that the Spanish authorities had never got round to finding out who sold the drugs to Sarah. Was there someone who Luke knew who could've done this?

With this thought, Frank went to the kitchen and poured himself a glass of orange juice, needing to take a brief break from staring into his laptop for so long. It was Christmas after all, and he was certainly in the minority of people working while on leave during this period.

'Stay focused on the goal and you WILL achieve,' McIntlock once taught Frank.

'To find the anomaly, you must become one.'

Years ago, Frank had known it was his focus and internal discipline that needed taming, not the prescriptive drugs. The Drax programme had saved many lives, but it had hurt souls over the years too, with some initiates losing all contact with their families during the course of the programme.

During the couple of minutes break from all the information gathering, Frank wondered about his estranged partner – what would *Leanne be up to now*? *Would she be seeing someone else*? He thought long and hard. Sending a Christmas greeting to her shouldn't be a problem. There were no rules about an estranged couple being in mutual contact, maintaining a respectful relationship, albeit a fractured one. He found himself staring at his phone for roughly five minutes, contemplating what to say to her, trying not to offend her, to at least show that he still cared and she was in his thoughts during this festive period. Frank sent his message and turned the phone off, not wanting to see if she replied or not, knowing Leanne was always very responsive to her phone. The fear of rejection and of being ignored crept over him once again. *What would she want from me?* Frank thought.

19

Ahhh, don't you just love the smell of freshly ground caffeine in the morning? One of those drugs that scientists say can be safely consumed regularly, although not too often because it's a common cause of insomnia. Lord knows how many sleepless nights I endured drinking coffee at Luciano's on weekdays while helping Molly out with her homework back in the day. This is the same drug that doesn't make you drowsy or hallucinate about things that aren't even there, so they say. I disagree with this, because there have been plenty of times where I've had an espresso and then, shortly after walking into work, had the sudden urge to shoot and kill my boss with a nail gun, then maybe even take a selfie with the body, send a picture message to that French supermodel wife of his (his third), and then send his son Jimbo 'the cunt' Turnbull one too. But no, most of the time, a hot cup of coffee brings all my attention to the now and I get on with the day.

Today, however, isn't like any other day. I might actually die tonight if I don't pay my debt to Ian, or end up in jail if I do. While my mind ponders on unrealistic expectations of how tonight may pan out for me, I yawn and pay attention to my immediate surroundings – I think I'm lying on a leather sofa. Or maybe a couch; I can't tell the difference, but it's the spiffing whiff of coffee that wakes me up. Susie's fruity shampoo smell used to welcome me in the mornings whenever I managed to spend the night with her. Right now, as I groggily look around, it looks like I'm in an open-plan apartment with oak floors and white walls covered with some rather creative graffiti art. What grabs my eye in particular looking around is an image of the black silhouette of a bird – the same image I saw on the back of Jacob's business card. I've finally decided that this bird must be a falcon – it's the only bird that kind of suits Jacob, I think. There's some weightlifting equipment, a treadmill and a training mat in the corner of the room too. There are multiple stacks of books, vintage items, African-looking sculptures all around the place, with candles lit and a dining table where I notice Jacob consuming a hot drink, which must be the coffee I was smelling but I'm unsure.

As much as I would like to call this place a bachelor pad, at the same time it isn't, simply because it doesn't look like one you'd like to show off to your folks. I also notice a double bed, presumably where Jacob sleeps, although it looks like it hasn't been slept on in a while. I only notice this after holding onto my ribs and jaw – enduring pain does certainly take some getting used to. It's the pain that wakes you up. *Pain is temporary, suffering is optional.* I can also just about make out a small stack of books near his bedside table, and I make my way over there to feed my curiosity. I notice *The Great Gatsby* at the top of this pile, and as I scroll down I see *The Prince*, *Things Fall Apart*, *The Art of War*, *As a Man Thinketh*, and *The Power of Concentration*. Looking at the condition of these books, it looks like he's studied them intensely from cover to cover.

I look at my phone to see the time but it's run out of battery. At this moment I can imagine my dad giving me a lecture on the usefulness of analogue watches and how useless smartphones are – hence why he doesn't own one. Well, I assume it's about 10am, the sun looks crisp, and it'll only be up for a few hours until it gets dark again, so now's a good time to stop thinking and start moving.

'Morning, sunshine!' Jacob greets me right on cue with a bright smile, like last night's events had no effect on him. He's wearing a pink bathrobe and round thick-framed glasses as he looks to be working on a replica pyramid of some sort. It looks pretty cool, but I have no idea how he's doing it. I'm sure if I asked, the answer he'd give would be too complex for me to comprehend. He's also got replica models of the Houses of Parliament, Tower of Pisa and The Shard. Jacob definitely knows a thing or two about building structures. *What can't he do?*

'Morning, mate, you live here by yourself?' I ask, while groggily rubbing my eyes. I certainly had a good night's sleep, but I'm dreading it every time my mouth wants to yawn, as it'll just bring on the pain in my jaw.

'Don't worry about the pain, it'll heal before you know it, and yes I'm on my own. I like the silence. It brings a lot of stillness,' Jacob says.

'Sure. So this is where it all happens eh?' I ask while yawning and then smiling, expecting him to come up with a wild story about how many sex orgies and Victoria's Secret Angels he's probably spent time with in here. Instead, I get a watchful, gentle glance that turns into a cheeky smile of optimism. *There might be hope for you yet, Luke.* He then returns to his model, deeply immersed in the pyramid he's building, which is almost at the point of completion.

'Help yourself to a coffee or tea, and may I also cordially remind you of the stakes that are at play for you today?' Jacob says, while still working on his pyramid.

'OK, OK, I'm up. Do you have a coffee machine? Charger, Wi-Fi at least?' He then glances up at me as if irritated by my question, then points over to a plug socket with a charger in it. *No Wi-Fi!*

The great thing about a good mug of coffee (preferably a Luciano's) is that when it does wake you up, it wakes you up good. Life comes to fruition again.

'I don't know much about that detective you met last night, but your best bet is to sort out your business with McAllister sooner rather than later. Rest assured he's already done his research on you, who you hang out with and all of that, just in case you try to play it smart and run away,' Jacob says, to which I catch myself kissing my teeth and groaning at my current predicament.

'This is all bloody insane!' I say. Jacob seems startled at my description of my present circumstance.

'Really? What makes you say that?' Jacob replies.

'Everything that's happened so far … you know, it … just doesn't usually happen to people like me.'

'And what usually happens to people like you?' Jacob asks, to which I realise I have no real tangible answer.

'Not this,' I say

'Well, maybe your sense of sanity is insane,' Jacob says.

'Huh?'

'Self-creation is true freedom, mate. Looks like you've been following the rules for way too long, Luke, and look where that got you. People will do whatever they can to protect the established order'

'OK, my girlfriend's gone and I'm in trouble with a gangster, cool, but I still have a good job, a car and I get paid all right too.'

'So these are things that define you, do they?' Jacob asks, while I let the kettle boil. 'You see, that's the ironic thing about this amusement park called 'life'. Our need to be noticed. "*Look at me, everyone, I'm here, please notice me!*" That's what's killing us, not the weed, not the heroin, but the self-destructive urge to glorify our existence. That's the disease we're all infected with. We've successfully nullified ourselves into stagnation,' Jacob says, then he focuses back on his model while I focus on hearing the kettle finish boiling. 'Anyway, I could be wrong. Who knows, we all might live happily ever after,' Jacob says. I once again find myself pondering Jacob's reflective words.

Following society's rules, doing what the world expects of you – serving your master – this is all considered sane. This is the status quo. What benefits does this give us? A company car, social status, public acceptance, but all at a cost: *your life*. But quitting your job, showing your master the middle finger, committing yourself to ideals – this is considered insane, but what can you gain from this? *Your life*. The more and more I think of things like this, the more I feel heartbroken and betrayed. Not by Susie, not by Jimmy, Pill or Tamera, but by how it took an extenuating circumstance like this to realise the cold-blooded lies and deception that are thrown around. Jacob looks like he has a principled, blissful approach to what is around him. Everything that he encounters has to be studied and appreciated. If I'm to sort this mess out by tonight and still live to tell the tale, then I need to have a plan, a method of action that'll have to succeed with as little bloodshed as possible.

My mind continues to ponder Jacob's philosophical question. I certainly have an acute sense of what it's like to overthink situations, but this one is unique in many ways. Before when I overthought, it was usually about what to wear to the club, or making sure I arrived on time to meet Susie or Pill and the gang. I continue looking around the apartment, this living area with books and replica models, which to me looks to be a place fit for a man liberated from *anyone's* opinion.

Best attend to the kettle, make myself a brew and let Jacob do his thing. As much as I would've liked to use Jacob's weightlifting equipment, there's obviously no time to waste here. As I move towards the kitchen area, each step towards the kettle on the other side of the room is laboured with aches and pains around my ribs, abs and biceps. I felt physical and emotional pain yesterday, and even though my body is stinging along with my morale, I feel … kind of great.

'Cleo reminded me of a colleague of mine who works with me that can help. He should know a little more about where we can get the money. We call him the "Oracle". If there's anyone who can help you it's him' Jacob says.

'What about Ian?'

'What about him?'

'You know the whole "feed my dick to pigs" thing?'

'Well that's the whole point of the Oracle. We'll find a way.'

'Can't I call Ian? You know, try and find him?' I ask.

'Nope. You can't call him. He finds *you*.'

Having forgotten to stir my coffee, I head back towards the kitchen area to grab a teaspoon while thinking about my current dilemma.

'Just wondering, Jacob, why do you call this guy the Oracle … Jacob? Jacob?' Just like that, the assertive, charming, pragmatic

Jacob Brown is fast asleep at the dining table, with his pyramid still unfinished, like a child taking a nap break from his Lego model. *Is he dead*? I go over to him, check his pulse just to be safe, and then he suddenly wakes up again. Weird but funny at the same time, it looks like my dear new friend Jacob is a narcoleptic.

'Are you OK?' I ask, trying my best not to burst out laughing.

'Yeah I'm fine, why?'

'You just went to sleep, mate.'

'Oh, sorry, I do that sometimes. I sleep whenever my body tells me to.'

'Do you sleep properly at all?' I ask, to which he immediately raises his finger.

'It's what you do while you're awake that's important.'

I drink my black coffee with more purpose now, then I instantly feel the effects of the caffeine shoot through me. Is it the whole "owing the big bad gangster money or your life thing" making me appreciate the warm beverage even more, or is it because I haven't had a good cup of coffee for a while now? Decisions, decisions.

20

Detective Chief Inspector Frank Walker, December 24th, 12:15pm

While deciphering the information on the evidence board leading to multiple dead ends, Frank, while frustrated at not finding the missing piece to this whole conundrum, remembered to put his phone back on, forgetting why he turned it off in the first place. Then, right on cue, he received a phone call from a private number. *Who could this be?*

'You have fun last night, Treacle?'

'Hel— Excuse me? Oh, Winston, I thought you didn't do mobile phone calls?' Frank asked.

'There's always room for compromise. So what the hell happened? Actually no, don't tell me, we need to meet.'

'This better be good, Winston. I think I'm going somewhere with this,' Frank lied.

'Meet me at The Huntington – one of your favourite gaffs I hear.'

'I'll see you there,' Frank sighed.

*

The apartment above the club where Frank and Leanne used to reside was now abandoned – though Frank thought maybe that was to allow for refurbishment – and he knew that the boxing establishment below was being threatened by the local council with being shut down. This was a place that was beneficial to the local community. Usually, young men and women came here to blow off steam and avoid the local gangs in the area. *Maybe Turnbull could 'turn' this old scum bucket around.* Frank smiled to himself when he thought this en route to The Huntington. Hopefully Winston would have some valuable information to hand. With the investigation hitting a brick wall all of a sudden, it was looking like he'd have to hope Luke could do what was required of him.

Approaching the cobbled road to the familiar old arches, Frank walked into the club and immediately noticed a young boxer training by the dumb-bells with push-ups. He walked slowly, observing the now dilapidated boxing club that he used to call home. He wanted to be out of there as quickly as possible; the old memories were creeping back up on him. He went to the reception office, the whole room looking a lot more decrepit – not much work had been done to this place since the last time he was here. *This place looks exactly the same.* There was an old miniature Christmas tree with lights around it that weren't on. *Saving money on the electric bill. Typical Richard.*

The office was empty and cold, clearly in need of attention, with Frank deep down wishing that he could do something to improve its current condition. The computer was still the same, along with the CCTV video monitors just under the desk.

'You've lost weight.' An old familiar voice greeted Frank from behind.

'And you haven't aged.' Frank greeted his old boxing trainer Richard Reid. He was wearing that trademark flat cap of his, and the gold at the side of his teeth went with an old sad smile. Frank had heard that his wife was losing her battle with cancer and his children were growing further apart from each other - certainly not the information that he wanted to hear about his former trainer.

Richard had owned The Huntington Club for decades now, but it hadn't been the same for the past couple of years, probably caused by the financial recession and the tragedy of his wife affecting him.

Richard would've been one of the few men he knew personally that would happily work during Christmas Eve, most likely to distract him from his wife's condition.

'What brings you back here, Franky? You don't look like you're up for a spar, or are you?' Richard asked with an eyebrow raised.

'Here to see a friend. I have an investigation I have to finish. Is that your next new star?' Frank asked, while glancing at the young boxer, now committing himself to abdominal crunches on the floor.

'No, he just came here to train. It's still early in the day. The kids want to commit to the summer body after Christmas. Some, as you know, come here to escape trouble, release their anger somewhere else. Come January, things should pick up again anyway.' Richard said this with hope and optimism, but Frank suspected otherwise.

'Look, Rich, I know about—'

'It's OK, Frank, she has about three months maximum. My boys are there for me.'

'All right then. If there's anything, just let me know. How's the first one? I always forget his name'

'You mean Orlando? He's doing what he can for the place, but he's struggling though. We'll get by – us Reids always do.'

'I can count on that.' While Frank had the utmost sympathy and respect for his old trainer, today wasn't a good day to stand and chat about old times. Richard had a concerned look when he glanced at the CCTV camera feed. It was the only piece of equipment that actually looked like it was being taken care of regularly, and its use right now seemed beneficial.

'Frank, you couldn't do a favour for an old friend, could you?'

'What's that?'

'There's a man just by the back door of the club waving to the camera. Who's that?'

Frank gazed into the CCTV monitors to see that it was Winston by the back entrance of the club.

'That'll be him. Thanks, Richie,' Frank said.

Frank braced himself before enduring the Christmas winter cold again. Not because of his encounter with Winston, but because it was certainly the coldest Christmas in years, with snow actually falling when the Hollywood movies said it needed to be.

'You have a funny way of announcing your arrival,' Frank said.

'I like making an entrance.' Winston had his hands deep inside his bomber jacket pockets.

'Why don't you come inside?' Frank asked.

'I haven't got much time. I have an errand to run then I'm supposed to be back at the Cock and Bull soon. Any update on this Kraken business? Tell me what happened last night.'

'The annoying little shit disappeared on me. I couldn't find him,' said Frank.

'Are you sure? His name's Louis, rough-looking, always walks around with his mates who are just as ugly-looking. Louis knew his lady friend would be attending a party in Chelsea, and I thought Louis would've known about the whole Kraken thing.'

'Shit.' *Thanks for remembering now.*

'Listen, did I not say I was coming onto something?' Frank said. 'I met this other kid instead, not ugly or rough-looking, a good kid, and he told me he had already met Ian before the party last night.'

'Who's that?'

'He looked roughed up, like he was in a fight, confused, a little lost, called Luke. Did you see him last night?' Frank said while Winston's face suddenly turned to a grimace.

'Argh, shit.'

'What?' Frank asked.

'Yeah, we saw him. You know Johnny Turnbull? Well, Luke played terrible poker last night and racked up his son Jimmy's debt.'

'How much does he owe?'

'About ten grand. Ian's serious about it too. He needs that money tonight.'

'Why tonight? Why not in the new year?'

'That's just how he is. He's always been very short term, you know that.'

Frank had already known all of this information from Luke. He only needed to hear it from Winston's mouth to confirm that Luke's story was accurate, and it sounded like it was.

'Well, I spoke to Luke and he said a similar thing. He's doing what he can to get the money back and I trust him.'

'I would trust him too except I don't know why he'd go to a party straight after meeting us though – he probably thought "Fuck it, I'm gonna be dead this time next month anyway",' Winston said sarcastically. Frank hoped that Luke was making progress on his end. Winston didn't appear to have any intention on harming Luke, but judging by what Frank had observed so far, it looked like Winston wouldn't be able to stop Ian even if he wanted to. *You can run but you can't hide.*

'Ahh, why didn't I think of this before?' Frank asked himself rhetorically, rubbing his hands together, wishing he'd remembered to bring out his winter gloves. 'I was on Turnbull's website earlier. There's a charity ball happening tonight at St Augustine's Drive, all the big cheeses will be in town. I'm surprised you and Ian aren't invited.' Frank smiled as he said this, hoping Winston would be in on the joke, but the cold was clearly getting the better of him, driving his intent to get out of there.

'I'd imagine Turnbull would need to be there. It's in one of his properties in Knightsbridge. We might get to him from there maybe. I'll find a way,' Frank said, hoping Winston would be satisfied enough with this information so that he could warm himself back up and carry on the investigation.

'OK, mate, this is enough. Let's hope Ian isn't too intimidating to Luke then,' Winston said.

'What do you mean?'

'Knowing Ian, he'll probably go ahead and get in contact with him in some way, depends on what mood he's in.'

'You need to make sure that he doesn't do anything too rash then,' Frank said, in the hope that McAllister hadn't already been in contact with Luke.

'Just keep your phone on,' said a very relieved-looking, but very cold Winston.

'Likewise,' Frank said, and the two men went back to their respective roles. Winston had to keep a close eye on Ian and act like nothing was wrong, for he knew how paranoid and neurotic he could be. Frank had to be sure that Luke knew what he was doing out there today. The next step was getting in contact with him and keeping tabs on any activity on the Kraken drug.

Walking back into The Huntington Club through the back entrance, Frank had a look at his phone. He now remembered why he'd turned his phone off in the first place. Usually he tended to ignore messages and phone calls from random numbers, but looking at the tone of language that this text message had, he knew exactly who it was:

Hey, I'm fine, thank you. You messaged my old number. I hope you have a good Christmas tomorrow too. It's been a while since we've spoken ... Don't forget your EarI Grey! Hope you're OK, Lea x

21

Jacob and I are walking towards this distinctive-looking vintage/junk shop in Hoxton. I should be concerned about where in the world he's taking me but I'm more concerned about the cold wind and the snow that's falling again. Each step we make leaves footmarks on the pavement with that distinctive crunching sound. Wasn't yesterday enough? It's pretty busy around here on the high street – presumably everyone is occupied doing their last-minute shopping and scrambling for last-minute presents.

A part of me wishes I was back in that life again, wondering, contemplating about what I was going to get Susie and my family for Christmas. Dad's presents usually were any paraphernalia that had something to do with West Ham FC, and if I felt mischievous, a Tottenham Hotspur souvenir just to deliberately piss him off. Either way, I would keep the receipts for his presents just in case he never used them – which was usually the case.

Another part of me, albeit a small fraction, is kind of glad I'm not involved in that life today. I guess this is the hidden curse of getting into routines and traditions: once it's broken, you feel like you're in hell, but beyond that, it feels great in a weird way. Jacob now has a look of excitement on his face, the look of someone who thrives on the adventure and suspense of life as we get closer to the store – *strong, confident, capable Jacob.*

'If there's anyone who should be able to help you out, it's this guy,' Jacob says.

'The Oracle?'

'He hates being called that, but yes, the Oracle. We work together in my shop. He's been there and done it all. I'd hate to dispute his special credibility and all that, but he's my go-to guy.'

'Everyone has a bit of special in them, I guess,' I say in my attempt to show off my limited philosophical knowledge. Jacob gives me a grin walking up to the front of the store.

'If everyone was special, there would be no such thing as "special",' he says.

Usually, I would imagine that those eccentric folk I see wearing weird clothing on nights out downtown get their attire in shops like these. 'Hipsters' the media dub them, supposed rebels. I just think it's plain weird looking at people wearing those oddball outfits – fur coats, multicoloured leggings – and I'm just concerned whether they ever exfoliate or not. I don't believe anything is going to prepare me for what I might witness today though.

There's a sign on the shop displaying 'Stuff You' in neon with the consonant 'Y' and vowel 'O' not lit up, leaving the U shining brightly. There's a striking model in the shop window with a stuffed polar bear on it, which makes Ian's one back in the Cock and Bull fairly redundant – presumably Jacob's handiwork too.

'That's my best work so far,' Jacob says, which then answers my thought about what he does for a living. Jacob Brown – taxidermist, vintage seller by day, poker enthusiast at night. Not the usual job description for your average narcoleptic, but at least it pays the bills for him. The shop itself is in the same vein as Jacob's apartment, an extension of sorts if you like. There's a chilled essence to this place, with seventies soul music playing in the background and the welcoming musty smell you normally get from a basement where you keep your junk. The music sounds like classic Isaac Hayes or James Brown maybe, I think, because it's music like this that Dad used to say he got bullied in school for liking – 'darkie nigger music'.

There are models of famous landmarks along with vintage clothes that obviously no one wanted back in the eighties and nineties, all collectively laid out for any new-age modern fashion enthusiast to feast their eyes on. Jacob politely greets the sales assistant behind the counter, a small, cute Afro-haired girl with freckles that I'd imagine my sister Molly would like to get in touch with.

'Hey, Mia, is Oracle in?' Jacob asks.

'He's always in to see you, Brownie Bear. How was my sister last night?' the girl says, who brings out a comic book while gently nodding to the background music.

'How'd you know I was there last night?'

'Well she IS my sister and word gets round quickly too,' Mia says while Jacob looks around nodding his head to the music.

'Good job on the playlist, and yes, Cleo was as charming as ever. She's happy you're here though.'

'Yeah, well good for her.'

'Peace and love, Mia,' Jacob says to her, who I can safely assume is Cleo's baby sister. He continues looking around the shop, presumably checking that it's up to standard. He then looks back towards Mia like a proud father. 'Keep shining, princess,' Jacob says.

'Thank you, Brownie,' Mia says. If only Cleo was as welcoming.

We walk through a beaded door curtain behind her – those real annoying doors that, as a child, you used to get stupidly excited over because you never thought to move the beads out of your face each time you walked through them.

A welcoming smell of incense greets us, contrasting with the musty smell in the shop. We walk into a room that is awash with ultraviolet rays. The walls of the room are covered with posters of old cartoon characters that I used to idolise as a child (my old Halloween Spider-man costume is still at home somewhere). There's a video games console on the floor, with a web of cables attached to a television, with stacks of old VHS video tapes all around the room. I suppose this is the Oracle's 'Batcave' of some sorts.

A big figure of a man, black and bearded, appears suddenly from the corner of the room. He's wearing a video games console headset, perfect for communicating with other online nerds. Straight away I'm thinking 'get a life', but if this is the so-called Oracle that Jacob works with and trusts, then it'd be wise to hear what he has to say.

'Ahh, the black Gatsby returns. Morning, Jay, I would've thought you'd take the day off,' Oracle says.

'Yeah, well, I've never expected anything from good old St Nicholas. Anyway, this is Luke, Luke, this is Oracle.'

'Hey, what's up, man?' Oracle greets me with a street handshake, his hands warm and sweaty, presumably from playing video games all morning – I hope. He strikes me as a thirtysomething (maybe older) who hasn't escaped the clutches of the noughties or maybe even the nineties for that matter.

'Is this that rich bastard who's gambling away his dad's money, Jay? … No, you have to head into the secret realm of Golem … because I've already reached level fifty on the sacred dungeon, ahh shit … I'm sorry.'

Oracle, clearly in two worlds, within his headset in the virtual world and his eyes on the real one, removes his headset and sits down on his office chair – his 'throne' for being 'King of the Underworld' in his video game.

'Sometimes I wonder what I pay you for,' Jacob says with a benevolent smile.

'I wonder the same thing. I got your message, but you need to break everything down for me, like going off to see that Cleo girl again. I swear there's something about that girl that makes me wonder why you—'

'I only went there because I thought going to a party would've helped Luke out at the time … besides, at least she doesn't play Sons of the Knights Realm or Moorish Invaders all night,' Jacob retaliates.

'You really want me to believe that? It's nice enough you have her sister here. You know what resources I have, plus you know I got your back, come rain or shine, brother.'

'Believe what you want, mate. She reminded me about you anyway'

'I don't know why you two don't just seal the deal and make it official already!'

While Oracle and Jacob are clearly in some need of catching up, I grab a seat on the sofa (or couch) in front of the television. I listen attentively to what Jacob has to say. He explains the situation accurately, as well as last night's events, to Oracle, hoping he'll gain an understanding and provide whatever level of mastery and wisdom he can obtain in this nerd shack of his.

After hearing Jacob explain the situation, Oracle gets up and opens a mini-fridge, the fridge light contrasting with the UV.

'I understand. Sounds like you have quite a dilemma there, Luke my boy. While Jacob was spicing up Cleo and you were getting your arse kicked, I baked a cake – care for some? It's gluten free.'

'No thanks,' I say, hoping he'll expedite his explanation sharpish so we can crack on with sorting this out without me having to indulge in consuming any saturated fat.

'Are you sure?' Oracle asks.

'Yes, I'm fine, thank you.'

'OK, so your so-called friend is Johnny T's boy,' Oracle says to me while slicing his cheesecake into pieces. 'And he's put you in debt with McAllister, but McAllister needs this debt paid by tonight. This detective – 'Frank', he calls himself – also needs you to bring down McAllister by paying back this debt but would also like you to lead him to Ian, which will probably get you killed.'

'What's worse?' I ask, struggling to find the lesser of two evils.

'Keeping you alive with no bollocks? Sounds like you're fucked either way.'

'That's right, I'm in a shit storm,' I say, now reconsidering Oracle's cheesecake offer.

'So it looks like you either do what Big Ian says you should do and keep your balls but go to jail, or you do what the policeman says, not go to jail but risk your balls. Then it's also the question of how you're going to get the money?' Oracle says, taking a slice of the cheesecake, clearly indifferent to my situation, like it's an everyday thing for local gang geezers to violently threaten young guys like me. Jacob, though, looks like he's coming up with something.

'I had a client come in the store last week. Russian, looked to be a little dodgy, he wanted about five stuffed rabbits all at once. Oracle, you told me once that this guy was supposed to be in charge of a drug ring or something, didn't you?' Jacob says.

'Allegedly, but yes, he was very steely looking, definitely not to be trusted. He's also supposed to be in possession of some blood diamonds too,' Oracle said, clearly enjoying his cheesecake baking skills.

'Well, he was very interested in buying some of my artefacts from the store. I told him it would be hard enough finding the specific one for him so I sold him a Fox for half price on a deal that he'll that he'll pay me back, but he hasn't returned yet. Good thing you kept tabs on him, right?' Jacob asks. I really want to step in and ask where this is all going, but I continue to listen.

'Andrei? Yeah he's supposed to be involved in that Kraken stuff everyone keeps going on about,' Oracle replies, with something that strikes a chord with me. *Where and when have I heard about this Kraken before?* 'Well, I've heard it's supposed to be the purest form of crack out there now. One hundred per cent pure.'

'Yeah, the philosopher's stone of crack cocaine … Maybe we can somehow grab a sample and perhaps use that as leverage against Ian, maybe frame him, but this Frank fella might already have it,' Jacob says. As graceful and as warm as his aura is, that sounds like an extremely harsh thing to do, but for my sake it sounds necessary.

'Shrewd idea, Jay, but I think I already have an idea about who's supplying this Kraken stuff. Have you ever read *Moby Dick*?' Oracle asks me.

'I've heard of Moby and I've certainly got a—'

'DON'T finish that sentence, for everyone's sake!' Oracle exclaims in a snap, which makes me catch myself smirking, knowing full well my immaturity is threatening him, but I assume he's more annoyed at how lame he thought the joke was. The television screen flickers on when Oracle starts typing something on his keyboard. The screen displays a whole barrage of images all simultaneously coming together. What comes up is an eerily familiar 5cm x 5cm plastic transparent bag with white powder inside it, which makes my heart drop as soon as I see it. *Where have I seen this before?*

'The Kraken is a mythological creature, a giant squid that's been represented plenty of times in modern pop culture,' Oracle tells us, while Jacob sits down on a stool and brings out a lollipop, which makes me want to have one all of sudden.

'So whoever out there is selling this, and distributing a pure version of crack and calling it Kraken, clearly knows a thing or two about history … and great books. There's this Russian mob that's been making quite a name for themselves lately. They might've been those dudes involved in all that diamond thieving in Africa. Have a look here.' Oracle zooms in on the bottom right corner of the packet:

Кракен

'That's Russian for Kraken,' Oracle informs us.

'So what's your point?' I ask impatiently.

'I'm getting to that!' Oracle snaps back. I don't think the 'Grand Wizard of Hoxton' likes me very much. We had waltzed into Jacob's shop expecting answers from this post-year2K, millennium-bug hippie, who's clearly desperately hanging onto the last ounce of youth he has left.

'I would bet my life that this Andrei is the front runner in selling this Kraken product. Perhaps if you had enough product, or if you find a worthwhile artefact for him, that's your ticket to paying back Ian.'

'But what about the police?' I ask.

'That's your decision to make there, buddy,' Oracle says while licking the remnants of the cheesecake away from his fingers.

He continues to fiddle away on the computer screen to find a possible location for this Andrei character, my only lead to getting me out of this mess today. Then, suddenly, as if the peaceful-mellow energy has drifted away with the snow, I hear what seems to be a scuffle back in the shop.

As Jacob and I head back into the shop, through the beaded door curtain (without my hand moving the beads away), I notice a man by the front counter raising his voice to the already spooked Mia. His appearance makes me think he's homeless. Either that or he's got a peculiar way of flaunting himself, but as we approach him at the front of the store, the sudden stench of urine and faeces confirms my assumption that he's definitely homeless. What a pathetic wretch of a human being this quasi man-thing is. Why must society go out on a limb to look out for these excuses of walking, talking flesh? The planet's overpopulated as it is.

Jacob has a concerned look on his face, as does Oracle as he appears through the clinking of the curtain beads against each other, though I feel they've both come across this character before.

'I don't know what to do anymore,' Mia weeps.

'It's OK,' Jacob says, reassuringly. 'Come on, mate, I've given you what I can for Christmas. How much have you had to drink now?'

'Flying with birds is no easy feat. You have to wonder what possesses the dreaded animal to do its thing. Is it nature? Or God? When I was a little girl, my first period was a rather turbulent experience. I had just popped my cherry to …' That's all the gibberish I can muster from him. The stench feels like it's overpowering – shame none of the Turnbulls are here.

Jacob brings out some notes from his wallet and gives them to the poor guy and Oracle eventually manages to persuade the old homeless man to leave the store, taking his smell with him. The previously amiable vibe of the shop has turned to a hushed quiet. The stench is still present and Mia looks crestfallen. She's a little shaken, leaving Jacob to reassure her that everything's OK.

'What happened last time?' I ask.

'He came in once before, but he was less aggressive – thought I'd give him some free clothes, you know? He obviously needed them, poor guy,' Jacob says, while Oracle brings out an anti-odour spray. Lord knows Stuff You needs it.

'Any chance of sending him a bar of soap next time?' I say, smiling. Oracle and Mia don't acknowledge the blatant foolish ignorance of my joke, but Jacob, for the first time since last night, has a look of disapproval, and it makes me regret committing myself to such a comment.

'Well, being a heroin addict can be a bitch. He's more free than you think he is,' Jacob replies.

'I was only joking, mate,' I say, as if to reassure him.

'It's the second time this week. He always comes in with some crazy story about how he was a little girl in his previous life and shit,' Mia said. *Maybe he was.*

I have a sudden mental sigh of relief when I realise that I don't say this out loud. I've already said enough today.

'Is there anything else we need to know about Andrei, Oracle?' Jacob asks, now readjusting the stands around the shop.

'You're lucky you pay me, Jay. You know how much I don't like being called that.'

'Come on, you're like the number one hacker I know. It gives you an added mystique. Besides, anything's better than Percival,' Jacob says, reviving that grin of his.

'Yeah, I still haven't forgiven my mum for that name yet. Anyway, I have some leads on where this Andrei guy might be today.'

'Great, we haven't got much time, or, rather, Luke hasn't got a lot of time.'

At this point, I want to emphasise that I'm still here. We go back to Oracle's office and he gives us some more information.

'I think I found what you're looking for, and looking at the location, it makes perfect sense. . Elephant and Castle.'

'Perfect. Sounds like this is a job for PC Plod, Luke,' Jacob says.

'Who?' I ask.

'That police guy you were telling me about. This is something he needs to be made privy of, savvy?' I think it charming and bewitching that in order to sort this mess out we're going to have to infiltrate an alleged European drug ring in South-East London. *This just keeps getting better and better.*

Oracle then, for some odd reason, proceeds to go on about government conspiracies – how HIV/AIDS was manufactured in the United States and how the mainstream imagery of Jesus Christ was being used as an indoctrination technique to justify some of the world's atrocities – European slavery in particular. As culturally disturbing as this all sounds, I'm sure that if I had time to waste I'd stick around and listen, but there's much bigger fish for me to fry now.

I've never really cared about how the country's being run. Everyone finds out eventually that it's the money that does the talking out there – yet another lesson that's deferred until later on in our lives. Men don't date women and women don't date men. Today, people date lifestyles and ideas – just ask Susie. Her and Jim's blade is still stuck in my heart somewhere. What I've realised now is that, without pain, without sacrifice, we aren't really worth anything to anyone, even ourselves. We attach to situations, people and things we believe make sense but end up becoming saddened when it runs away from us. I guess everything eventually disappears at some point. I can only imagine what that crazy homeless guy was thinking or going through. Whenever I go past other homeless people and occasionally give them money, there's no catharsis, no removal of guilt, only the mystery about where my sterling is going to. After all what's the point of living if you aren't comfortable?

All I know now is that everyone has their pressure points or centre of gravity. Pill is a master bullshit-a-lot who continues to search for acceptance and Jimmy is just Jimmy, privileged and rich, so to him your opinions mean nothing. Jacob, however, may have sleeping problems and hangs with odd people, but looking at how he's living, not having to answer to a boss, he's clearly got a method to his subtle, gentle madness.

As Oracle does a little more digging into this Andrei chap, I come to a realisation that, ironically, poor people represent the rich without the perfume, the expensive dresses, suits and the butler. So what is it all worth? I'd much rather be rich than poor, but since my life is on the line today, all the money in the world won't amount to anything if I'm dead.

Jacob's apartment looked like a reasonable enough place to live despite having no television or even a Wi-Fi connection, only stacks of books, stuffed animals, artwork and replica models. My house is definitely better than his, or rather, if I had my way it wouldn't look anything like his place, but let's throw away my elitist sense of thinking for a minute here. The characters that I've met so far all carry within themselves a sense of liberty, like financial prosperity isn't an issue, or even an ideal for them, and if it were, buying the latest technical mumbo-jumbo wouldn't be the baseline or sole purpose for their achievements. Oddly enough, even though I feel a slight sense of detachment from these folks, it certainly seems like I'm one step closer to sorting all of this out.

Jacob's methodology seems to be that being fearless is the only smart way to be liberated, the only path for freeing yourself from the social paradigm of what the world wants you to be. Before last night, I *thought* I was happy, but I was really dead. Now I'm dumped in this situation, this 'death-ground' if you like, and I'm more alive, more prepared for when the shit hits the fan, but I doubt I'll be prepared for tonight's events and what might become of me. It is all a mystery right now, because when you die, your hopes, dreams and aspirations burn with you.

Jacob now decides to sort a few errands around the shop, and I, more than anything, need some time to catch my thoughts, so I decide to stand outside next to the road and observe the opaque innocence of the snow. Better enjoy it now before heading into good old Lambeth. As I head into an alleyway right next to the store it looks like the pedestrians seem to have dispersed – that morning shopping rush has passed its peak around here.

'Luke? A message from Ian.' An ironclad voice comes out of nowhere from behind me, together with a WHACK to the side of my face, as if last night's battering wasn't bad enough. An intimidating figure of a man, who's clearly made a fair investment into workout supplements, gives me another blow to my stomach – my insides giving way.

'That was for Louis, you cunt.' Whoever this guy is obviously knew who Louis was and knew about Ian. As I get myself back onto my feet, my attacker continues to look at me, his eyes snake-like, with only scorn and hatred reeling out of him.

While I'm trying to catch myself, I vomit in the side of the street, my mouth gushing a red and yellowish goo, clearly from the herbal tea and the alcohol I had last night as well as my blood. My assailant still stands there inquisitively watching me with contempt, reaches into his pocket and brings out a phone, makes a phone call and then gives it to me. I barely manage to say hello, but the voice that responds is disturbingly familiar. The man on the other side of the connection is probably hearing my wails.

'You haven't forgotten about me, have you, Luke?'

'Who's this? Oh shit, no I haven't, Ian. I'm still working on it.'

'Good, listen, I like you, Luke, I really do. It's just that we're in a desperate time now, me and you, so come back to the pub tonight. Just remember I'm always watching,' Despite his threatening tone, Ian sounded like he had company.

I hand the phone back to the henchman, now recognising him as one of the guys that held me back when I wanted to get even with Louis last night at Cleo's. What an ugly bastard. He walks away and I stand in the street, with the snow falling, my disparate sense of realism hitting me on the face once again – literally. I start to feel my eyes water, while my mouth quivers as I think again of my dear beautiful and intelligent sister Molly, and then I burst into tears.

22

Detective Chief Inspector Frank Walker, December 24th, 1:05pm

Despite meeting up with Winston earlier, his attempts to contact Luke proved to be unsuccessful: *Your call has been forwarded to the voicemail service of ...* That was a line that Frank couldn't bear to hear anymore. For Luke's sake he hoped that he hadn't decided to flee the country; he had seen that happen a number of times before. Spooked illegal drug couriers attempting to outsmart their clients – all of them failing to flee the country for good, all of them reported missing shortly afterwards.

Frank decided it was best to drive back towards Scotland Yard. Perhaps there might be some documentation that may prove to be useful to him in his office, maybe even another method to take down both McAllister and Romanenko all in one night. Tonight would be the perfect opportunity to achieve just that – the ideal opening to prove that Drax was still relevant to today's modern, social media and lifestyle-obsessed, driven world.

Even though he was still a Drax operative working within the London Met's SOCA Unit, collaborating with members of outside forces other than Drax was deemed as risky behaviour, simply due to the strong possibility of any classified intel being leaked. *Desperate times call for desperate measures*, Frank thought. He then contacted Marlon after his failed attempts to call Luke.

'Merry Christmas, Chief. You missing us already? It's only been a week …'

'Afternoon, Marlon, it sounds busy over there. Good to know it's not like the *Mary Celeste* today.'

'Ha ha, it could be worse, Chief, believe me.'

'Marlon, I need you to do me a favour. Can you head upstairs and check if McIntlock is in?'

'I haven't seen him yet today. It is Christmas Eve, Frank. What's this about?'

'You don't know him like I do. Could you head upstairs and check? I'm on my way. I'll explain everything when I get there.' Frank knew that if McIntlock had even a sniff of him being there, that would be an automatic dismissal from the Drax programme. McIntlock had a reputation of ruthlessness towards other colleagues, but he always had a soft spot for Frank, something that he had never taken advantage of.

As Frank made his way to London Victoria station, he was slightly relieved that the roads weren't busy. The snow had clearly convinced some people to do their shopping online, not making them endure the travel difficulties thanks to the snow today.

*

Meanwhile, back at the station, Marlon, fully appreciative and even uplifted by Frank entrusting a task to him, a simple one at that, was on his way to the upper division of SOCA, before he was stopped by one of his colleagues to confirm a few details. After that brief intermission, he proceeded upstairs to witness an almost familiar balding head that almost looked like McIntlock. He continued towards the office noticing that it was Sergeant Banahan of the forensics division only just leaving the meeting room. There had been a departmental meeting between the heads of each division that had just closed. Marlon wondered whether DSU McIntlock had been in attendance or not.

As he proceeded to the office, he could see that all the staff were still fully occupied on their computer screens. Marlon looked around the room, the energy still tense and serious – what you'd expect from a sensitive department such as this. Matthew Paul McIntlock III – Detective Superintendent of SOCA Operations. Marlon knocked twice on his door. No response. He decided to go in, just to be sure.

'Hey, what are you doing up here?' If there were a prize for startling someone in a tense situation, Kyra would certainly receive top draw for that.

'Just checking if the chief is in.'

'I think I saw him … not sure if it was him or not though.'

'Sergeant Banahan?' Marlon said, slightly annoyed now.

'Hmm, not sure, they're both losing their hair. Anyways, I've got us tickets to *The Lion King* show on New Year's – I'm well excited,' said Kyra quietly, trying not to disturb the sombre atmosphere in the department.

'I thought you wanted to see the Michael Jackson one?'

'Yeah, I changed my mind.'

Marlon felt his phone vibrate. It could only be Detective Walker sending a text message:

Any sign of him? ETA 10 mins F

'I really need to go, Kyra. I'll call you soon for lunch,' Marlon said quietly in haste, and he walked quickly out of the office back down the stairs – perhaps there was something in Detective Walker's office that he didn't want McIntlock finding? He walked past his own workstation and into Frank's office. He was startled by a figure rummaging through Frank's filing cabinet and drawers, papers scattered all over the room. It was McIntlock.

'Can I help you, officer?' The DSU asked inquisitively.

'I … er … just wanted to see if Detective Walker was around,' Marlon said hesitantly.

'Walker has taken a leave of absence. You know how hard that man likes to work.' McIntlock gave an ironic smile.

'I certainly do, sir.,' Marlon said.

As McIntlock gestured, indicating to him to leave the room, Marlon nervously left the office, reeling at what he'd seen. What was he not being told? He wanted to give Frank a call in confidence to explain what was going on but was afraid that might compromise him. He decided to head to Victoria station, just a little way away from headquarters and sent a text letting him know where to meet him.

*

To Marlon, the man approaching him at Victoria station appeared somewhat younger; it was the first time that he'd seen him wearing casual winter attire.

'You look very ... festive, Detective,' Marlon said with a tired smile.

'Thanks. Did you manage to find the chief?'

'Yeah, err ... he wasn't in his office, Frank. He was ... in your office, looking for something. Do you mind telling me what's going on?'

'Shit. Sounds like he's desperate. OK, you need to keep this to yourself. The raid we did the other day, the lead we had on Romanenko, this whole Kraken business? While I've been off, I've continued working on it.'

'I wouldn't have thought you'd be doing anything else, sir,'

'Thanks, Marlon.'

'Kraken is going for a stupid amount of money out there. I imagine whoever controls distribution of the product is making a fortune, and no, I meant that as in it wouldn't be like you to simply give up on a case just like that,' said Marlon graciously, reaffirming his confidence to Frank. 'After all that madness at Whitechapel, anything's possible.'

'I know, Marlon. I've also found another lead on McAllister too. He's looking to get into retirement ...'

'And you still think Kraken and McAllister are linked somehow?'

'Very, very loosely, but I doubt he'd want to get himself involved in that. He may have the reputation but he hasn't got the resources to actively control such an operation, but there's something I'm missing. Another piece to the puzzle – that's why I wanted you to have a look at anything you can find in my office, but it sounds like McIntlock beat you to it.'

'What do you need me to do?' Marlon asked, his hands deep in his pockets, wondering whether he should take an early one for the day – it was Christmas Eve after all.

'Act like nothing's happened. If you don't go back, that may raise a few eyebrows. No doubt other people saw McIntlock go into my office, and then saw you go in there after him.'

*

As Frank said this, there was a vibration on his phone. He looked and saw a missed call. It was Luke.

23

I feel pathetic and useless right now, as I sit down on the side of the alleyway, contemplating my relevance to this life. With my mouth tasting of blood and my stomach still stinging, my head continues spinning before an ice-cold gust of wind wakes me up. The snow seems to have died down a little and it's pretty much a ghost town on the high street. A couple of bystanders drop me a few pennies with a *Merry Christmas* greeting. I've only been here for about ten minutes, I think, and I've made about five pounds. *Not a bad hustle.*

'Not a bad hustle indeed,' a raspy voice suddenly says right next to me.

'What?' I say, as I notice the same homeless man who came and outraged Jacob's Stuff You business with his smell. What does this guy want from me?

'You'll be surprised at how often people talk to themselves. Look at me, for example. I wasn't always like this. A lot of fucked-up things happen to fucked-up people, and this is the result.'

'Why are you telling me this? What you said earlier didn't make any sense.'

'What makes sense to you? Trust me, mate, I've been through some shit. I'm not crazy,' the man says, with his breath reeking of lager and malt, which suggests otherwise. 'Are you friends with the gaffer in there?' he asks.

'Who?'

'You know, the boss, the owner of the shop?'

'Oh, Jacob? Sure, I know him.'

'Well, I'm authorised to tell you this. Look at me, do you think I want to be here?' the man says defiantly, after which he starts laughing maniacally.

I should really be on my way. The biting cold has gotten to my fingers and my backside feels a little damp now from sitting here for nearly half an hour.

'The world doesn't give a shit about your problems. There's no messiah, no saviour, no bloody nothing, but that's the beauty of it. I think I'm more authorised to tell you that than anyone, even the boss man in that shop.'

'OK, I'm sorry,' I say, while bringing out my phone. The only logical thing to do now would be to call Detective Frank, and it coincidentally looks like he's been trying to get hold of me for a while too.

'Sorry for what?' The man grumbles, as he looks even more disgruntled, like he's had enough of this life, and who can blame him? I don't believe he would've chosen to live like this if he had options, but looking more closely at his face I notice a strong greyness to his eyes. He was looking at me, but not right at me.

'Sorry for you being … like this,' I say, as I conclude that the man's blind, making me regret even more what I said earlier about him in the store. Ignorance truly is bliss.

Everyone in the store is probably wondering where I am now, so I get back to my feet and wipe the dry remnants of the crocodile tears off my face and dial Frank's number. Whatever Detective Frank has been trying to get hold of me for hopefully should be good. The first time goes straight to voicemail, but if he's called me this many times then it must be serious. Before walking back towards Stuff You, I have one last glance at the homeless man and I see just a trail of footprints to the end of the alleyway. I try Frank again while walking back into the store.

'Luke! Happy you called. We need to talk.'

'We certainly do.'

'Where are you? You sound down. What's happened?'

'One of Ian's guys gave me a subtle reminder of tonight's objective.'

'Ian got to you first then. Are you OK?' Frank asks. The warmth of the Stuff You store welcomes me as I walk back in. Mia seems to be occupied tidying up shelves as I walk through the beaded door curtain and delve back into Oracle's room.

'I've been better. Look, we've found a way to get Ian's money back. We're gonna go to this bar in Lambeth. Apparently some dodgy European guy owns it.'

'Who's that?'

'Romany, Romaneeeko? Roma-something.'

As I'm trying to pronounce this correctly, Oracle whispers loudly to me, 'Who's that?'

'It's that police guy again,' I say.

'Oh, it's Romanenko.' I give Oracle a thumbs-up. I think I'm in his good books now.

'It's Romanenko, Frank.'

'Andrei Romanenko, Luke?'

'Yeah. Sounds about right.'

'Ha ha ha, you must be joking!' Frank sounds a lot happier all of a sudden. I think I made his day somehow.

'No, I'm definitely not joking. Apparently he owes Jacob some money, so we're gonna see if he can get something done then head to Ian's and you can do what you want with him.'

'You have no idea what this means, Luke my boy. Good man! I'll meet you over at the Elephant and Castle. We can all brief each other on our approach. I'm not too far from there now. I can meet you in, say, twenty minutes?' Frank says very excitedly.

'I'll let you know when we're close,' I say. I hang up my phone, mentally noting that Frank's day must clearly be a contrast to mine.

'Shit, what happened to your face, bro?' Oracle asks.

'I had a rude awakening.'

174

Ikenna Nwimo

I catch Jacob sleeping on Oracle's couch, with the same lollipop stuck in his mouth – his narcolepsy doing me no favours once again. How he's been able to maintain a business with his sleeping pattern is beyond me, but it looks like he's done a pretty swell job so far. Oracle looks solemn now, perhaps even sympathetic to my facial injuries.

'Sorry, dude, we have a plan in place to get into Romanenko's.'

'Great,' I say, not knowing what this plan is yet.

'You know, you remind me a little bit of what he was like years ago,' Oracle says, glancing at Jacob's peaceful slumber.

'How?'

'Well, he's certainly paid his dues, believe me. Considering where he's come from to then build all of this? It's exceptional.'

I nod as I struggle to disagree with Oracle. He then goes over to Jacob, as if him sleeping at this time of day is embarrassing.

'Sorry, he does this all the time,' Oracle tells me.

'I noticed.'

Jacob wakes up from whatever dream he was in and yawns while holding his lollipop. He glances at my face, seeing the extra bruises.

'Are you OK?' Jacob asks groggily, while trying to get his question across and his tongue wrestling with the lollipop.

'Yeah, I'm fine,' I say.

'You sure?'

'I just had another *wake-up* call, that's all.'

'Funny. I get it,' Jacob says, smiling while staring at my newly damaged face.

'Get what?' I ask.

'You're not supposed to talk about it, right?' Jacob hands me a tissue from the coffee table. 'Use this to wipe the blood off your face then. You're officially one step closer to freedom. From now on everything will taste much better than it used to. Trust me.'

I guess there's no shame in having some scars.

*

As we make our way to the Romanenko location, what shocks me the most is how quickly the day has gone. My time at the Stuff You

175

vintage/junk store obviously took longer than expected, and I still feel like God took a massive dump on me and asked me to sit with Hades in the Underworld right by the 'douchebags only' section.

Right now, my sister and Julia would more than likely be getting the house decorations together for when the guests arrive tomorrow for their annual (free) Christmas dinner. After all, Santa Claus didn't sacrifice himself for our sins for us to eat alone now, did he?

Before entering Old Street station en route to Elephant and Castle, I message Frank letting him know we're on our way, to which I receive a quick acknowledgement from him. Amidst all the chaos of today, I wonder what everyone who was supposed to be close to me might be doing right now. I doubt that ex-girlfriend witch of mine will be doing anything like what my dear sister might be doing – probably doing her nails or talking behind Tamera's back again. What a let-down she was. All those times I provided her with a shoulder to cry on and then she just decides to vanish, like there was nothing between us.

A more self-respecting man (probably Jacob) would've walked away from that emotional vampire ages ago – no matter what *Alpha Digest* tells me. Once again it's pissing me off that it's only now that I'm realising how wrong I was about a lot of things. Lord only knows how I'd react if I saw Jimmy again. Well, Jacob's very much a doer. I'm sure he'd have the nail gun in his apartment somewhere.

As we pass by Borough station on the Underground train, my eyes water a little at how little time I've spent with Molly recently. Recently it's only been a 'good morning' and a 'where are you going?' type of dialogue, which normally results in 'out with friends' or no reply, all topped off with the weekly chat the morning after a night out on the town or her dealing with my marijuana-influenced behaviour on my 'high-days'. After last night, sadly I've learned the hard way that the deception of a female isn't one to contend with. They are supposed to be the civilising force in this society, the standard of common sense, justice, order and love. The overbearing affection a mother has for a child, that warm fuzzy feeling you get when you meet a woman you're attracted to – this is what makes their manipulations even more ugly and horrifying.

24

Winston went to the post office to send his daughter and wife a Christmas package, reassuring them that he'd make some time to see them again soon, hopefully by New Year's Eve. Tonight, however, was a different business. He needed to keep a closer eye on Ian to ensure he wasn't going to commit to any rash actions before Luke got Ian his money. He made his way back to the Cock and Bull pub, expecting another delivery of alcohol, albeit with some delays due to the festive period.

This would've usually been the duty of some of the other employees at the pub, but to keep himself over there today, he'd made sure that they all took the afternoon off, sending them all a text asking them not to worry about today's delivery and to save their energies for tonight's shift. Customers tend to let themselves go the night before Christmas, particularly younger consumers, all wanting to dare themselves to wake up with a Christmas Day hangover. *Happy Holidays*!

After signing off the delivery and allowing the suppliers to bring the alcohol into its usual location through the back door, Winston looked for Ian. As thorough as he was, experience taught both Ian and Winston to be very meticulous with their movements. Ian was in the habit of disposable phones, leaving no trace of himself anywhere – if he needed to disappear and make himself scarce, this wouldn't be a problem for him. Winston went up to the bar for a normal check on the place – all neat, tidy and ready for another evening of business. The Christmas tree was up, it's constantly changing lights already gracing the bar – the cleaner this morning obviously put in extra effort to ensure the place was spring-cleaned for tonight.

Ian could only ever be in one other place. It would make sense to see him before the employees came in to commence their shifts. The downstairs lounge/bar was empty, cold and silent, its leather seats and snooker table all clear, like nobody had stepped in there for a while. The silence that engulfed the basement lounge came with a strange alien-like eeriness. Something wasn't right. He went into Ian's office to check everything was still in place, but the room reeked of Scotch whisky.

The stuffed bear in the corner of the room looked more threatening than it usually did, with the desk light on and the leather chair right opposite the main desk. Ian's chair was facing away from the desk though, was the only thing that was out of place.

'Ian?'

Nothing was to prepare Winston for what he saw next. As he turned Ian's chair, he saw that the front of it was covered in blood, his old friend's eyes and mouth wide open, his wrists and his neck slit. Winston gasped in horror at Ian's lifeless body.

Winston shrunk down next to his dear old friend's body in shock and with regret that he hadn't been at the Cock and Bull earlier to perhaps prevent this from happening. Sadness then overwhelmed Winston. *Who could've done this?* There were a number of jealous rivals who Winston could think of, but not at this time of year; even his most hated foes wouldn't have taken the risk of attacking a competitor on Christmas Eve. It was disrespectful. Winston adjusted himself and got his phone out to contact Frank. Only he would be able to find out who did this, as well as being the only man he could trust now.

25

It's already way past lunchtime as I make my way into the underbelly of the Elephant and Castle, past the Ministry of Sound nightclub, walking further as I enter the stairs of the underground public tunnel. It reeks of urine and helplessness, and sadly there are a few homeless people lying here whom, after the minor altercation earlier, I now wish I could save this Christmas, but I *need* to get through this. We met Frank outside the station, eager to get the low down on settling this thing, but before I was even able to make a formal introduction to Jacob, the phone call Frank received sounded like the shit hit the fan. He reassured me that he'll get in contact somehow, which I'm sure he will, but we've come up with a plan on how we'll approach this anyway. *Now or never. Here we go.*

My heart races even more on reaching the market area. Each stall is selling something I would never dream of buying. One stall is selling counterfeit Louis Vuitton belts, the type you'd normally see wannabes wearing in Club Eros. Another stall is selling Snapbacks, two for ten pounds. None of them are worth buying because none have the colour that I would require anyway. Clearly these market stalls are desperate for customers on their last-minute quest for presents. The whole market is filled to the brim with customers. All around the market there are senior citizens carrying their roller baskets to fit as much useless shit in as possible, which slows my journey to Romanenko's.

'*The bar should be easy to identify*,' Oracle mentioned before we left. I just wanted to know in what way should it be easier to identify? Somehow the cold was a little easier to endure due to the weight of the situation at hand now. I then notice an establishment that looks like it was supposed to be shut down, with no shop sign and an array of different lights – pink and blue – inside the store. This could be the place that Oracle meant.

I shift through the crowds of people in the market without saying sorry as I would normally do, to which I receive a number of negative looks and grumbles, but I don't care. From outside the bar I can make out about ten people, I think. I don't believe an establishment this small would be able to hold many more people than that anyway, but I imagine it would make a perfect front for an alleged European diamond thief and drug baron.

There isn't anything particularly threatening about this club, I don't think, although from the outside I can tell straight away that it's not supposed to be for people like me. Outside the club I see some promo girls with bright, sparkling dresses, Santa Claus hats and Rudolph red noses who seem to be unaffected by the cold.

I walk up to someone who looks to be the bouncer. I can tell because he's built like a wrestler and bald. I'm guessing he's about six foot five; he has a goatee and a no-nonsense mug for a face.

'I'm here to see Andrei? I think I'm at the right place,' I say, with my arms shaking, desperate to head inside to get out of the cold.

'Andrei here not, not here,' says the bouncer, which answers my question about this being the correct bar. Another bouncer comes out of nowhere, identical build, similar face, height, but without a goatee, starts saying some things out loud in another language. He then stares at me – I assume he's checking if I'm a threat to him.

'Errr, I'm sorry for my friend. He's not very smart. He's what you British call "retarded",' the second bouncer says, while the other simply looks at him, emotionless, and says a couple of words in a non-English language – me hoping there would be a set of subtitles somewhere so I could understand what they're saying, but I couldn't care less right now. The conversation they're having seems to have gone from opinionated to heated and then to a full argument now, so I slip past them and make my way inside the bar. Part of me wishes both the twin bouncers would settle it soon though – it is the time of giving, after all.

There's what appears to be a little booth to the side just before another pair of double doors, which I assume would be the cloak room, and the lady in there – big hooped earrings, cheap red lipstick, with her hair gelled and tied in a bun – greets me with a fake smile..

'Hello, handsome, two pounds per item please.' Her accent is also foreign, but at least her English is better than Dick and Dom outside.

'No, I'm fine, thank you. I'm here to speak to Andrei,' I say.

'Andrei who?'

'Romanenko? Kraken. You know the guy who does Kraken?' I ask.

'Ahh yes.' She smiles at me again and is this time much less fake and more welcoming. 'We have plenty of this here, pretty boy.' She looks to be a bringing out a bag of Kraken, to which I gesture that I'm not interested. I need to walk away before this woman makes me cringe any further.

'Have a drink and enjoy yourself.'

'OK, thank you.' Conversation ended. Thank goodness.

Even though the crowd is small, the atmosphere in here is somewhat sombre. Everyone looks to be having a good time, and there's some laughter, but no one's dancing or anything. *It's not my scene*. Commercial eighties disco music is playing in the background. I'd better get a move on before I hear a song that I really don't want to be hearing right now. Either way, if I was Detective Frank, I would say this would be the perfect ruse to be keeping something in here that shouldn't be here, so I hope Jacob plays his part well. I head over to the bar to grab a drink, hoping that the alcohol will ease the tension. A single straight shot of vodka should do the trick. If I'm leaving Planet Earth tonight and joining God in the heavens, please let me leave here intoxicated and have heaven see me at my ugliest. I bloody well hope whatever Frank is up to now is worth it.

The music all of a sudden sounds a hell of a lot louder as the vodka slightly vaporises my sense of being as I shuffle around the club reaching for what I assume to be the toilets but instead is actually a flight of stairs – the vodka is playing mind tricks on me already. As I climb them, I notice some kind of golden ornament by the top of the landing, but with my new-found Dutch courage intact, I continue up the flight of stairs.

'Oi, boy, where you going?'

The voice behind me couldn't have frozen me any more than it has. I turn around, sheepishly hoping that I'm just hearing voices. It's one of the twin bouncers – the 'retarded' one with the goatee.

'That's private office. Toilets over there. Can you hear what I'm saying? Over there,' he tells me.

I start clearing my throat a little, then force myself to raise my voice so he can understand my impatience now amidst the loud pop music.

'I. AM. LOOKING. FOR. ANDREI.'

As rude as that may have sounded if I was completely sober, I couldn't have gotten my point across any more clearly than that. He gives me a real steely look afterwards.

'Come.'

He then goes past me up the stairs and I follow him. We enter an office, real lush, with expensive antiques and paintings around the room. The black marbled floor complements the black marbled desk. I presume this is where Andrei has been spending the diamonds he's been stealing from Africa. He certainly has expensive taste, hence why Jacob is inclined to get his money back. The office contrasts with the rest of the club in terms of its interior decoration. Johnny Turnbull would be impressed, I would imagine. The bouncer who's now added 'gangster's henchman' to his job description takes his radio and blurbs something.

'Andrei will be here soon,' he tells me.

'Good, I haven't got much time. It's Christmas you know,' I say.

'Huh?'

'Never mind.'

I could have a career visiting local gangsters now, although I don't believe I could get used to it. I'm sitting down on a leather chair once again but this time it's in front of a black marble desk. I take a quick scan of the room, hoping I can find something that could be worth at least ten thousand pounds. Shouldn't be too difficult. There's a stuffed model of a fox that must be the one Jacob mentioned – not bad, but I much prefer the bear over at the Cock and Bull better, you can see the anger in its eyes. Hopefully I can find something small enough to take for myself if I get out of this alive – I haven't managed to buy anything for anyone this Christmas yet.

After a brief scan of the room, I'm rewarded with the presence of a man, about average height, dark-ish hair, sharp eyes, medium build, with a three-day razor stubble. He clearly hasn't heard of exfoliation, but this thought is overcome quickly by what he says to me.

'Tell me something, are you British all fucking stupid? Did he send you as well?'

As much as I just about made his sentence out, this man's English is much easier to understand than Dick and Dom or the cloakroom lady, but I'm still flabbergasted by him, his accent making his sentence sound more menacing.

'I haven't been sent here by anyone. I need something from you. I presume you're Andrei?' He gives me a real awkward look, as if taken aback by my approach. He then begins murmuring to his retarded henchman. He proceeds to laugh maniacally – that evil kind of laugh you usually hear before the villain reveals his master plan for world domination.

'Yes, I'm Andrei. You think you can just walk in here and make such demands? I run legitimate business. I take from previous guy and make club nice,' he says, sitting comfortably in his chair – all he needs is a cute white cat for him to start petting.

'You took something from a friend of mine, and all I want is some money. Let me take the fox – how much did you pay for it?' I take a deep breath and clear my throat as Andrei watches on. 'I didn't come here to insult you or fight you. These past two days have been hell for me. I've been through some shit. I've spent time with a lot of shit people and it's only now that I'm asking why – I DON'T know why. All I know is that for me to sort out my shit, I need the shit that's going to get me out of this shit!'

My fundamental pattern of speech went straight out of the window. I'm in a desperate situation and I *need* a way out. He looks at me for about ten seconds, studying me as if I'm just another human being begging to be sleeping with the fishes. His attention then turns to some shouting and loud voices outside the office. Andrei tells the bouncer something in Russian, presumably to find out what all the fuss is about outside. I turn around to see what he does, just to be sure that my assumption's correct, and just before he motions to open the door, there's an enthusiastic knocking on the door. He talks foreign again, opens the door and my heart races to see the familiar young man, this time in a sheepskin winter jacket, who greets Andrei in Russian. Jacob. *About bloody time.*

'Ahhh, Mr Brown. Season's greetings! How can I help you on this Christmas Eve? You're the third person who I wasn't expecting a visit from today,' Andrei says, smiling, looking like he's genuinely happy to see Jacob.

'And this guy's supposed to be the second?' Jacob says, looking at me with scorn and then a wink. S*tick with the plan and follow my lead*. They both exchange handshakes, then Jacob walks over to the stuffed fox.

'Have you given him a name yet?' Jacob asks.

'I'm at a crossroads between Django and Scarface. Reminds me of the stories my grandfather gave me back in the old country. I'm very happy you gave this to me Jacob. It gives me ... inspiration, you know? Like Machiavelli's *The Prince* – have you read it?'

'One of my favourites! "*One must be a fox to recognise traps and a lion to frighten wolves*",' Jacob says, smiling. I'm intrigued by the conversation but sincerely hoping they'll both just get straight to the point now.

'Precisely. My friend, is there any chance of having a lion's head? I want to put it just over here, just above my desk,' Andrei says while getting out a cigarette.

'Oooh, that'll be a challenge, Andrei, but nothing I can't handle, which is kind of why I'm here today.'

'And what does bring you here then, Mr Brown. Do I smell a trap?' Andrei says, looking at me suspiciously.

'Is this what you've stooped to now? Taking defenceless young men into your office? You know why I'm here. I'm chasing payment,' Jacob says. *Charming, intelligent, impetuous Jacob.*

Andrei chuckles to himself and says a couple of lines in Russian to Jacob, non-threatening though, like they have an in-joke between themselves. Fair enough, I suppose. Judging by how the past forty-eight hours or so have gone, I should expect anything weird and unexpected.

Andrei, walks out of the office with the bouncer, leaving Jacob and me alone. Jacob then goes over to Andrei's desk and shuffles through his drawers. *What's he looking for?*

'I would've really loved it if you told me what you were going to do before you do it!' I whisper loudly.

'This is precisely why Oracle and I didn't tell you the whole plan. You wouldn't have agreed with it,' Jacob says, whispering loudly while rummaging through the desk.

'How? You were supposed to come in behind me in the club!'

'And watch you get wasted over a shot of vodka? Yeah I saw you. I've seen enough entertainment from you today – sshhhh!' Jacob says, holding a finger up to keep me quiet. He then finds a small black leather pouch.

'What are you doing?' I ask, hoping he won't give me a complicated answer.

'Remember, I'm a collector. You can thank me later – just play along.'

'Sure, play along with a guy who I thought was supposed to be one of the good guys and who actually works with some drug dealer!'

'Would you just calm down. I don't work for—'

The door opens and Andrei walks back in with a grin on his face and a bottle of Vodka in his hand. He oddly enough doesn't say a word, which makes the situation very awkward indeed. He reaches into his drawers, hopefully not noticing anything misplaced on Jacob's part, and pulls out two shot glasses.

Feeling a new sense of fear in me now, it looks like this is it. The end is nigh for me. Here it goes.

'You know what? Ever since I've heard of you and your little crew, I must admit I've been a little impressed, maybe even scared walking in here, but I have to say that this is outrageous.' I feel Jacob gazing at me, forgetting, unfortunately, that *I'm* in this situation and not Jacob. I'm not even supposed to know him – in essence I'm an unwanted guest, but I continue.

'Yeah, sure, you all *look* like bad people. The big creepy Gothic office overlooking the club, the scary but retarded bouncers. I must say, for being a well-known drug lord, Andrei, you're pathetic,' I say.

'What the fuck are you talking about?' Andrei says.

An odd silence falls. I can even feel eyes staring at me from behind. I look behind me to see Jacob having a 'What the fuck' look on him. He smiles again and says something amusing to Andrei, which makes me look stupid, but it's maybe for my own benefit.

'Ha ha ha ha, you think I'm the one responsible for Kraken?'

'Err … yeah?' I say.

'That's what I was trying to tell you, old sport,' Jacob says.

At this point I'm unsure what it is that I hate right now. Is it the fact that I still don't know anything about what's going on? Or the deliberate aloofness from Jacob?

'I thought Andrei was—'

'You thought wrong, my friend. I tell you I run legit business here.' Andrei laughs, like my questions were just entertainment for him. Andrei and Jacob start sharing the vodka between themselves.

'You looking in wrong place, my friend. I was told a policeman was looking for me. When Yuri told me you walked into my office, I thought he was you.'

'So who or what is Kraken then?'

'Kraken is sold just like any other drug out there, on the streets, in the park, in the offices, boardrooms, anywhere. Somehow, because I Russian and not Ukrainian they think I'm the big man. If Home Office want to come, let them come! OK, sure, we sell in club, but the other club is just as bad!'

Call it luck or coincidence, but it was fortunate that Frank had been detained. Jacob trades a few more laughs with Andrei and reveals to us that Kraken is something that they'd heard of even in the old country. Andrei's going to pay Jacob doubly back for the stuffed lion's head that he requested from him earlier. Either way, whatever was in that black leather pouch that Jacob took from Andrei, it better had been worth that ten grand or maybe more. At my sudden relief at the revelation, I take one of the shot glasses and take two more shots of vodka, knowing that I've just gone past a major hurdle. All that's left is sending Ian whatever's in Jacob's pouch and getting this all done and dusted.

*

As we leave the bar, I see that the market stalls have all disappeared, with people dispersing into the underground tunnels and into the train station as the icy wind continues to buffet the city. It's gone dark all of a sudden, so everyone's either in the bars getting their final drinks before Christmas Day tomorrow or having a warm night in with their families. As much as I wish I was doing one or the other, embracing the ever more cold presence of Ian McAllister and his good old buddy Winston is something that I still dread but something that I have to go through anyway.

26

Detective Chief Inspector Frank Walker, December 24th, 5.45pm

Frank walked at a blistering pace, hotly anticipating what lay in store after the shock of Winston's phone call earlier. He was excruciatingly close to finally finding Romanenko, but it was up to Luke to sort this out. If he made it out of there alive, then he would at some point have to make his way back to the Cock and Bull pub anyway. As he walked along Shoreditch High Street towards the pub, he once again recalled the telephone conversation:

'Who's this?'

'Frank? It's Winston. You need to come here quickly, it's Ian, something's happened.'

'What's that?'

'I can't say it over the phone but you're the only man I trust right now. Can you please get here? It's a bloody mess. You'll find the back door opened for you.'

Frank heard Winston's voice tremble with fear and desperation. Whatever it was, it sounded damn serious.

He briskly walked into the pub through the back door, as directed, and closed it behind him slowly. Whatever 'mess' Winston spoke about on the phone would certainly contrast with what was in the main bar. This was Frank's first visit to the Cock and Bull. He'd had enough reports in the past suggesting that this was the McAllisters' base of operations, but he'd never paid an official trip here though, for there would've been a strong chance of Winston being spooked by Frank's presence. This still wouldn't necessarily be classified as an official trip, though he'd been summoned here out of desperation from a trusted informant.

The main bar was empty, and an eerie silence seemed to beckon him. Public places like these needed to have people in them, hence why the silence seemed unnatural. Frank went behind the bar, through the back door and down the stairs, each step eliciting creaking from the old wooden steps. Off of the basement landing, he found a very well-decorated lounge. Yet another bar occupied the back wall, with a snooker table in the middle of the room. The area itself was complemented with Chesterfield leather armchairs and a darts board. There was a half-open door behind the snooker table that enticed Frank's curiosity. He went through the door and noticed a medium-sized poker table with cards, dice and chips neatly stacked next to each other in the middle of the table. This must've been where Luke had been down on his luck. There was no sign of Winston in there.

He left the poker room and noticed a corridor just past the other side of the stairs, with doors on either side of the wall. He proceeded in this direction and detected the familiar whiff of Scotch whisky. It got stronger the closer he walked towards the door.

'Frank?' a solemn voice said.

Frank froze when he saw what was in front of him. Winston was on the floor, curled up, his face red and eyes watery – presumably from all the tears.

'You should see this, Frank.'

He looked into the front of the room and saw a leather office chair covered with blood and there was a hand poking out at the side. He went round the chair and saw Ian McAllister's lifeless body.

'What in the world happened?' Frank asked.

'I just found him like this. I've no idea who would've done this to him. No one had any reason why they would want Ian dead, Frank. What do you think we should do?'

'I need to take a proper look,' Frank said, as he stared at his former target's hands and feet. There'd clearly been a struggle. Ian more than likely knew his killer, but he hadn't gone down without a fight.

'His neck's broken,' Frank said while observing Ian's jawline. There were red marks all over his neck, right above where his throat was cut open.

'Are you sure no one would've wanted Ian dead tonight? Romanenko maybe?' Frank asked, still in a daze over today's turn of events.

'Kraken did slow business down a little over here, but we were still having enough people coming in for poker,' Winston said, still reeling from shock.

'That still doesn't explain why he was killed,' Frank said. 'There must've been for something Ian might've known about, something he might've heard?'

'He never usually had any whisky bottles in here,' Winston said, pointing at the near-empty bottle of *Jack Daniels* left by Ian's desk. Frank's attention returned to the strong and familiar smell. A past taboo that had caused him plenty of pain was about to cause him another headache.

'How much of a drinker was Ian?' Frank asked while examining the half-empty bottle.

'Sensible. He never really drank in here, only by the bar in the lounge if he fancied one. This was his sanctuary. Only for handling "business", if you know what I mean,' Winston said.

'OK, have you communicated with anyone since I arrived?'

'I've cancelled everyone's shifts tonight, and I wanted to let the lads know to keep on their toes, but I wanted you to come down first.'

'Good idea. Call the police. You need to be calm and tell them everything.'

'I can't bring them around here! A dead body found in an illegal underground den? I'm gonna call the boys to hide it,' Winston exclaimed. 'It's a bloody great time of the year to start a gang war, isn't it?'

The unforgiving wail of a police siren was suddenly heard throughout the Cock and Bull.

'Shit, sounds like someone already has,' Frank said.

'Fuck knows who did that.'

'OK, I have to go. I'm onto something with this. You'll have to sort them out, Winston, have a chat with them, try and act like you're oblivious to this. Where's your fire exit?'

'Right by where you came in. I'll show you.'

They both exited the office and raced up the stairs. Hoping to avoid any missteps with the authorities, Winston quickly escorted Frank towards the fire exit. As Winston forcefully opened up the door, a gargantuan screech befell the once silent Cock and Bull pub again. The back door fire alarm had gone off.

'Well at least the alarms are working,' Winston said with irony.

'Listen, if the worse comes to it and they take you in, tell them nothing,' Frank said.

'This isn't the first time, so no need to tell me, mate, and if I don't see you again, Frank, thanks for helping me.'

'I'm sorry, Winston.'

'Don't be. Let's be honest, I had it coming anyway,' Winston said with a tired and sad grin.

Frank quickly left the area, avoiding the police. When he looked back, he noticed there was already a crowd of people building.

What was most puzzling to Frank wasn't the death of Ian McAllister. With the type of work that a man like Ian was in, sadly, a brutal death was always on the cards. It was a question of who he rubbed the wrong way to provoke his murder. While the police would more than likely arrest Winston and take him in under suspicion of manslaughter, it sounded like someone somewhere else was pulling the strings. It was safe to assume that Romanenko, to Frank's knowledge, wouldn't have the wherewithal to want to kill an

East London loan shark. They weren't necessarily in direct competition with each other and it would be extremely unwise for either men to want blood on their hands over a festive period.

Whoever had done this was a different type of animal, someone who had connections, money and power. It was a loathsome thing to comprehend, but McAllister's murder looked to have been committed by an expert. Someone wanted Ian shutting up by any means necessary. Frank, in the blind hope that nothing had happened to young Luke, messaged him to meet at the one place where no one would likely be tonight – Turnbull and Partners Ltd.

Part 3

Exodus

27

While en route to the Cock and Bull pub, Jacob and I decide to make our way to Luciano's not far from the pub on the High Road for a soothing hot chocolate – call it celebratory if you like, but I feel like I damn near deserve it. I'm not sure what it is, but something is telling me that tonight isn't over. Despite my vodka shots taken at Romanenko's, I still feel rather coy about my performance earlier.

For a brief moment, I actually believe that's it. What is it about the fear that compels me? Is it the threat of having my genitals being fed to pigs? Despite the fact that Ian could still instigate this, either way, I'm sure there are other ways to make a man suffer than that. With the adrenaline still very much pumping in me, the vodka shots earlier certainly hit the spot, so Jacob and I decide it's best to continue walking down Shoreditch High Street, back on course to the pub. The hot chocolate and marshmallows can wait.

'How do you feel?' Jacob asks.

'Bloody stupendous,' I reply sarcastically.

'Good. That's what freedom feels like'

'Freedom from what?'

'Do you not think that you've lived with more intent in the past day or so than you ever have before? This is what's supposed to govern us. No more lies or play acting,' Jacob says.

'You stole that pouch from Andrei's office,' I enquire, slightly off-topic. 'What's in it anyway?'

'People have been slaughtered for what's in this pouch. I'm only taking back what's rightfully ours, and no, Andrei's still not accustomed to how we do things over here. Take a look.'

I look inside the pouch to see something sparkling and glistening inside. It was one of the most beautiful sights I've ever seen – so small, innocent and priceless. Jacob had stolen a bag of diamonds.

'Those are gorgeous,' I say. Perfect for Susie. 'But won't Andrei come after you once he realises that they're missing?'

'Nope. Despite his love for antiques, paintings, and my artwork, he actually can't see past his own nose. In due time he'll probably end up killing Yuri anyway. It's always good to know your customers,' Jacob says, winking. Despite Andrei playing innocent earlier, Oracle wasn't wrong about him. That club of his is indeed the Kraken hotspot, hence why the cloakroom lady was so casual with offering me some.

Intelligent. Astute. Forward-thinking Jacob.

'So we give those diamonds to Ian and call it a night?' I say, as my body finally gets accustomed to the cold.

'You can say that, but Ian's been acting weird these past couple of weeks. Winston doesn't say much to me, but something's definitely up between those two. Makes me damn glad I don't work there,' Jacob says.

'They had a disagreement when I was with them last night after the poker. It kind of sounded like they clash on things often. Do they normally have heated arguments?' I say.

'You were in Ian's office, weren't you? Well, when I sold him my bear, Winston thought it was a waste of money. He thought Ian could use that money for savings or to improve the bar upstairs.'

'Yeah, I never really got a good vibe from either of them. Winston seemed to be the more rational one, whereas Ian was more harsh,' I say.

'They've always been like that. If they were to clash about anything it would be the interests in their "business". Ian is known for excessive spending, whereas Winston thinks more long term. I honestly think the pub's only been kept afloat thanks to Winston,' Jacob says.

'Well, Ian sounded the same when I spoke to him earlier,' I say, trying to remember the conversation I had with him.

'You spoke to him? When?' Jacob asked intently, as if concerned for his old customer.

'Just before Oracle showed us where that Romanenko guy was back at your shop. After that homeless guy came in, I needed to grab some fresh air. A guy I recognised from Cleo's last night came out of nowhere.'

'So he had someone following us the whole time just in case you were trying to mess him over. Must've been the bloke that gave you that sucker punch last night,' Jacob exclaims.

'Louis? No, it was one of his friends.'

'Whatever his name is, that also explains the blood on your face earlier. Sorry, old sport, I thought you slipped over a banana or something,' Jacob says, while I catch myself chuckling a little over his remark.

'Well … yeah. He gave me a phone and it was Ian. I guess that's his way of giving out reminders. It sounded like someone was there with him though.'

'Hmmm, you know it's obvious who's behind all this,' Jacob says.

'Who's that?'

'Your owner – I mean boss – Johnny Turnbull.'

'How?'

'He's rich, ignorant and doesn't give a damn about anyone else. Sounds like the perfect villain to me.'

'We can't know for sure,' I say.

'I'm only connecting the dots, dude,'

While trying to ignore Jacob's outrageous suggestion, now the whole thing with Louis last night made sense. He was working with McAllister all this time. That would explain why he dropped out of uni early last year. Tamera always did like bad boys. Maybe all that talk of me being in trouble with Ian was why she seemed so open to me? Or maybe not. Who knows with women.

As we approach the Cock and Bull pub, we notice there are a couple of police cars around the place. I then receive a message from Frank:

There's been a change of plan again. Meet me at your workplace, Turnbull and Partners. F

Of all the places in London I would rather avoid, Detective Walker asks me to meet him at the T and P plantation. What in the world would T and P have that would prove beneficial in this mess? Out of sheer curiosity, we go over to the crowd of people by the pub, seeing police and paramedic vans. When we get to the pub, I see a figure covered in a white sheet being carried off on a stretcher. What the hell happened? I then notice the deflated figure of Winston standing handcuffed next to the police van.

'I hope he didn't do what it looks like he did,' Jacob says with his arms crossed, looking just as puzzled and concerned as everyone else here. If my eyes don't fool me, I can't help but think that his eyes lock with mine briefly. Shame my telepathy isn't that great tonight, but it seems like only Frank would have an answer to this.

We turn around quickly and go back to Liverpool Street station. Jacob seemed a little stunned, and I can't help but feel a sense of guilt there. The last ten minutes walking to the pub has sadly brought up that gut-wrenching familiar dread of Marbella once again – only this time I haven't witnessed the body or wished that it was me cloaked in white sheets on the way to the morgue. What I saw by the Cock and Bull was uneasy to say the least. A human life had been taken and I could only feel that we were connected to this somehow.

Could this be the reason why Detective Frank wants to meet over by T and P? Jimmy did owe Ian McAllister money. Maybe Johnny got wind of his son frittering away his dad's fortune and decided to take it upon himself to sort the problem out. No. It can't be. Johnny wouldn't want to commit such an act. Ten grand shouldn't be a problem for Johnny – his property portfolio is too prestigious. After I show Frank's text to Jacob, he gives me that '*I told you so*' look; my mind goes back to thinking mode. We need to get to my workplace and see where this takes us. Once again, I don't think I'm going to like how this night is going to end.

*

It's coming up to about dinnertime now and my family will be worried sick about my absence at home tonight. Hopefully Molly's relayed my message to Dad and Julia. Despite my objections to them, they don't deserve to be embroiled in this. While walking up the stairs to the exit of Bond Street station, I catch myself smiling. It feels like I'm going to work but this time under different circumstances – not because I have to go to get paid, but because I need to go, and in essence I'm not really going to work, I'm going because someone's life has been taken and I feel that we are in some way indirectly connected to that death. Now is the time for answers.

'What's it like working around here?' Jacob asks, as if slightly awed by the Central London zone 1 metropolis. He's the last person I'd imagine who would be working a normal, 'proper' job.

'There's this real decent Pan-African restaurant called Ashanti. They're small, but they do the best jollof rice, jerk chicken and salt fish in the city. A perfect source of protein for lunch,' I say enthusiastically – part tourist guide, part nutritionist.

'What's their plantain like?'

'Oooh, it's their specialty.'

'Good. Nothing much worse than overcooked yam and plantain,' Jacob says as he looks around and observes the capitalist infrastructure around him.

'No Starbucks before work?' Jacob asks.

'Nah, I prefer Luciano's. I usually make myself an espresso at home before heading to work anyway.'

'Sounds exciting.'

We walk along Bond Street, which is lined with sparkling Christmas lights. Fashion retailers from Selfridges and Zara's to Tiffany & Co are all beautifully decorated. The street itself is still reasonably busy, consumers making their last-minute dash for gifts in the blind hope that their loved ones will love them even more after receiving that gift. If Susie hadn't dumped me last night, I would've been here doing the exact same thing as everyone else, as usual.

While walking along the familiar path to Turnbull and Partners Ltd, I see a dark, lonely figure standing just outside the main door of the building coughing up cigarette smoke. Virgin lungs.

'I haven't smoked a cigarette since I left college years ago. The first time was when I was told that I wasn't going to see my parents again. Apparently they were "bad for my development" anyway. I take it you got my message, Luke?' Frank says with a glint of sadness and guilt in his eyes.

'Yeah, we were coming up to the Cock and Bull when I got it. There were police vans and shit there. Ian's friend that I met last night too … Winston? He got arrested.'

'Shit,' Frank says, shaking his head in disapproval.

'What the hell's happening?' I ask desperately.

'When I left you at the Elephant and Castle, that was my informant that called me. Winston. He said it was urgent.'

'You know Winston?'

'Yeah, I've been working with him for some time now. He was going to leave Ian, quit that life and look after his family. The only way that was going to happen was to find a way to bring down McAllister indirectly.'

'So you thought you'd kill him instead?' I ask.

'No, of course not! That was the emergency. Winston found Ian murdered in his office. You know the one with the big bear?'

'You're very welcome,' Jacob cuts in smiling. Facetious to say the least.

'Frank, are we involved in this somehow?' I say, needing him to just get to the point.

'I was getting to that. Not entirely. As discussed last night, you were supposed to bring the money to Ian somehow, then that would've been perfect for bringing him down, except someone else wanted him gone more than I did. You did nothing wrong.'

'What about Winston? Apparently they weren't getting on recently,' I say, relieved.

DRAX

'Well, Ian needed the money tonight so he could walk away from that life as well. Ever since his father died, the burden of carrying on the McAllister tradition became too much of a burden for him.'

'Doesn't explain why Winston would want Ian dead though,' Jacob says.

'Exactly. It doesn't make sense. The police have got the wrong guy, but since they found a dead body with him inside the building, they'd have no choice but to take him in.'

'OK, so why are we here then?' I ask. The office wasn't supposed to be open until the next working day in the new year. We can't possibly need to go inside there, do we?

'I think Turnbull's involved somehow. His son Jimmy obviously got you into this mess through a debt that he had with McAllister. We need to go inside, head up to Johnny's office and see if we can find anything in there that could help.'

'All right then. How comes you haven't gone in yourself?'

'Because it's closed and I don't know the code to get in.'

'Oh.'

I press the four-digit passcode to enter the building and then allow Jacob and Frank to enter first, keeping an eye out for anyone who shouldn't be here other than ourselves. Even though I've had my fair share of late nights in the office, double-checking planning applications, tender documents, observing the architect's drawings and whatnot, being here at a time when I shouldn't still makes me feel uneasy. Frank takes out a torch and hands it to me while I look for the light switch in the reception area.

'So where's your master's office?' Jacob asks.

'Just up the stairs. I'll have a look in Jimmy's office. You can have a look at Johnny's if you like, Frank.'

'No, that's fine. You should go on ahead.'

'Erm ... OK, why?'

'I've done my digging on Turnbull, and on you, Luke. I know about what happened in the summer with your friends. Sarah Hewings? You all went to uni together.'

'She was a good friend,' I say.

'I'll have a look at what I can find down here. But before you go upstairs, I need you to think back. Did you find anything suspicious about Jimmy that night?'

I think back slowly, past my indiscretions, the lies, my infidelity with Tamera, Sarah's dead body, Club Nino, the predrinks we had, Olivia and the hotel, giving Phillip a nickname – it all makes sense now …

'Before we went to Club Nino, Jimmy *did* do something quite strange. Just as we were about to leave, I went into his room and saw him with a couple of small bags of that Kraken stuff, I remember the symbol of the squid thing on it … you mean to tell me that he did that to Sarah?'

'Well, her autopsy did show that she overdosed on some form of cocaine. It was vague, but Kraken's been growing more and more popular so quite possibly so. Try and think back. When you were at the club, did you see Jimmy in there?'

'No, he and Sarah just disappeared. He offered me some back at the hotel,' I say, my mind now enveloped with the knowledge of the strong possibility that my former best friend Jimmy Turnbull may have killed Sarah.

'Shit. Sorry, Luke. So … could his dad Johnny T be responsible for the Kraken thing then?' Jacob asks.

'Tonight would've been the perfect opportunity for him to eliminate competition. Everyone's guard is usually down at this time of year. Romanenko was just a front, I suspect – the product is most likely sold in whichever city or country he operates, Like that bar you went to at the Elephant and Castle. If I'm a successful drug dealer and I know McAllister is in the way of me making more profit, I'll do whatever it takes to stop him.'

'I know Johnny's always had a taste for the theatrical. Why tonight though?' I ask.

'Tonight is that charity ball over at St Augustine's Drive. I'm confident Turnbull will be there. I can nab him over there, but I need your help.'

'Why weren't you invited?' Jacob, for the second time, looks at me aghast, like working for a modern-day capitalist such as Johnny Turnbull was a crime against humanity. The annoying thing is that I remember Jim mentioning to me about how Alexander Pierce might be attending and … blah, blah, blah.

'Sounds like you work for an arsehole of a boss,' Jacob continues.

'You don't know the half of it, mate,' I reply, remembering all the times I've had to do things I'd never wanted to do in this building. Answering phone calls that Jimmy didn't want to respond to, organise documents and files that Johnny's PA didn't want, making and serving the drinks for every meeting in the boardroom – that was bloody annoying – all without a thank you, only just a rare '*good man*' or '*you're a legend, mate*'.

With this new revelation, I don't feel anything. No anger, no happiness, simply a slight state of catharsis. I guess the truth really does set you free. Whether or not I can get used to this is yet to be seen, but when you realise you've been raised on beautiful lies and fake smiles your whole life and the house has been burning for a while, you're glad that someone, anyone, had the decency to wake you up and get you out before it's too late.

'Jimmy would always be up for an opportunity to try and upstage his father. I'll go ahead and check in his office space upstairs to see if there's anything we can use.'

Jacob follows me up the stairs to the important offices, while Frank stays downstairs to search and keep a lookout for anyone turning up. While I feel like I'm supposed to be shocked at the current revelations, to some extent I'm not. I always thought Jimmy was capable of doing something horrific. I've seen examples of this in the past. On Sarah's funeral all I got from him was the impression that he didn't want to be there in a 'I fucked up big time' kind of way. The look I saw then was the same one I'd seen from him on the morning after her death – guilt. At the time I was so focused on grieving with Susie that I hadn't realised that I was still having after-work drinks with a narcissistic anarchist.

All that sob story yesterday evening about how he and his dad don't get on and how he's stalling in giving him more power in T and P was all garbage. I should've punched him in his snivelling little face when he mentioned me walking away from the situation like my real mother. He and Susie were the only people I told that Julia was my stepmother. I trusted him and he abused it. He used my natural affinity to his advantage to get out of trouble with a local gangster and now another life has been taken because of it. First Sarah and now Ian, which by the way could've easily been me if it hadn't been for Frank's intervention and Jacob's help.

Do you ever envy the dead? Being sat at God's high table among all the other lost souls of the world, watching down on everyone, observing, pondering whether the people we love will ever get out of the cesspit of humanity? All it takes is one bad day, one moment, for everything to simply snap and then break off and you've either woken up to enlightenment or you're on the downward spiral to an eternal oblivion. Who have I been I trying to impress all this time? Attempting to gain acceptance from folks who never accepted themselves. This is the thing about it all. Despite Darwinism and the natural process of evolution, we're all in a power struggle that's been in existence since the dawn of time, and no one, and I mean no one, has the answer as to why we can't fully understand each other. Henry VIII damaged Ann Boleyn. Cleopatra played Caesar. It's an ongoing cycle. People like Pill spend their lives trying to impress folks with a fake personality and it never works until they start earning a few and hanging with the 'right' people. It's as if, tragically, that selling yourself out is the solution.

'What are you thinking about?' Jacob asks as he heads into Johnny's office.

'Some stuff.'

'You're thinking too much. The problem isn't the problem, the problem is that there's too many options to solve the problem,' Jacob says.

'I'll have a look in here. Please don't mess anything up.'

'You can trust me,' Jacob says with a wink and a grin, the type of smirk that teenage girls would fall head over heels for. A teenage girl's wet dream.

Looking into Jimmy's office, everything seems reasonably tidy, as expected. On the wall there's a picture of both of the Turnbulls and a big fish. Catch of the day. Or rather a picture showing a rare father–son moment, probably Johnny's recompense for all those board meetings with contractors and hedge funders instead of spending time with his son. On his desk are a multitude of documents – invoices, printed emails. *Looks like Jimmy actually did some work.* There was also a familiar brochure: *Cliveden Place – The Roadmap to the Future.* This must be the brochure that Johnny kept putting everyone under pressure about. I'm sure this is what that the design meeting was all about on Monday; this must be the finished article.

Now that I've seen some information about things that I should've been made privy to, I decide to do some more snooping about those invoices. I'm not much of an accountant, but a recurring name appeared in the account of J&J Holdings, (Jimmy and Johnny, I assume): an 'MM'. I imagine whoever this is must be running the show for Cliveden Place – both Turnbull and whoever MM is will be reaping the profits after the development is completed. *Whoever pays the piper, plays the tune.* Perhaps Johnny wants to make T and P part of Pierce Enterprises. It would make sense considering he's continuing to get this funding from MM, but that's for another time.

I sit back in Jimmy's chair (which is way more comfortable than mine downstairs) and wonder what it must be like to live with inherited privilege. When your father's already a multimillionaire and you haven't got a care in the world, success is handed to you from birth. I stare briefly at the lone photo of me, Jimmy and Pill on our first night in Marbella that he has on his desk: one super-rich kid, a junior planner, and whatever the hell Pill is. *How cute.* While sitting back comfortably, I open up his desk drawer and find an array of stationery, an opened condom packet, and an envelope – Jimmy's never been the tidy type, but I guess if you've always had someone to clean up after you, why should you be?

I open up the envelope and find two elegantly designed tickets:

CHRISTMAS CHARITY BALL
24th DECEMBER
St Augustine's Drive, Knightsbridge, London
Champagne at 8pm, followed by supper

In aid of Great Ormond Street Hospital. There will be a charity auction and raffle.

RSVP Kelly Bridges   *RSVP Jim Turnbull*
k.bridges@turnbullandpartners.com   *jim.turnbull@turnbullandpartners.com*

Ticket: £300 per person   *Dress Code: Black Tie*

Right now, I have no idea what's more surprising, the fact that I wasn't invited or the price of admission to the place. Either way, I've found something that we can use tonight. If there's any chance of Frank nabbing Turnbull tonight, it could be this. Believing that I've got what's necessary from Jimmy's office, I'm curious to know what Jacob might have found from Turnbull senior. Heading through the door and into Johnny's office, past the CEO's office door, it's only now I'm realising that this would be the second time I've ever been in here. Full-height double doors, solid oak walls, a soundproof floor with full-height windows, this room illustrates Johnny's preferred taste in style. Elegant but atmospheric, the luxury homes that he's developed and sold followed in the same style. It's obviously selling to his target market, but I'm not sure having Jacob sleeping on his leather seat would help sell it. I walk up to Jacob and wake him up.

'Did you find anything in here?'

'Find what? Oh shit,' Jacob says groggily. I think I've kept him up longer than he's supposed to.

'What's the time?' he asks

'About seven thirty.'

'OK, I should be alright for now. No more sleeping,' Jacob says, rubbing his eyes.

I have one last look around the room. So this is how the other half live.

'Luke, I've decided your boss IS an arsehole.'

'Why's that?' I ask, while Jacob stares at Johnny's photographs of himself and a number of celebrities behind his desk.

'Who in their right mind decides to take a photo of himself and Gary Lineker and frames it? What a loser.'

'You should see the one with him and Donald Trump and Bill Clinton on their golf trip,' I say.

'I haven't even met this guy and I don't like him,' Jacob says with a disapproving smile.

'Well, we need to get to this party. I think I have a plan,' I say, while noticing Jacob staring at Johnny's wall of achievement. He fixates in particular on the press release of one of Johnny's grand developments: Coleman Place. I wasn't involved with this project, but through the media attention this development received, it propelled him to be one of London's finest.

'Ten million pounds, so that's what he got from it,' Jacob says solemnly to himself.

'What do you mean? ... Oh, shit.'

Ten Coleman Place only got the media attention it did because it was part of the regeneration plan of the whole of East London. Part of the scheme was the tearing down of the local orphanage that was there. This must've been Jacob's orphanage.

'I'm sorry, mate. I had no idea,' I say sympathetically.

'It's OK. You said you have a plan?'

'I'll let you know with Frank downstairs – come on.'

'All right, just a minute,' Jacob says while stretching. All of a sudden he steps in front of Johnny's desk, unzips his trousers and begins to urinate all over it!

'What are you doing?'

'Consider it your resignation.'

28

Detective Chief Inspector Frank Walker, December 24th, 7:38pm

While still deep in thought about tonight's events, Frank knew that now wasn't the time to feel melancholy about Ian and Winston's demise. Tonight isn't over yet. While patiently waiting by the front entrance of Turnbull and Partners LTD for Luke and Jacob, he revisited what he'd seen at the Cock and Bull. Ian's eyes and mouth wide open, his neck and wrists slit, filled with blood and a bottle of whisky splashed all over him at his desk. The sharp, biting smell of the whisky continued to plague him: '*he never really drank in here, only by the bar in the lounge if he fancied one. This was his sanctuary. Only for handling "business", if you know what I mean*'.

Why would Ian all of a sudden decide to have a drink if he wasn't a big drinker? Festivities? *Only by the bar if he fancied one. This was his sanctuary.* Frank recited Winston's words once again. A sanctuary is supposed to be a place of safety, away from danger –

peace, for him at the very least, anyway. Someone had brought the bottle to Ian. If that office was his 'sanctuary', why on earth would he decide to drown his sorrows all of a sudden in there?

After his brief thoughts, Frank, with his phone in his hand, knew that a successful infiltration into Turnbull's Christmas fundraiser would be the next step. However, to achieve this he would require some help. He went back inside the building over to the bottom flight of stairs.

'Are you all done up there?' he asked, raising his voice after hearing a slight echo.

'Yeah, just a minute,' Luke replied.

After leaving T and P and going back out into the cold once again, Frank was eager to find out what Luke and Jacob had found up in the offices.

'Check these out.' Luke showed Frank a pair of elegant invitations. 'I know Jimmy isn't responsible enough to keep something as prestigious as these to himself,' Luke said, grinning.

'I doubt he'd need admission to his own father's party,' Jacob replied.

'Exactly. Nice work, guys.'

'I'm sure Johnny will love the surprise we left for him upstairs,' Jacob said, laughing.

'OK, I won't ask,' Frank said.

'I have a plan. Take a look at this ticket,' Luke said while Frank watched closely. 'Notice that Johnny's name isn't even on the invitation.'

'But Jimmy's name is. Who's Kelly?' Frank asked.

'She's Johnny's PA. There've been rumours that she and Jimmy have had something going on, but anyway, I think this is Jim's night. The perfect opportunity for Jim to show that he's capable of running the company someday after his father. What better way to strike at him than tonight,' Luke said enthusiastically.

'Great, but that's the reason why you can't show your face,' Frank asserted.

'Why's that?'

'Because if he didn't invite his "best friend" to his event and you show up all of a sudden, there's a possibility he'll get spooked and suspect something's up,' Frank said in full detective mode.

'Jacob, do you have any smart clothing at your place?' Luke asked. Which Frank found very astute from Luke. Jacob would be the only person who could pull off a cunning infiltration into London's elite tonight realistically.

'Depends what you're looking for.'

'It's more for you, but I'm sure we'll find something. Jimmy might recognise you, but that's it. Other than that, it'll just be a whole bunch of rich old people and some celebs.'

'What are you asking?' Jacob said, grinning. Frank found that the two young men had chemistry between them that would prove useful.

'I'll explain on the way.'

Frank knew that revealing what he knew about Turnbull to Luke would've been a risk. He had no knowledge about what the relationship between the two young men was, only that one had betrayed the other for his own personal gain the previous night. In a short space of time, though, Frank had seen what Luke had gained from being outside his comfort zone. He didn't look like the insecure troubled boy that he'd pulled to one side from the house party last night. He was a little more self-assured. Perhaps his revelation, the exposing of his former friend's deceptive behaviour, had made him aware of the folks he kept around him. He was still unsure about Jacob, however. What was his goal? Frank could see that he was intelligent, sharp and strong-minded and exceedingly charming, but he couldn't pinpoint why he would go with Luke to risk his own life. Today's events had answered and also opened up a multitude of questions and, so far, as long as Jacob was happy to carry out Luke's agenda, justice might be served and ultimately the Drax initiative may be saved after all. All Frank needed was a little assistance from a trusted friend to continue with his own agenda tonight.

*

'Whatever this is, Chief, it better be important. My aunt's got me on the stuffing and the turkey now.'

'I'm sorry, Marlon, but once again you're the only man I trust right now to see this through. I wouldn't have come here unless it was critical,' Frank said with authority. 'McAllister's been murdered.'

'What?' Marlon said, shocked and confused.

The whisky bottle found in Ian's office earlier in the evening continued to disturb Frank. As unsettling as the idea was that someone out there was perhaps trying to frame him, today's events had driven Frank to conclude that there was only one possibility for what was really going on.

The snow had settled on Marlon's front porch. Marlon, dressed in a Winnie the Pooh Tigger onesie, looked at Frank with slight embarrassment at his front door.

'Family tradition?' Frank asked with a smirk.

'I pulled the short straw this year, Chief.'

'I have some more information. Critical, but I'm going to need your help to solve this tonight.'

'What is it, Chief?'

'I think I'm being framed. At the Cock and Bull pub, Ian's body looked like it had been staged to make it look like he'd been in a struggle.'

'What makes you say that?'

'Just a feeling. Someone knew I was going to be at that pub at some point tonight.'

'With respect, Chief, you want me to believe that you think someone's trying to frame you only through a "feeling"?'

'When I was at the Cock and Bull, after observing Ian's body, I asked Winston to contact the police. Then I heard the police outside.'

'So someone had already called it in. I was on my way out of the office when I heard what was happening. Who do you think did it?' Marlon asked.

'Winston said that Ian was never much of a drinker, and I found a bottle of whisky over there conveniently placed in the office.'

The moment was broken by Marlon's aunt. 'Niiiiick, who's that outside?'

'Just a friend. Gimme a minute,' Marlon wailed.

'Are you sure about this, Frank?'

'I haven't been more sure about anything for a long time. Come on. You're driving.'

Marlon, trusting Frank's suggestion, took a deep sigh. 'OK, I'll bring my badge. My aunt's been the best cook in the family for years and now I have to tell her that work has stopped me from learning her secret jerk chicken recipe.'

'Tell her I'm sorry, Marlon, and, erm … you might want to change outfits,' Frank said.

*

While driving, Frank felt indebted to explain himself a little more to Marlon. He knew exactly how he would've felt if they were in opposite positions. That frustrating feeling of not being told everything that was necessary. Frank, grateful for Marlon's loyalty to him, was determined to put this all to bed tonight. There had been one too many twists and turns, and the last thing he needed was another one.

'You know, I've always been told my jerk chicken's been a killer since day one. You could've asked me,' Frank said, trying to make conversation.

'What are you not telling me, Frank?' Marlon asked, who looked disappointed at having to leave his aunt's.

'And what was the deal with the onesie? You're in your late twenties. You're lucky I wasn't Kyra—'

'Frank! Where am I driving to?'

'My home. I'm going to give you everything I have on Kraken, McAllister, Turnbull, Romanenko, the lot.'

'Why's that? And for your information, Kyra has a Miss Piggy onesie.'

'I'm supposed to be on suspension. If there's evidence that I've been handling an investigation against direct orders from above then I'm finished. That's why you're going to handle this case and get promoted. Merry Christmas, Marlon.'

Nearly driving through a red light, Marlon, still bemused, was grinning.

'But we've been working on this case for a while now, Chief, why throw it all away?'

'I'm not. I've seen enough in this life to know that everything can be taken from you at any moment.'

'Why does this sound like a farewell?'

'Because I'm tired, Marlon. How long would it be until the person you've trusted ends up becoming the culprit you're trying to put away?'

'Wow, that's pretty deep, Chief.'

'Anyway, tonight is Turnbull's charity ball. I have two young men already on Turnbull keeping tabs.'

'What's he done?'

'Do you remember that story in the summer about that holiday death? The girl that overdosed at a nightclub.'

'Yeah, *"Kraken Strikes"*. They had it on the news. Kyra was looking into that when it happened.

'Well, Turnbull's boy was in possession of Kraken and coerced Sarah to take it, making her overdose.'

'And you've got evidence of this at home?'

'No, I've had someone help me with this. A young kid. He was a friend of hers and with Turnbull's son too. He's been able to get evidence for me that should be able to get them away tonight.'

Frank, while happy that he was able to disclose such information to Marlon, couldn't help but notice his face was filled with dread.

'Chief, how did you get the evidence?' Marlon asked slowly, hoping there would be a good explanation.

'We broke into Turnbull's office and collected it.'

Marlon's response surprised Frank.

'Excuse my French, Chief, but that's fucking gangsta. I guess it's just like what you taught me …'

'The world is never changed by reasonable people.'

'Exactly.'

'And don't you dare forget it, kid.'

Over at Frank's apartment, Frank realised that his home, although it was tidy and liveable didn't have any Christmas decorations. *Would he think I'm a loner?*

'As much as I would like to say "make yourself at home", don't. We haven't got much time,' Frank said, going over towards the lounge area to get his evidence board. Frank found Marlon looking around curiously, his expression not impressed with his superiors surrounding. Before he made way to bring out the investigation board, he went around to the coffee table and looked at the picture of himself and a woman of a chocolate complexion. She had beautiful brown eyes, thick lips and a wide smile to complement it. They both looked young and hopeful, ready for whatever challenges that would await them in the future. Sadly, this wasn't to be.

'Not a bad place, Chief,' Marlon said.

'You don't have to lie to me or call me Chief,' said Frank. 'DSU McIntlock is the chief.'

'Everyone in our unit looks up to you though, sir. Whenever McIntlock comes down, everyone stays frightened and quiet.'

Frank smirked to himself, thinking about McIntlock's history with him in the Drax programme.

'Yeah, well, he's always been like that.'

Frank presented the board to Marlon in the hope of explaining the whole case to him as clearly as he could – he was the teacher, Marlon was the student. Tonight's potential success would rest on Marlon's understanding of the current situation. Frank needed the confidence that it was Marlon and not Frank who had been building a case against Turnbull privately.

'So what has Romanenko got to do with it?' Marlon asked while looking at the evidence board.

'I get the impression he was a red herring to keep me, or rather you, off the scent, but either way, the Kraken produced in Southwark is reportedly the source of the product that has been sold at his place of operations.'

'Which is?'

'Just by the Elephant and Castle. I only received this intel earlier this afternoon.'

'OK, so you believe that Johnny Turnbull got Ian McAllister killed over his son's gambling debt?'

'That's my hunch, yes.'

'But there's no proof or evidence to show that your theory is true. Only drug possession, which is an allegation strong enough to arrest Jimmy, but not Johnny.'

'Except this,' Frank said, while he pulled a document out of his pocket. It was the document that Luke had found while back in the office.

'This is a balance sheet …' Marlon scanned the document of numbers, current assets, liabilities, capital. 'Turnbull's had a good year … who's "MM"?'

'Precisely. Ian never liked the name his father gave him.'

'What was that?'

'Marshall. Marshall Ian McAllister II. Marshall named his son after him. Used to serve in the military. Ian used his and his father's initials to cover himself. Winston said that Ian would always spend money that wasn't there.'

'So McAllister was loan-sharking to Turnbull?' Marlon asked.

'McAllister is too small time to be dealing with Turnbull directly, but if I was Ian, this would give me every reason to put his offspring indebted to me. The figures look like he did just that. Then he'd get his revenue back from profits made on the properties sold.'

'This is more than enough to bring both Turnbulls down for questioning at the very least!' Marlon said, while Frank felt his enthusiasm. 'You said they're both going to be at that charity ball?'

'They should be down there right now as we speak. It's at St Augustine's Drive, Knightsbridge. Head to the office, you need to assemble a squad, grab a warrant and call it in. I'll stay in the car – remember, I'm not there,' Frank said, making clear his intention to stay incognito.

'Understood, Chief – if I can call you that?' Marlon asked.

'That's fine, officer. Let's take the board to the office – you'll need it,' Frank said with an ironic smile. Everything was finally falling into place tonight. With Frank's agenda back on track, it was sad to him that his perseverance on this case would pretty much be squandered for the success of his younger colleague. All he had now was the fleeting hope that Luke and Jacob would play their part with Turnbull.

29

We left Frank outside the T and P building to go back to Jacob's place to suit and boot up for the charity ball. Frank said he needed to take a call, so we went on our way. Why hadn't I thought of urinating in Johnny's office? Maybe if I was a little more free-spirited I might have excreted in there and then seen how Johnny would've liked it in the new year.

Anyway, back at Jacob's place in East London, his book collection and artwork greeted me again as he put the lights back on. What is even more shocking as we go into the other side of the apartment is the sheer size of his wardrobe. In front of me is an array of clothing, from Bugs Bunny pyjamas to oversized sweatshirts and a multitude of boots, smart brogues to trainers. Once again, I can't honestly see myself wearing most of this clothing but, frankly speaking, right now it displays my helplessness. I'd take a rough guess that the clothes in here probably cost at least half of the clothes I have in my wardrobe. Some of them haven't even come out of their packaging yet. I guess this is a perk of owning your own vintage store, or rather your own company – you get to keep the best merchandise.

As Jacob re-arranges his main wardrobe, I take another look at his studio apartment. Rather impressive if you ask me, considering what he's probably done to get all this. OK, it isn't some high-end Chelsea apartment, but it isn't bad at all.

'Just give me a minute, mate, I just need to make sure I have your size,' Jacob says.

'No problem, mate. How do you manage to hold all this stuff together?'

'Everything's a masterpiece in its own respect,' Jacob replies, excited, like tonight's adventure is just another challenge yet to be conquered. While he sorts out whatever he needs to do, I notice an old Polaroid photograph on a counter beside the wardrobe. I see a blurry image of a young golden-brown-skinned, innocent-looking woman joyfully holding a child.

'Pretty, isn't she?' Jacob says, with a whole array of clothes scattered on the floor now. 'I think I found your costume for the night, dude.'

'Great!' I say, as I flip to the back of the photo to find a message in expert handwriting:

Me and my 'Prince' Jacob
I love you.
10th July 1994

Jacob hands me a pair of smart black trousers, a blazer, shirt and bow tie. I put the photograph back on the counter as I put the clothes on. They fit perfectly – coincidentally – and look pretty sharp on me too. That will do me nicely, but Jacob is going to have to be the star of the show tonight, especially with my face being the state it is.

'Be careful, that's all custom fabric,' Jacob says.

'I can certainly feel that. Are you sure you wouldn't have anything back at the store?' I ask while adjusting my tie, while he stares at his juggernaut of a wardrobe. I see Jacob has a familiar problem to most of us. *What the hell should I wear tonight?*

'No. I remember a client sold me this outfit for occasions like this. I never thought I'd have to use it until now ... ahh, here we go,' Jacob says, while ripping the plastic off a tuxedo that would do him just fine.

'Perfect. Will it fit?' I ask, to which I receive a '*I look good in anything*' look.

'Now, I'm sure you have an idea about what type of people you're going to have to be dealing with here?' I ask, cautioning Jacob.

'Yeah, the elite of London's upper class, who spend most of their time debating on policy that benefits no one other than themselves. While drinking tea, crumpets, and eating crab Rangoon, the world around them crumbles and their prejudicial inhibitions turn into a self-fulfilling prophecy. So yeah, I know what I'm dealing with,' Jacob replies with a smile. *What in the world is a crab Rangoon?*

While I spend a fortune on clothes and things that I don't really need, someone somewhere is reaping the benefits of my money – hard-earned, because that would be the money I receive monthly from T and P. In my case, Susie benefitted from me in many ways, but it isn't about her now. Sometimes I think we're just cursed with memories. If something painful happens to you, why on earth would you want to remember it? You can't simply un-remember events, whether you benefit from the experience or not, it all just becomes a joke in the end, a funny way to end the anarchy.

With that in mind, I'm pleased I took the liberty of taking the documents that were left on top of Jimmy's desk and handing them to Frank just in case my thoughts about the Turnbull's attempt at world domination is actually true. Waste not, want not. While Jacob and I make our way to Knightsbridge, I can honestly conclude that Jacob would probably be better off being on that front cover of Alpha Digest, maybe even Melanin Beauty and Black Star magazine too. I raise my white flag with dignity and with due diligence. *At least you went down with your arms swinging, Luke. Articulate, respectful, charismatic Jacob.*

On our way to St Augustine's Drive, I send our friend Frank a message, letting him know that we're on our way to the ball. While on the Piccadilly line, neither of us look out of place or overdressed on the Tube. The other folks in our carriage look fabulously smart as well, probably heading in the same direction as us or towards Holborn. There are plenty of bars and nightclubs to drink your life away over there.

Going past Leicester Square, I see an aristocratic-looking Arabian family – mum, dad and their daughter (Ten years old I'm guessing) – looking enthusiastic on the train. I'd imagine this is the first time they've been on an Underground train. I suspect they're on their way to Winter Wonderland in Hyde Park, not only because they can probably afford it, but they'd likely want to take the experience of winter in London back to their homeland. *Wish you were here, Insha' Allah.* The little girl gives me an innocent, guiltless smile as they disembark at Knightsbridge station with us.

Jacob has an inquisitive look to him.

'I was just thinking. Would you ever trade places with Jimmy, or Johnny for that matter?' he asks.

'To dress in tight suits and pretend to like it? Fuck that,' I reply grateful for my survival up to tonight. *It's been a blast.*

Whenever you mention Knightsbridge to anyone, they only every reply with 'Oh, that's where Harrods is'. I assure you there's a lot more to it than just that. The area epitomises the aristocratic elegance of this city. One of those places where you can either indulge yourself in the high-end spectrum of the demographic, or, at the very least, enjoy the socio-economic turnpike of the modern-day upper echelon – the settled snow being the icing on the London cake.

Jacob watches the buildings around him. *How can something be so ostentatious and elusive at the same time?*

'Let's get this over and done with,' he says.

'Agreed.'

St Augustine's Drive was the first project I was on when I started working at T and P. A luxury three-bedroom house so luxurious that I've completely forgotten how much it was worth. This was a conversion of two semi-detached houses in the middle of Belgravia to form one property. Usually when foreign investors decide to invest in property over here, they do it as a refuge for whenever they visit the city, either for business or pleasure. Foreign oligarchs and sheiks buy property in London not so much for their families, but for their mistresses, sex escorts and whatnot – morbid, I know, but true.

The property shark that is Johnny Turnbull bought the semi-detached houses and decided to convert them into a single house. The problem was that the market didn't necessarily buy into his open-plan design.

The project certainly wasn't a pleasant time for us in the office. I'd only just got my feet in the game and already I was on the late nights, liaising with several architects and designers, good ones as well, coming up with ideas on what might be profitable for the market. Johnny had a connection at the Borough of Kensington and Chelsea, so getting planning permission wouldn't necessarily be an issue, it was just selling it and making a profit. It eventually became an arts centre, which the council approved of simply because it would complement the Belgravia area and all the other smaller luxury fashion stores. The consequence of all of this for me was barely spending time at home for my sister and Friday night after-work drinks with cuntflap-face Jimmy along with cock blocker Pill and Saturday night dates with 'Medusa' Susie.

As we walk up the familiar pathway towards St Augustine's Drive, we head towards a placard sat on a neatly placed tripod outside the venue that neighbours the newly opened art centre. I can see a multitude of paparazzi just outside the building, presumably to grab a snapshot of any celebrities in attendance today along with many other upstanding citizens. Bankers, fashion designers, Members of Parliament, company executives, high-end fashion models, you name it – men and women who are all deemed valuable to the status quo.

*

As Jacob went into the main foyer, he was given a Venetian mask. As overwhelming as the whole scenario was for him, he continued to enjoy the moment. Entering the grand hall, there were several guest tables, each with elegantly dressed people on show, already noshing down on their dinner plates while trading niceties and jokes with each other – *No crab Rangoon in sight*, he thought. The decorations on display were very festive, and a gargantuan Christmas tree was set on the main stage of the hall, along with a chamber orchestra playing classical music.

Jacob gave the grand hall another scan to see if he could spot anyone familiar other than the TV stars, politicians, actors, directors, fashion models and socialites. He looked at them indifferently: *Who dares wins, each one to themself,* Jacob thought.

'Hello, sir, whose table are you on?' A petite female concierge suddenly approached Jacob.

'Hello, I'm with James Turnbull. My name is Jacob Brown. I'm representing Pierce Holdings,' Jacob replied while she was checking on her clipboard of names.

'Alexander Pierce?'

'Precisely.'

'Oh my goodness. I thought Mr Pierce wasn't able to attend?'

'He sends his deepest regards,' Jacob said, smiling.

'OK. Mr Turnbull hasn't arrived yet, but Turnbull senior will commence his opening speech soon. Can I show you to your table? I'll let him know you're here.'

'That would be great, thank you.' The young concierge escorted Jacob towards his table while he still scanned the room, partly in awe of the hall's beauty. He noticed a chocolate fountain on display. *What a waste of milk.*

'I didn't catch your name, madam?'

'It's Kelly, sir.'

'Thank you, Kelly, Merry Christmas,' said Jacob. Kelly walked away, appearing to blush. She was impressed with the way the young man carried himself – the warm regal aura expected from a man of supreme wealth and dignity. There was no one sat at the table, but this didn't faze young Jacob. He dropped his Venetian mask on the table, glad that he didn't have to wear it for a while.

As the guests mingled, the chamber orchestra took a brief pause. A man in a very well-tailored tuxedo approached the main stage with a microphone as the lights in the hall dimmed, highlighting the Christmas tree, to a sudden hush from the guests.

'Ladies and gentlemen, may I thank you all for spending your Christmas Eve with us here tonight. I must say everyone looks dapper and gorgeous this evening. Please may I introduce our main benefactor and host for our fundraiser, Johnny Turnbull!'

The hall erupted in applause, with some men and women up off their seats in appreciation of the average-sized man with broad shoulders, thinning hair and tanned face who slowly walked up to the stage waving in appreciation. Jacob was astounded that such a powerful figure could look so average. The man in front of him on stage had the appearance of someone incredibly self-conscious of himself.

'Friends, Romans, countrymen, lend me your bloody ears,' Johnny Turnbull said, with the guests bursting out in laughter.

'It's been a hell of a year, hasn't it, folks? Well, first of all I'd like to thank all of you for your attendance tonight. Your undying support will help the children at Great Ormond Street have a leg up towards recovery in time I hope for the New Year. Some, sadly, may not be able to go home to their families, but we're all here to do our part in helping them have a brighter future.' The crowd responded with a positive round of applause before he continued. 'I'd also like to take this moment, as a father, to give my strongest commitment to my son James. He's put a lot of work into making tonight a possibility and he's certainly been a changed man since graduating last year. It hasn't come without a few bumps and bruises, as with all things in life, but I'd also like to show my appreciation and love for him, as it's not easy raising a son on your own ... and it looks as if, just like his old man, he has a talent for timing – here he is now with his friends!' The crowd applauded once again, along with a collective '*awwwww*' showing their love for the king and the heir to the Turnbull empire, arriving with a small posse.

'Well, folks, please don't let me stop you. Keep your champagne and wine glasses full and a Merry Christmas to you all!'

Jacob clapped along with the crowd and kept his stoicism in check while the lights slowly came back on and the music resumed. He noticed Kelly speaking to Johnny on stage, pointing for him to come over and greet Jacob Brown, the so-called representative for Pierce Holdings. He turned round and noticed Jimmy Turnbull by the bar along with three other individuals getting drinks. Jacob put his Venetian mask back on, as if to hide from the crowd, but it proved unsuccessful when the man of the moment walked up to his table with an eye on Jacob while greeting the other guests at the table.

'A very rousing speech, Mr Turnbull, and a great party. I'm sure you would have been a superb Venetian doge,' Jacob said.

'My pleasure, young man, and you must be Mr Brown. I must admit, Alex hasn't mentioned anything about a Jacob Brown,' Johnny said, making himself comfortable at his table with an exceedingly attractive woman, a mid-thirties brunette.

'Mr Pierce sends his utmost regret for not being able to attend tonight. He has a number of personal issues to attend to, but he would like me to inform you face-to-face that the deal for Cliveden Place is back on and to, of course, congratulate you on your fundraiser tonight.'

Johnny looked to his female companion, who Jacob assumed was his wife, with a look of concern.

'Honey, can you get me a glass of champagne and get that ungrateful bastard son of mine over here please?' Johnny said quietly but with venom.

'Look, Mr Brown—'

'Jacob.'

'Jacob. Ha, that suits you. Look, that's great news and all but I have a very important investor here with me tonight. He hasn't shown up yet, but when he does, I'm going to have to explain to him why a representative from Pierce Holdings suddenly shows up uninvited'

'We've had a collaborative relationship for a number of years now, Mr Turnbull. Mr Pierce felt incredibly guilty about not attending tonight, besides, I'm sure your new investor would respect you for your hospitality to an old partner.'

'Well, my special guest tonight is not exactly an old partner. You don't understand, he's … ah, son, there you are. I'd like you to meet Jacob Brown of Pierce Holdings. He has some news for us.' Jacob and Jimmy exchanged pleasantries while Jimmy handed a bottle of champagne to his father, both of them exchanging unpleasant looks with each other.

'You look familiar. Have we met before, mate?' Jimmy asks.

'Just one of those faces,' Jacob says while smiling at Jimmy's entourage.

'James, care to introduce your friends? I don't think I've met them before,' said Johnny.

'OK, Dad, this is Pill, who you met at my graduation last year, and this is Susie, who you also met at my graduation.'

'What about that other one? The one who works at the office – Luke, was it?'

'Yeah, well he's gone off the rails for a bit.'

Disregarding Jimmy's behaviour at the table, Jacob decided to make himself known to the new guests.

'So how did you two know Jimmy then?'

'Well, we knew him from uni. We used to always hang and stuff,' said the blonde-haired girl with the deep blue eyes, whom Jacob now knew was Susie. 'Jimbo's never mentioned you though?'

'He wouldn't have. I work for one of the investors in the company,' Jacob said.

'But you're like … our age though,' said the scruffier fellow, whom Jacob also now knew was Pill.

'I apologise. He said your name was Pill? Is that a nickname?'

'Ha ha, yes. That's a long story, mate. How long do you have?' said Jimmy.

'Not long. I only came to give Mr Turnbull here a message,' Jacob said.

Looking away from the table, Johnny had squinted and noticed a tall, pale, balding man, middle-aged, walking over to the table, and he instantly adjusted himself. The man walked confidently, like he wasn't there to stand on ceremony, or for the celebration, but instead on a specific assignment.

'Ahh, Jacob, this was the investor I was telling you about …' The man gave Johnny a disdainful, emotionless look.

'Merry Christmas, John. I can introduce myself, thank you … and you are?' the man asked.

'Jacob Brown.'

'A pleasure. You can call me McIntlock.'

30

I'm hidden in this real flash toilet cubicle inside the art gallery, patiently waiting for Jacob's signal to come out. All this time, while I've been in here hearing and smelling men urinate and excrete, I've been thinking of the various things I would love to ask Jimmy:

Was our friendship ever real? Did your mum sniff Kraken while she was pregnant with you?
What did I ever do to deserve your lies? How often do you use the sunbed at home?
Ever heard of acid? You should drink it. Have you ever thought about fucking your dad's wife?

I overheard Johnny's magnetic voice earlier, greeting everyone with his self-aggrandising attempt to show how amazing and bloody special he is. How patronising. I'd much rather listen to some other bloke come in to piss and shit himself than listen to that overtanned orange bastard talk. I probably won't even look at his wife just to show the lack of appreciation I have for his choice in women. If he's been married and divorced as many times as he has, then there must be something wrong with him. You mean to tell me that with all that money you can't find yourself a decent, well-rounded woman to appreciate and cherish? I thought I had that with Susie, but I know if I had the money and power, that blonde spawn of Satan would come running back in no time. *Whore.*

Anyway, with the dirt that I found on Jimmy's desk, if Frank puts that to good use, it looks like I'll be having the last laugh. Who knows, if I hadn't ever been friends with Jimmy Turnbull, I may never have travelled to Mallorca, Tenerife, Cancun or even have talked of going to Vegas. I may have met Susie in different, more realistic circumstances, may never even have ever lost my virginity to her. Pill might never have been that annoying scruffy shit stain. Pill would still be called Phillip. I would probably be in a relationship with Tamera, or probably no one at all. Who knows? *Sarah might still be around.* It might have taken away the sadness that we'd all inflicted on each other over the past couple of months, and restored a life that was taken all because a young naïve woman's folly got the better of her by entrusting herself to a misanthrope.

Is that what this life is all about? Wanting happiness but driving yourself in a whirlpool of madness wherever you go? If there's anything that the past has taught me so far, it's that you're better off doing what you can to enjoy the madness wherever you are. The world watches with indifference, blood is spilled, we all laugh, most cry, and Planet Earth always finds a way to keep on spinning regardless. *No one gives a shit about your feelings.*

As I'm patiently sitting here in this toilet, anticipating the next middle-aged snob to come in and talk to his foreign mistress on the phone, I'm hoping that Frank might come and shut this party down like he did last night. I hear a familiar mumble and some laughter just outside the lavatory. It's painfully familiar because I'd recognise that voice anywhere. I quickly double-check that the door on my cubicle is locked (which it is), then slowly I lift my feet up off the floor and sit on the toilet seat with my knees hugging my chest. That horrid pretentious laugh returns to haunt me once again, while sitting here in one of the grandest properties in London.

Phillip 'Pill' Parsons enters the toilet with that same old pretentious '*I really want to be your friend*' tone of voice.

'Mate, you might wanna have a look at your dad's missus. She couldn't help but stare at that Jacob guy,' Pill says while I hear his urine hit the urinal. I know Jimmy is always edgy about pissing next to someone, and he tries to enter into my cubicle, the handle adjusting up and down to no avail. He then enters the cubicle next to mine and I feel my arms and legs tense up more.

'I could've sworn I've seen that guy somewhere, but I can't remember where. It's pissing me off now. Anyway, do you know where '*Anais*' came from? Dad met her at Paris Fashion Week last year. He said that usual line to her and before you know it she's all loved up and I'm having to accommodate having another bird at home again,' Jimmy says, pissing away, presumably, his dad's champagne. *Bottoms up.*

'What line did he use?' Pill asks.

'What do you think?'

I hear that automatic hand-dryer noise and I can't hear what they say next.

'Hopefully I'll be able to fuck her the way he couldn't tonight,' Jimmy says while exiting the room, with Pill laughing at his friend's vulgar comment.

As much as I want to know who in the world Jimmy is fucking tonight, it sounds like Jacob's doing – whatever he was doing – very well. Forty-eight hours ago I would've cared that Jimmy had invited Pill instead of me for tonight's event, but that's irrelevant now. I'm here anyway and I can't wait to see the look on their faces when they see me soon. *Come on, Jacob, when do I come in?* Another group of men enter the lavatory, so I clench my knees up to my chest while sitting on the toilet seat and continue to wait patiently.

*

'So, what are you, Mr Brown? What drives you?' McIntlock asked Jacob, clearly admiring Jacob's quiet force and intelligence.

'Liberation. What's the point of living if you don't aim for it?' Jacob replied, while looking deeply at Susie, at which point she slightly blushed. *Freedom is never free.*

'Liberate yourself from what? What is it about you that Mr Pierce puts his apparent faith and millions in? From what I hear from you so far, that sounds like a man who's already free,' McIntlock said. Jacob stared at the man in front of him coldly, like this was a job interview of some sort. Johnny, his wife Anais and Susie all watched with interest.

'I've always had a passion for trade and development. I feel if I can apply my expertise in a field where I can fully utilise myself, then I'm sure Mr Pierce can send me in the right direction,' Jacob said.

'Awww, I wish we had more handsome noble men like you, Jacob,' Jimmy's wife said, her French accent alluring.

'Je vous remercie, mademoiselle,' Jacob replied, smiling.

'Merci, bel homme,' Anais replied.

'What drives me?' Jacob continued. 'I suppose knowledge is power. You can get the information from books, but not the power. So to my understanding, for what it's worth, it's that they can never really co-exist. It's a contradiction, but obtaining knowledge of self and purpose, though, that to me is *true* power, I feel. That hunger, the *cancer* in you of powerlessness that pushes you forward – I guess everyone can have that drive in them.'

'Bloody hell, Jacob, you a poet?' Johnny asked.

'What about you?' Jacob asked, smiling at Johnny's attempt at humour. 'We all know Mr Turnbull's story, a very admirable one at that, but what drove you both to work together?'

Both Pill and Jimmy returned to the table, and Jimmy put a hand on Susie's leg, suggestively, to which she responded uncomfortably.

'Mutual interests. McIntlock works at Scotland Yard. He's seen it all – espionage, terrorism, the lot,' Johnny cuts in to answer, as if Jacob wasn't allowed to challenge someone like McIntlock.

'Ah, very John Steed. Well, the property market has always been of great interest to me also. What's not taught to most of us though, is the value in ones own investment. Jacob said, maintaining his stance among the unfamiliar group of people around him. 'Give a man a gun and he'll rob a bank. Give a man a bank and he'll rob the world,' Jacob said. 'I believe your ideas choose you sometimes.'

'Where the hell have you been all this time, Jacob? Alex has never mentioned you before,' Johnny said. 'Do you mind teaching my son a thing or two? Nearly ninety thousand in total for his tuition fees,' Johnny said while eating a crème brûlée.

'Dad, that's very cheap and unfair,' Jimmy said, reacting to his father's comments.

'It wasn't bloody cheap!'

'It's OK,' Jacob reassured Jimmy. 'There's no need to feel contempt for wealth, Jimmy. That's just another trick used to keep people in their place.'

'What does that mean?' Pill asked.

'It means "democracy" has taken a turn for the worst, Phillip,' Jacob replied, with a pang of annoyance at Pill's ignorance.

'Wait, hang on a minute,' Jimmy said, with a confused look. 'How did you know his name was Phillip?'

'You told me his name was Phillip,' Jacob said, caught out by Jimmy's question.

'No, I said his name was Pill.'

'I told him about how he got the name Pill, Jim,' Susie cut in, as if to break up two boys squabbling. 'I told him while you were both in the toilet.'

'All right, babe. Geez, just getting to know our new friend.'

'You'll have to excuse my son, Jacob. He likes to talk when he should be listening,' Johnny said, almost in embarrassment.

'Like father, like son,' McIntlock said icily, with a dagger straight to Johnny's heart and ego. What exactly did McIntlock have on Johnny that made him so conscious of himself? Jacob twiddled his thumbs on his mobile phone and, with perfect timing, the live band change their song, at which point Jacob, to avoid any more awkward questions being thrown at him, brought out his phone and appeared to send a message out. He then put his Venetian mask on and got to his feet.

'Dance floor looks a little quiet – may I?' Jacob asked Susie, offering a hand while observing the lack of people dancing in the hall.

'Errrm … OK?' Susie replied, blushing. As they both went to the centre of the floor, Pill and Jimmy look at each other with what appeared to be disdain.

In the midst of the crowd, while slow dancing to contemporary orchestral music with his mask still on, Jacob couldn't help but ask Susie about her attendance here tonight while fighting the temptation to mention Luke.

'Nice dress, is it tailored?' Jacob asked.

'No, I bought it online,' Susie replied, her arms resting on Jacob's athletic shoulders. 'How do you put up with them?' she then asked.

'With who?'

'The Turnbulls.'

'I don't have to explain all of that again to you now, do I?' Jacob asked, smiling at his own sense of humour.

'You and your boyfriend seem to be getting on fine,' said Jacob, while keeping in time with the music.

'He's not my boyfriend. We've just started seeing each other. I broke up with my boyfriend last night,' the girl who Jacob knew as Susie replied.

'Sorry to hear that.'

'I am too. I think everyone's looking at *us* now' Susie said clearly self-conscious of the moment.

'Why do you care?' Jacob asked.

'I don't know. Why do you think other people care?'

'Most people in this hall, only care about where others come from. I only care about where I'm going'

'Jimmy's on his way' Susie said, embarrassed, but again intrigued by Jacob view point.

'How do *you* put up with them?' Jacob asked rhetorically, as he noticed Luke appear at the entrance to the hall, and just before Luke could have locked eyes on the both of them, Jimmy appeared, flustered and frustrated.

'May I?' Jimmy asked, slightly out of breath from manoeuvring his way through the crowd without disrupting anyone.

'Be my guest,' Jacob replied, hoping Luke wouldn't catch him dancing with his ex-girlfriend. Noticing him by the bar, Jacob went over to join Luke.

*

Thanking the good Lord Jacob sent the message when he did, I finally escape that shithole (pun intended). I then proceed swiftly to what looks like the bar. As if telepathically linked, I see Jacob walk over to the same place, taking off his mask at the same time.

'Enjoying yourself double-o-seven?' I say to him, still a little in awe of the surroundings.

'She regrets what she did yesterday,' Jacob says to me solemnly, and, it seems, with a degree of sympathy. I'm confused, because I'm not sure what he's on about.

'What do you mean?' I ask. He then gestures to the dance floor, to the sight of Jimmy Turnbull and Susie, both elegantly dressed, slow dancing. They look so *damn perfect together*. A feeling of dread overcame me, repugnance – the ice pick was still stuck in my heart where she'd put it last night. Before Ian, Frank, Andrei, or even Jacob.

I find myself walking slowly over to the dance floor, not knowing what on earth I'm going to do. I receive a number of looks from some of the guests here; perhaps it's the result of me hiding in that toilet for as long as I did. I even see Phillip look at me with astonishment from what looks like Johnny's table, along with Johnny himself, his wife Anais and another middle-aged guy who looks like he's seen enough of tonight.

As I slowly approach them both and shuffle my way through the crowd, Susie looks unhappy. *The flawed beauty and the ignoble beast*. She looks at me with a mix of surprise and resentment. Jimmy, while still focused on the moment, looks in my direction with incredulity. *You're not supposed to be here.*

'Jimmy Turnbull. You are under arrest on suspicion of drug possession. Anything you say, can and will be used against you in a court of law.'

I turn to see a young-ish police officer and a crew behind me. *Right on cue.* The music stops and everyone stares in shock at Jimmy. The golden boy is going to have to go for bronze.

'FUCK OFF!' Jimmy says, with a look of despair. I look back over to Johnny and I notice him getting up off his seat in haste and confusion.

'WHAT IS GOING ON?' Johnny exclaims.

'Johnny Turnbull?'

'Yes?'

'I'm arresting you on suspicion of money laundering and murder,' the policeman says, arresting Johnny, his fake-tanned skin doing him no favours right now, making him look a hell of a lot uglier than on the T and P website.

'ANAIS? KELLY? GET MY FUCKING LAWYER, GET GILES ON THE PHONE!' Johnny exclaims.

The police escort both Turnbulls out of the building, much to everyone's shock and bemusement. I walk back over to Johnny's table and see Phillip looking like he's just seen a ghost.

'Go home, mate. You're just another person who he can blame his problems on,' I say, nearly feeling sorry for the poor kid. The middle-aged, serious-looking guy had disappeared, and Anais was still sitting at the table twiddling her thumbs on her smartphone. No lawyer would be working on Christmas Eve, would they? I can imagine the paparazzi and press having a field day right now. Goodness knows what the tabloids will conjure up. *Millionaire Property Tycoon Turnbull Swiped by Cops* … to be continued on Boxing Day.

*

Detective Chief Inspector Frank Walker, December 24th, 10:47pm

Frank waited patiently on St Augustine's Drive inside his car, biding his time to strike. The other group of officers didn't know about Frank being outside the hall, so after they went inside, Frank exited the car.

It was only a matter of time now. Outside the hall, Frank was grateful and proud that Jacob and Luke had played their part tonight. He received Jacob's message for the go-ahead and signalled for

Marlon to proceed. Moments later, Frank heard multiple loud voices, and the music from the hall went quiet. A swarm of paparazzi rushed inside, past the security and the concierges. *Any time now*. Moments afterwards, there were a multitude of disgruntled guests, famous people who Frank recognised from the papers, and important Members of Parliament. He kept his distance from the entrance to make sure his target wouldn't spot him.

And there he was! Frank walked along the cobbled pathway, following his prey onto the high street towards Hyde Park Corner station. The roads were still reasonably busy on this Christmas Eve.

'You've gone soft in your old age,' Frank said with his voice raised over the traffic. The tall, middle-aged man in front of Frank was the man that he'd hoped wouldn't have been the architect of these recent events. *Time to take the bull by its horns*.

'It was only a matter of time, Frank. Now, arrest me quickly and take me in. It's cold,' Matthew Paul McIntlock said with a venomous smile and a snigger.

*

I look back over to Jacob with relief, knowing that the madness is finally over. *...and they would've gotten away with it too, if it weren't for us meddling kids*! He holds a glass up in congratulations to me, walking over to the piano that I think he's itching to play. I'll have to thank him at some point, but I think listening to whatever song he's looking to play is a start. There's a small crowd around the piano listening to the beautiful melody that Jacob begins to play. If there was anything truly beautiful about the past couple of days, it's the realisation that I was a puppet and I finally know where the strings were being pulled.

I head over to Johnny's table, now deserted, with Pill obviously taking my advice. The entire hall is now filled with a mix of confusion and somewhat relief from the people that remain – I guess the rich and famous aren't that bad after all. Jacob continues to play on the piano elegantly as the onlookers continue to observe him with silent admiration. He finishes his song, which is received with a round of applause from the guests that are still in attendance. I watch them from a distance, hearing everyone's laughter and the conversations echoing around the hall.

'Your friend's very talented,' Susie says as she sits next to me, looking tired and dejected.

'I know, he has that way with people,' I reply. I'm indifferent to the baggage we have. I'm just simply happy to be alive.

'You know Sarah wasn't your fault,' I say.

'I know.'

'You know?'

'Yeah. It was obvious. We all just got caught up in the moment. Jimmy was being Jimmy. She was my best friend,' Susie says to me, her eyes watering. I want to put an arm around her, show her that I understand, but this is her guilt, her pain. Not mine.

'We both lost a friend that night. Friends?'

'Friends.'

My ex-girlfriend then hugs me and stands up, and I notice she's wearing the same perfume she used to always grace my presence with, and then she walks away.

31

Detective Chief Inspector Frank Walker, December 24th, 11:28pm

On the way to the station, Frank had a deep sinking feeling. Something was eating away at his stomach, a previous wound reopened. The ghosts of his past were returning for another haunting. Drax operatives must do whatever is necessary to achieve the goal. What on earth was McIntlock's goal? Frank had to arrive at the station before Marlon did, that way he wouldn't know that he'd arrested the DSU. Other people would know in the station, but he didn't want him to realise that he had betrayed his trust straight away. Not like this.

Driving past Marble Arch station en route to Victoria, McIntlock was chillingly calm in the back seat.

'Does this remind you of anything, Frank?' McIntlock asked. *It damn well does.*

'... I haven't physically hurt anyone before ... He thought he was strong and tough so I had to prove him wrong ...'
'By hurting him?'
'HE HAD MY MEDICINE!'

The painful memory of that afternoon in college crept up on Frank once again. However, the tables were turned this time. *The hunted had caught the hunter.*

'I remember it like it was yesterday. You were the only man I trusted, but you were counting on that, weren't you? I was depressed and upset and you found that was your way for me to contribute to the programme. What was that all about anyway? That whoever works under the big and nasty McIntlock ends up *becoming him*?' Frank said angrily. McIntlock continued to smile to himself.

'Poor is the pupil who does not surpass his master,' McIntlock said. 'You're an exceptional man, Frank, always have been. Do you want to know the contradiction of human nature? I'm sure you already know, but allow me to pick your brain for a minute before you attempt to question the morality of my actions. Humans are a predictable and consistently disappointing people. We bow and scrape for anything – manipulate, hurt, do whatever we can to get what we want, but you know what the funny thing is? We like to articulate this as ugly behaviour. It's all one big joke. You and I are simply agents operating under the same hypocrisy.'

'I doubt that,' Frank replied.

'You knew I was going to escape that joke of a fundraiser the minute you sent that Marlon kid out, did you not?' McIntlock continued. 'Honestly, I thought they were coming for me. Everyone *always* wants more power, never less, always more. Even if it's at a grave cost, and that's why some people will always be in the condition they're in – they lack the *will* to do what's right for them. Now that, Frank, that is what I found out about you at that college. Not the insecure, unstable child fighting against his emotions. No. You've always had that burning passion, that rage. You just couldn't stand the fact that you were powerless against that boy back then, so you did whatever was possible to show that you had power.'

'Then why put me on suspension? You could've kept your cards close to your chest?' Frank asked, still disconcerted by the sound words coming out of his former mentor's mouth.

'I'm done talking. Take me to the station so we can finish this,' McIntlock said.

*

Matthew Paul McIntlock III was left inside one of SOCA's interrogation rooms. It was dark and eerily silent but none of this would faze McIntlock at all. He'd dispensed with the bow tie and the first three buttons of his shirt were undone before he was caught. Frank opened the door and there was a screech from the steel security door as he entered into the room.

'What was everyone's reaction when they saw you bring me in for interrogation?'

'They'll be fine. They trust me,' Frank said with confidence.

'I'm sure they do, son.'

'DON'T call me that!' Frank said, feeling disgust at McIntlock's arrogance, like he was in control even though he was the one in the cell on handcuffs.

'You had to kill McAllister to put me away for good. You even used my whisky bottle that I hadn't used to make it plainly obvious that it was me, no doubt having my prints on there. I can tell because I ripped the label off and put it back on upside down on the bottle.'

'Oops.' McIntlock shrugged his shoulders sarcastically, then adjusted himself to sit straight. 'You were getting too close. Your gift is also a curse, Frank. You know this better than I ever will. You became a concern to the big cats in Whitehall, so I had to put you on leave to get you away. I had to deal with McAllister myself because I knew about your relationship with his friend, Winston, is it?'

'How did you know?'

'We have people everywhere, Frank,' McIntlock said with a smug grin. 'The report told me that even on leave you weren't going to let this go. If anything, I did you a favour getting rid of that ungrateful Scot for you. You're better off in prison than what's coming, boy'

'What's that?' Frank asked.

'London's reckoning. The world is changing faster than you know it, but tell me, after all these years you never actually asked me what my job was at Drax. I had to join you at SOCA because Whitehall knew I was the only man you'd trust.'

'What do you do then?' Frank asked reluctantly, feeling McIntlock was a step ahead of him once again.

'The same thing I've always done. The same thing all of us are here for. Even the average so-called "innocent" taxpayer. To maintain the stability of the current system. Do whatever is necessary to keep the status quo. Drax is only one tool of that.'

'You told me that it was shutting down, that they weren't giving us funding anymore.'

'Glad to know you still think you're one of "us". Drax has always had a systemic economic approach. It's been said around the board that Drax has been funded by the Ministry of Defence. This isn't true. Not many actually know of Drax's true purpose, but what's certain is that we've never been involved with any form of government. *We're an army of no nation.* We have always funded ourselves towards one objective. Clear out the clutter. A culling is what's needed in order to uphold the established order. This is much bigger than you and me, Frank.' Frank listened to his old mentor intensely. 'So yes, I had a relationship with Turnbull. His projects have been funding our programmes for years – without his knowledge of course ... until recently. As you should know, you only invest for a timely, handsome capital return.'

'So those were your initials on his balance sheet. "MM" – Matthew McIntlock, not Marshall McAllister'

McIntlock replied with a wink. 'Turnbull wanted to break away from us by changing his company name. I, of course, was one of his shadow investors, as you know – you do what's needed to be done.'

'But why kill someone else? Surely there must have been another way?'

'Knives are always more effective. Guns are too swift. There was a rather charming young man in the party who gave an interesting analogy on a gun actually.'

'You're sick,' McIntlock's former apprentice said.

'Stop talking like a cop, Frank. I trained you better than that. All those people in the offices may look up to you – the youngsters we had in Drax all looked up to you too, and still do, not because of your stance on morality and justice, but because you're fearless. You have the will to do what is necessary!'

'And you don't? Why didn't you just kill me? End this whole thing altogether?'

'If Drax didn't see you as a worthy asset, you wouldn't be here. Tell me, where are your parents, Frank? Where's Leanne? You sacrificed them for the good of the objective, did you not? Yes, you did so because it was obvious. You didn't do it because it was right and just, you did it because it was necessary. The chain of events from when I dismissed you upstairs, leading up to this moment, have proven that the Drax initiative is working superbly,' McIntlock retorted. 'It's all about getting your piece of the chaos that's left when it's all said and done.'

'And what's your piece of the Kraken chaos?'

'Hmph. I warned that Russkie you might be snooping around. Romanenko was a distraction too, to get you to believe that a former Russian mercenary was rising to become one of London's biggest drug lords with a drug that's been upholding the London and New York stock exchanges for decades.'

'Continuous consumption. If you control the drugs, you control the politics,' Frank said to himself, feeling deflated.

'More importantly, people – why control money when you can control the consumption?' McIntlock added coldly.

'None of this was an accident.' *Supply and demand.* Frank looked at McIntlock in disbelief. *Why is he telling me all of this?* 'Well, whatever you and the suits at Whitehall are planning is done. Turnbull's been taken in.'

'On what charges? Trading with McAllister? Well you know that isn't true, especially when Turnbull's lawyers catch wind and find out the accounts don't match. He'll be out by Boxing Day … and Turnbull's boy? You're accusing that spoilt brat of a death that happened in the summer with little or no evidence. It'll never stick with the lawyers they have, Frank.'

'Shit,' Frank grimaced.

'Indeed,' McIntlock said. There was a rumbling noise outside the interrogation room. Frank listened carefully to the noise that sounded like shouting. Marlon had finally returned with both Turnbulls.

'You better see that through. It's been a pleasure,' McIntlock said with a grin, the wrinkles on his face appearing more refined and apparent than before.

Frank was left bemused about McIntlock's confidence. He was handcuffed and locked in an interrogation room. *No way out.* He went to the main reception desk to see Johnny Turnbull, smartly dressed but now scruffy, his tie out of place and more veins popping out of his forehead than usual, along with his son, Jimmy, who looked absolutely petrified about being in a police station. Frank looked at Marlon proudly.

'Good job, Marlon. Put them in holding,' Frank said, smiling at his young protégé.

'Thank you, Chief. Their lawyers are already on their way.'

'Well, until then, make them feel at home.' The other officers took the two men away into the holding cells. Marlon was about to follow them until Frank gestured Marlon to meet him upstairs.

The upstairs offices by Marlon's desk felt very solemn, Christmas Day was but minutes away but people, of course, still needed protecting. Frank pulled Marlon into his office.

'I need to tell you something,' Frank said with a touch of guilt to his voice.

'What's that?'

'I haven't been completely honest with you. I had to hold back earlier to bring someone in.'

'Who's that?'

'The chief. He's the one that's been behind everything. McAllister, Kraken, the lot. I thought it best I told you about it rather than someone else.'

'But there's evidence proving it was Turnbull and McAllister?'

'No, McIntlock's been the one investing in Turnbull.'

'Where is he now?' Marlon said with a grimace.

'He's in the interrogation room. Don't worry, the evidence you have will still be useful to you.'

'Except none of it points to the chief. Frank, why didn't you tell me this earlier?'

'I wasn't sure until now. I recognised the whisky bottle at the Cock and Bull pub with its label ripped off. That was the same one I had in my office, and when you told me earlier you saw him at my desk searching, it all came together.'

'OK, I'll be back up. I'm going to see the Turnbull's get to holding OK.'

'All right, mate,' Frank said with a tired grimace, still caught by McIntlock's words, still caught by everything that he had done in his career so far.

He looked towards his office in a daze. What is it all worth? he thought. His morals – was it necessary to go to extreme lengths for all of this? He had saved a life once again – Luke, a young man whose life was ahead of him. *'You didn't do it because it was right and just, you did it because it was necessary'*. Frank stared at his office door, which was still wide open. How long had he been working under McIntlock's thumb? 'W*e have people everywhere, Frank.'* McIntlock's sniping words resonated with Frank. He checked his phone for the time: 12:05am. It was officially Christmas. Frank all of a sudden felt tired and was in desperate need of some sleep.

'What do we do now, Chief?' Marlon asked, walking back into his office. Frank put a hand on his junior's shoulder.

'Go back home. It's Christmas,' he said with a wry smile.

*

Frank sat down at his desk and continued pondering McIntlock's chilling words. He then gathered himself and went back downstairs to the interrogation room, only to find he was shocked at what he saw. McIntlock was gone. It was as if he'd never been there.

32

Even though it's only just gone midnight, and every part of my body wants to lie down on a warm bed, it's officially Christmas now. As Jacob and I walk along Brompton Road, Harrods is still looking as blissful as ever and the cold is just about bearable now. Despite Jacob's fine work tonight in charming London's finest, for the first time since meeting him yesterday, I can't help but sense an air of loneliness to him. To my knowledge, he doesn't have a family to go to, and that apartment of his near Hoxton is quite a way from here.

'What happens now?' I ask him, hoping he'll tell me he's not going to be alone for Christmas.

'What do you mean?' Jacob asks.

'Like, where are you going to go?'

'There's only one place I can go.'

'Cleo's?' I ask, to which I receive a wink in return.

'We're due for a proper catch-up anyway. Cab's going to cost a fortune right now though. You should be on your way home, old sport. It's been a journey, mate,' Jacob says with a sad smile. I could just about make out his eyes watering a little. Whether or not it's the cold atmosphere, though, I'll never know. *Everyone deserves a family.* 'We should grab a cab from South Kensington. It's not far from here, but it'll burn a hole in our pockets though.'

'Can't be as bad as going back to Essex for me.'

'Ahh well, such is life,' Jacob says indifferently.

I call up two cabs from South Kensington station. While we wait, patiently admiring the snow, Jacob begins to have that inquisitive look once again.

'You know the whole thing with you and that Susie girl? You shouldn't walk away with a bitter taste in your mouth.'

'I'm not. Why's that?'

'Jimmy nearly caught me out earlier. When I said something to that Pill guy, I accidently called him Phillip. You'd already told me everything I needed to know about your friends, so Susie backed me up when he called me out and she said she'd had already mentioned to me about the whole Pill/Phillip thing.'

'Why do you think she would've done that?' I ask.

'I don't know. It worked out in the end,' Jacob says, shrugging his shoulders as his cab arrives. 'Hey, I take it you've pretty much resigned from T and P, right?'

'I think it'll be a while before it's up and running again. What are you going to do with those diamonds?'

'Ha ha, give them to people who really need them, or maybe not. Anyway, come by the store when you're ready. I can do with someone who's sharp with numbers. Oracle has too much going on to be stuck on purchase orders and invoices all the time. Should balance the books a little in the store having you around. Besides, your clothes are still at my place anyway. I'll bring them to the store.'

'I'd like that, mate.' I then say my goodbyes, as my driver finally arrives and I go back to the place I'm grateful to call home.

Christmas Day

Last night was the best sleep I ever had. Usually after an intense workout I used to always look forward to sleep. When the adrenaline wears off and the lactic acid decides to do its work, I used to always assume that a good night's sleep would be the answer, the solution to essential muscle recovery. More often than not, however, this wouldn't be the case. I'd only receive neurotic feelings of sadness while scrolling down everyone's social media page on my phone.

Hotly anticipating having to spill the beans to my sister about my death-defying endeavours, I get a jolt of excitement about the day, to which fatigue eventually overtakes my body again. Back to sleep. *You wouldn't believe what happened to me, Molly.* Right now, though, I only feel serenity – during my sleep I can't help but hear a number of peaceful light-hearted female voices – Julia and Molly no doubt resisting the urge to wake me up for opening presents.

'... what happened to his face? ...'
'... is your brother OK? ...'
'... he's fine ...'
'... we'll have to wait till he's awake then ...'

Today is simply a requiem for my near-death experience, the autumn of my ebullience. I wake up with aches and pains all over my chest, arms, legs and my face, but I do have the consolation of feeling the underfloor heating beneath my feet. I stretch my arms to their fullest, almost reaching the ceiling. I put some clothes on quickly and make my way downstairs to the living room. Then I take a brief look at the photograph once again of my younger, hopeful self with my sister. The photograph that once symbolised my naïve ambivalence now stands as a time capsule to the past. I take a moment to look and reflect at this photograph before heading into the lounge – a sight to truly behold and be thankful for.

'Good afternoon, son. Merry Christmas!' my dad says, looking intently at the bruises on my face. Then he grins. 'Wild night?' He's putting the finishing touches to the Christmas tree.

'You have no idea, Dad.'

'All right, son. I'm nearly done with this tree. Do you mind finishing off the dishes? Jules has taken your sister out for a walk to enjoy the snow before it dissolves. You'll also be surprised to know that we'll be spending Christmas alone this time.'

'No one else is coming round?'

'Nope. Unless it's Estaban Rodriguez from FC Barcelona coming over to West Ham, then no. No one this time.'

'That's not if Spurs get him first.'

'I bloody hope not. Probably Arsenal. Not to Spurs in a million years.' We both quietly laugh together in unison.

'Thank you, Dad.'

'For what?'

'I don't know. Just thank you.'

33

Frank Walker, December 27th, 09:25am

Frank Walker   Diary Entry:DR520-2
Day: 27th December   Time: 9:25am

Dear Reader,
With all due respect to you, I must confess that the past couple of
days have been, to put it lightly, one of the most educational
experiences in my career so far. All my life I've always loved and
taken pride in solving crimes in various forms. Even during my time
working for the Drax Intelligence/Counterterrorist Unit, although I
had experienced my fair share of traumatic chaos, I had the fading
hope that one day, maybe, our children would be able to live in a
safe world, a just, democratic world.
However, what the past couple of days have shown is how little I
actually really know of the world. Of how contradictory it is to
believe that the answer, the only way to achieve freedom, justice and

equality, is through violence and deception. With all my expertise, and of course not to mention my past failures, all it took was the help of a few good young inexperienced men and a certified criminal (the least likeliest of individuals, I must add) to show me that there is hope, that it is possible. The candle was close to dying and all it needed was someone to light the flame again.

As mentioned earlier, the past couple of days have been what the kids might call today 'quite a trip'. As much as it would please me to say that the assignment was a success, every passing minute that I think about the events on Christmas Eve – although victory was achieved – I can't help but think that it was only a Pyrrhic one.

I couldn't shake the feeling I was walking on a minefield the minute I decided to persevere on the Kraken case, and with McAllister so close to leaving, I can only be grateful for the cooperation I received from Winston. The intel I received from him with regards to McAllister's operations were useful and, as it turns out, it was by all means critical. It was only about finding the right moment to strike. This would not have been made possible had I not mistaken young Luke for one of McAllister's upcoming lieutenants. It turns out the young man whom I thought I was looking for was affiliated with the man who sadly inflicted the violence on Luke the next day.

One can only imagine what it must be like to grow up in this day and age where everything is under surveillance and posted online, and then your self-affirmation and social standing is at the mercy of a few hundred followers' 'likes'. George Orwell's biggest nightmare, to say the least, I must say. Young Luke eventually proved to be useful in this operation, as much as I'd like to think that the leverage I had in taking him in for assault charges would be conducive. I also believe that having his feathers ruffled also worked to his benefit. Before taking down his employer Turnbull at his grand hall, I noticed a slight change to his personality. He was the one who instigated the plan of infiltrating Turnbull's charity ball. Although dependant on his associate Jacob, his fabrication as a representative of one of Turnbull's investors wouldn't have been made possible if it hadn't been for Luke's in-depth knowledge of his former employer's dealings. Impressive to say the least, although I couldn't make out why he would want to stay hidden out of sight. I could only assume *he wanted his former friend and employee to see him and lock eyes before being taken in – I'll leave Luke's personal difficulties to himself.*

All of this made me believe that Luke, and in particular his 'new' friend Jacob, may be useful for initiation into Drax, but I'll leave that decision until after the New Year – everyone deserves their space. Where they both go from here, though, I'm not particularly sure, but I'll be sure to keep an eye on them from time to time.

As for Winston, despite his arrest under suspicion for McAllister's brutal murder, he's been let go due to the evidence being inconclusive about whether Turnbull or Winston were involved. Plus, Winston, being who he is, was able to talk his way out of the suspicions about what went on in his basement bar. A search has been put out to look for members of McAllister's old club, and I'm sure Winston will make the search as difficult as possible for SOCA. Now that Winston is 'free', I imagine he and his family will move back to London, but it'll be interesting to observe his activities. Time will tell whether he decides to continue with the McAllister activities or whether he'll do what he can to be a family man. The Cock and Bull pub has been closed until further notice and will likely be abandoned soon, so this is his lifeline. For his sake I hope he chooses wisely.

Despite my initial inclinations about Romanenko and his supposed link to the Kraken distribution pipeline to the UK, I've done some digging into his network. He had a few complications with his entry into the UK but he appears to be pretty clean. However, I'm confident that with the information I've leaked to the Home Office Romanenko would do well to escape his fate. As you can imagine, it's difficult to analyse and determine how a drug as popular as Kraken is distributed. I do have faith that SOCA will get their act together after McIntlock's disappearance, but with enthusiastic and honest men like Marlon on board, I'm sure they'll pull through.

Never say die.

*

Frank was finally in good spirits. Even though he believed his future was once again uncertain, he realised that this was what made his career worthwhile. He turned to make himself a cup of his favourite Earl Grey tea and allowed the soothing caffeine enhance his senses temporarily.

Spending Christmas Day dinner with Marlon's family gave him a chance to taste his junior's jerk chicken – much to his pleasure – but what was most delightful today, however, was a phone call he received, a private number once again. The second he heard the voice he knew exactly who it was.

'Hello … erm, Frank?'

'Hey.'

'Do you know who this is?'

'I wouldn't forget that voice from anywhere, Lea.'

'Oh, OK. You don't usually answer new numbers on your phone'

'I would if it's from you, Lea.'

'You know you're the only one who's ever called me that,' Leanne said.

'I know. I hope it stays that way.'

'I'm sure it will.' They both chuckle to each other over the phone, happy to hear each other's voices, albeit from a distance.

'How was your Christmas? I forgot to ask,' Frank asked.

'I spent it at my mums this time. The same old same old.'

'Ha, your Uncle Mensah spreading those good old Black Star stories about his time in Ghana?'

'As always. How was yours?'

'Spent it at a work colleague's house. Afterwards I told him this was goodbye from me to him. He won't be seeing me at the station anymore.'

'Oh my. Why not?'

'Creative differences come to mind. Long story. Not one to share on the phone'

'I can imagine, the minute I found out McIntlock was going to join you at SOCA; I knew some dodgy stuff was going to go down. You need to tell me all about this'

'Yeah … it's a long shot, but it'd be nice to catch up with you, you know' Frank said.

'Sure, I'd like that',

'Great,' Frank said with a warm smile. 'Let's arrange it.'

The End

DRAX

Acknowledgements

Firstly, I'd like to give a shout-out to some of the great personalities, artists and writers of the planet whose work and history have provided inspiration and knowledge to me:
Frederick Douglass, Marcus Mosiah Garvey, Haile Selassie, Nnamdi Azikwe, Elijah Muhammad, Dr Martin Luther King Jr, Malcolm X, Dr Carter G. Woodson, James Allen, Niccolo Machiavelli, F. Scott Fitzgerald, George Orwell, Robert Greene, Dr Frances Cress Welsing, Neely Fuller Jr, Dr Claud Anderson, Theron Q. Dumont, Don Miguel Ruiz, Baltazar Gracian, KRS-One, Dick Gregory, Chinua Achebe, Sun Tzu and E.Franklin Frazier.

I would also like to give a personal thank you to my friends, family, associates and in particular my parents Tochi Nwimo and Magella Kakie - Nwimo and their siblings.

Also to the memory of both my Grandparents:

The Late Martin and Eugenia Nwimo and The Late George Nwachukwulor Kakie and Mrs Anna Tohon Sosam - Kakie…

… and last but certainly not least, I give praise and thanks to almighty **GOD**, the infinite intelligence of the Universe, for Heaven is not a place we go to, it is what we can become.

www.ikennanwimo.com

Blaque Falcon
P U B L I S H I N G

www.blaquefalcon.co.uk

#0052 - 120418 - C0 - 210/148/13 - PB - DID2170668